Cath Staincliffe moved to Manchester (all red brick and rain) from her home town, Bradford (hills and stone) to start a job. And stayed.

After many years living communally, she and her family went nuclear. Cath and her partner both work part-time and share the care of their children and the domestic chores. As a result, they are pretty permanently skint.

She is an avid reader of crime fiction with a well-used library ticket and an addiction to reading at bedtime. *Looking for Trouble* was inspired by the books she loves to read.

She is currently working on the next Sal Kilkenny mystery.

Cath Staincliffe

LOOKING FOR TROUBLE

First published in 1994 by Crocus

Crocus books are published by Commonword Ltd, Cheetwood
House, 21 Newton Street, Manchester M1 1FZ.

Commonword gratefully acknowledges financial assistance from the
Association of Greater Manchester Authorities, Manchester City
Council and North West Arts Board. Commonword also wishes to
thank Guardian and Business in the Arts: North West for their
invaluable support.

Crocus books are distributed by Password (Books) Ltd,
23 New Mount Street, Manchester M4 4DE.

Cover design by Hemisphere, 47 Newton Street,
Manchester M1 1FT.
Produced by Commonword and Caxton's Final Film, 16 Nicholas
Street, Manchester M1 4EJ.
Printed by Shanleys, 16 Belvoir Street, Tonge Fold, Bolton.

British Library Cataloguing-in-Publication Data. A catalogue
record for this book is available from the British Library.

Thank you to all the people who helped me write this book: to Annie who was there from the beginning and shared all the ups and downs along the way; to Mo, who kept telling me I could do it; to Brenda, for great chunks of free child-care; to the novel writers' group past and present, Ailsa, Christina, Jay, Livi and Maggie for encouragement, support and the pleasure of learning together; and to my children, Daniel and Ellen, for their sweet inspiration.

For Tim

CHAPTER ONE

I get a kick out of following people. There's a childish excitement in trailing the unwitting suspect, in not being caught doing something shady. It's rarely easy. Fate conspires to fix the traffic lights, spirit up needy strangers seeking directions, wayward dogs and road-works. Actually, I can't blame fate for the road-works; that's down to the city council. They'd only just finished digging up the whole of Manchester, to replace the rotting sewers, when they started digging it up all over again to lay the tram lines.

Of course, in between the thrill of the chase there's the stifling boredom of waiting. Waiting for the woman to emerge from having her hair permed, for the couple leaving the hotel, together or separately, or for the bloke to finish his stint at the pub.

But that Friday morning back in June, I was lucky. Vernon Wainwright, supposedly off on a business trip to Amsterdam, left the airport ten minutes after his wife dropped him and took a cab to the Trust House Forte hotel in nearby Northenden. There he was joined in the foyer by a young woman. They booked in and took the lift up to their weekend of bliss. The Trust House Forte hotel would hardly be my idea of the perfect setting for a weekend of forbidden passion (couldn't he at least have taken her to Amsterdam?) but then it's so long since I had any passion, forbidden or otherwise, that I'm hardly *au fait* with these matters.

With my adrenalin buzz fading, I drove my old Mini back to face the less than pleasant task of telling Mrs Wainwright that her suspicions were well founded.

I've found they usually are. Women know. They spend an inordinate amount of time blaming themselves for being paranoid or insecure, giving hubby the benefit of the doubt just one more time – then, at their wit's end and fearful for their sanity, they approach someone like me. It's my job to prove to them that they're not going loopy.

Mrs Wainwright took the news in her stride. Politely, even. She thanked me for doing the job. I was relieved. I've been on the end of a whole heap of anger and bitterness before now. Don't shoot the messenger.

I sat back and tilted my chair at a dangerous angle. What now? My desk was clear. No work in the pipeline. Should I struggle on as a private eye or launch myself on another career? I'd never actually had a career. I'd had a broad and fairly useless university education, a stint as a desk-potato in a tax office, a baby (now a four year old) and eighteen months as a self-employed investigator. 'Women returners' screamed the ads in the local paper, but what had I got to return to? Being re-educated didn't appeal. And my fantasies of an alternative career ran along the lines of jazz-singer, investigative journalist, film star. None of which featured on the summer school syllabus at what was left of the adult education college.

I sighed, righted my chair and took a turn round my office. It's a cellar room I rent from a family who live round the corner from my house. Well, not *my* house

– I rent that too. From a brain-drain lecturer who's over in Australia.

The office looked decidedly jaded eighteen months in. The leak from upstairs the previous winter had left ugly water stains over most of the ceiling. Two corners sported an interesting variety of fungus. Random coffee stains and what looked like bits of old food peppered the walls. I've no idea how they got there. I have no recollection of ever throwing food and drink around. Faced with no useful employment and time on my hands, I decided to do something practical. I'd redecorate. There would be paint left over from the kids' room. Pale lilac. It would be an improvement on what I was looking at.

An hour later, clad in dungarees, I was back in the Dobson's cellar with step-ladder, roller and tray, paint and dustsheet. I shoved the furniture into the middle of the room, rolled the edges of the carpet in and covered the lot with the dustsheet.

I paint fast and messy. The ceiling was done in twenty minutes and I was speckled lilac like some rare bird's egg. The phone rang just as I was scraping the excess paint off the roller. I dived under the dust-sheet to find it.

'Hello.'

'Is that Sal Kilkenny?' The woman's voice was soft, a glottal Bolton accent.

'Speaking.'

'I got your name from a friend of mine, Audrey Johnson.'

'Yes.' I remembered Audrey Johnson. She'd been less than civil when I'd told her what Mr Johnson was up to.

'Could I come and see you?... if you're able... you see... oh...' She was floundering.

'Yes, of course.' I tried to put her at her ease, sounding confident and reassuring. 'When would be convenient?'

'Well... now. You see, I'm in town, I thought...'

'Fine.' I was getting horribly hot under the dustsheet and why not seize the moment? 'The office is in a bit of a mess,' I apologised, 'but I'm sure we can manage.' I gave her my address and directions from the city centre.

I ran round like a blue-arsed fly, clearing up and replacing furniture. I left the door ajar to let some of the overpowering ammonia fumes escape. I hadn't time to go and change my clothes. I managed to get most of the lilac spots off my face but my hair bore witness. Hopefully, Mrs Forgot-to-ask-her-name would be more concerned with the business in hand than my appearance.

The bell rang. I clattered upstairs. I might have been lucky with Vernon Wainwright but all that was about to change. It was a Friday in June. Given what I know now, it should have been Friday 13th. It wasn't but it should have been.

CHAPTER TWO

She was a plump woman, middle-aged, average height. Short dark hair streaked with grey. Sallow complexion, broad face, brown eyes. Large eyes. Eyes full of fear. She was dressed conservatively, neat and tidy. Tan skirt and jacket, cream blouse, court shoes. Tiny studs in her ears. No other jewellery, no make-up. We shook hands; hers were clammy. From nerves I guessed.

'Come on in.' I closed the door behind her. 'My office is downstairs. I'm in the middle of re-decorating – that's the awful smell.' She followed me down and sat across from my desk.

'I'm sorry, I didn't get your name.'

'Hobbs, Mrs Hobbs.'

'And how can I help?'

'It's my son, Martin. He's missing. I want you to find him.' I nodded and began to make notes as we talked.

'How old is Martin?'

'Sixteen. It was his birthday at the beginning of June.'

'How long's he been gone?'

'A month now.'

'And he's not been in touch at all?' She shook her head.

'Has he ever done this before?'

'No.'

'Any idea why he's left?'

'No, that's why I'm so worried.' She twisted the straps of her handbag round her fingers. 'He'd just gone one morning.'

'Did he take anything with him? Clothes, money?'

'He'd no money. I think some of his clothes had gone.' She didn't seem very certain. Maybe when kids are that age you lose track of their wardrobe.

'He didn't leave a note or anything?'

'No.'

'Have you been to the police?'

'Yes, the local police, in Bolton, but they didn't seem to take it very seriously, with him being sixteen, you know – it's not like he's a little boy. They put him on file, made a few enquiries, came round to the house to take more details. That was about it. They said if I hadn't heard anything in a couple of months, to go back. I'm sure they thought I was making a fuss about nothing.'

'And you've not heard from them?'

She shook her head. 'I'm sure they've just filed him away. It happens all the time these days, doesn't it, kids running away? How can they possibly look for them all?' She had a point. But surely they could have done a bit more in this case. It wasn't as if Martin had been in the habit of running away. And he hadn't even told his mother he was leaving.

'What about friends, people he spent time with?'

She sighed. 'He were a loner really, he loved his fishing, there was no-one close. He liked to be on his own.'

'There must have been someone, a schoolfriend?'

She bit her lip, gave a small shake of her head.

'Which school does he go to?'

'St. Matthew's.'

'Tell me about Martin.'

Her account was sketchy though there was no mistaking the love in her voice. Martin was a quiet boy, doing reasonably well at school. His passion was angling. There'd been no rows or unusual events at home. He'd not talked of leaving. He'd not been in trouble. She told it all slowly, in that thick blurry accent.

'What about drugs?'

She shook her head.

'You're married? How did Martin get on with his father?'

She considered her reply.

'Okay. They're both quiet, never that close.'

'Was Martin lonely, Mrs Hobbs? Was he unhappy?'

Maybe it wasn't the most sensitive question to ask. But I was trying to fathom out a reason for Martin's disappearance. He was a loner, not close to anyone except Mum. Adolescence was a terrible time – even when you had close friends; without them it must be intolerable. But why leave home? An attempt to break away from Mum? Had Martin perhaps blamed her for his loneliness?

She covered her mouth with her hands, shook her head from side to side. Tears welled in those brown eyes. 'I don't know,' she sobbed. 'I don't know.' Guilt and grief.

I tried to bring her back to the task in hand.

'Think for a minute. Is there anywhere Martin might have gone – relatives, a place he knew well, friends of the family?'

She pulled a lace-trimmed hanky from her bag, wiped her nose and eyes, took a shaky breath.

'No, I've racked my brains. We've no relatives round here, we're a small family. I'm so worried, it's just not like him. Will you look for him?' Her eyes were pleading.

'Mrs Hobbs, there's so little to go on. If Martin wants to stay missing, he will.'

'But you'll try?'

'Look, I can ask around a bit. A lot of youngsters drift into Manchester initially... but after a month... If I don't get any leads in the first couple of days, I really don't think it would be worth pursuing. You'd be wasting your money.'

'Thank you.' The hanky came out again.

'I need a recent photo.'

'Yes.' She fumbled in her bag. 'I'm afraid I haven't any good ones. We had a fire you see, last year. The lounge got the worst of it, the albums...'

She handed me two snapshots and a newspaper clipping. Both photographs were outdoor shots, full-length, taken from a distance. In one, a slight dark-haired boy in school uniform stood by a bus-stop; in the other, the same figure, in a waxed jacket, sat at the edge of some water surrounded by fishing tackle.

'That's up at Lostock. Rumworth Reservoir,' she said. 'He liked it there.' It was a better shot of the reservoir than it was of Martin.

The newspaper cutting showed a smiling Martin holding up an eight pound carp. It was faded and grainy but it showed his face more clearly than either of the photos. There was an elfin look to him; pointed chin, slight nose, cap of dark hair. His face seemed lit up by that smile.

'I'll get copies done of these, then you can have them back.'

'I brought some money.' She fumbled with the clasp of her purse. Drew out an envelope. Cash. A thousand pounds.

'This is far too much,' I protested.

We wrangled for a while. She insisted I keep the money and, if I did end up resigning after two or three days, I could send her the difference. Oh, well. It'd be a pleasant surprise for the assistant bank manager, with whom I had such a lively exchange of letters.

I made a note of Mrs Hobbs' phone number and told her I'd be in touch early the following week, unless I had any news before then. She thanked me about twenty times on the way to the door. I began to wonder whether she might have been Martin's problem, finding it hard to let him go, not knowing how to give him the space to grow up and away from her. Perhaps. But, for now, my task was to find out where he'd gone, not why he'd left.

I jotted down a few starting points; hostels, his school, the reservoir at Lostock, Manchester. Impressive, eh? I rang my friend Chris, who works in the housing department and, after the usual exchange of pleasantries, asked her to give me a list of the hostels in the city, particularly any popular with young people. And any other places she knew of where a runaway might end up. She was about to start a meeting and promised to pop round after work with the information I wanted.

I rang St. Matthew's High School to check what time lunch was. It might be tricky trying to book appointments with form teachers, trying to establish over the phone what lessons Martin had liked best. I reckoned the best bet would be to just turn up unannounced, ask around the staff room and the playground. People would give more away if they were caught unawares. No time to provide neat cameos of the truth. It'd be Monday before I could get up there but the hostels would be open all weekend.

I looked bleakly at the drying ceiling. The remaining walls were begging to be given the same treatment but I'd lost my momentum. I'd try and find it again some time next week. There'd be no chance over the weekend. Some activities don't go with children and decorating's one of them.

I shut up shop and left a note on the Dobson's kitchen table apologising for the appalling smell. The fumes seemed to have risen through the house with a vengeance, strong enough to make my eyes water.

After nipping home for a bite to eat, I swapped my Mini for my pushbike and hurried to deposit the money in the bank. I was certain to be mugged before I got there. Couldn't everyone tell I was carrying a grand in my rucksack? A thousand pounds. When I draw money out, they always trot off to check the computer while I sweat it out, trying not to look worried. This time I expected a little respect and admiration. A smile perhaps, a financial nod and a wink. No such look. Bland indifference. Perhaps they sensed the money wasn't truly all mine – not yet – probably not ever, if the case was as fruitless as I expected.

I needed photocopies of Martin's photographs. There was a photocopier at the library. The library was shut. Industrial action. The council had promised to regrade the staff years before; the staff were still waiting. And fed up to the back teeth. So was I.

I cycled over to the newsagent's that had a photocopier and got five of each of the photos and ten enlargements of the newspaper cutting. It was time to go and collect Maddie from nursery school. My working day was over. Paid work, that is. The second shift was just beginning.

CHAPTER THREE

Home is a large, slightly shabby Victorian semi in Withington, south Manchester. Solid red brick with crumbling stained glass, high ceilings, big rooms and a wonderful garden. Withington houses a mix of people; families, students, workers from Christie's hospital. The area has an old-fashioned swimming pool, a library, a health-food shop and its very own fleapit-style cinema.

Maddie and I share the house with Ray and his little boy, Tom. It's a strictly platonic arrangement. We rent the attic flat out to a lodger.

Tom's a year younger than Maddie, a fact he's never allowed to forget. He's developed the resilience of a second child. The four of us get along pretty well, though Ray and I have our moments, a bit like the kids. Just like the kids. Resentment and squabbling, usually over the chores. Ray sulks, I bully, he flies off the handle and flounces off to do whatever hasn't been done (it's always a one-way nag) and peace is restored. Life is humdrum, domestic. We take turns babysitting but neither of us paints the town red when unleashed. We just shuffle along to the local for a couple of pints with old friends. Every few months Ray meets a new woman and takes to wearing aftershave and trimming his moustache. But it never seems to amount to much and he appears more or less content with his lot. He potters around, building furniture in the cellar, which is a labour of love rather than an economic proposition, and spends hours hunched over his computer. Ray's doing a part-time computing course at Salford Tech. He hopes it'll help him earn a decent income. To date, all it's generated is a lot of indecent language.

I made tea for Tom and Maddie and let them eat it picnic-style in the garden, then slung some vegetables into a pan with half a jar of Nazir's Vindaloo Sauce for Ray and I to eat later. Chris arrived in the gap before bedtime. We sat in the kitchen, tea in hand.

'How's the new lodger?' she asked, raising her eyes heavenwards.

'Don't ask.'

'That bad?'

'I think so. No sign of improvement. He's away till Thursday. But then... we're going to have to do something. We can't go on like this. It's getting so I dread coming into the kitchen in case he's brewing up. It's your fault,' I rounded on Chris. 'If you hadn't moved out, we wouldn't have ended up with him.'

Chris giggled. 'I've got the stuff you wanted.' She foraged in a battered briefcase and drew out a large manila envelope. Inside were lists of hostels.

'These are the two direct access ones: the Direct Access Centre and Peterloo. I've marked them with an asterisk. They take people straight off the street, always keep a few beds free, sort people out with Welfare Advice the next day, try and get them into a B & B. The rest are the general hostels, men's and women's; some are church-run. Most of them expect payment, unlike the direct access ones. What do you want them for?'

'I'm on a case, missing person. He left home with no money, nowhere to go, as far as his mother knows. It's possible he came to Manchester, stayed in a hostel. I can check these... '

'No chance,' Chris interrupted. 'They won't tell you anything. It's confidential.'

'But if I explain...'

Chris shook her head. 'It doesn't matter, they have to protect people. No-one's given that information.'

'But all I need to know is whether he's stayed in any of the hostels, nothing else.'

'They can't tell you that, Sal. They won't even tell family. It's a strict rule. It has to be.'

'Shit!'

'C'mon,' Chris remonstrated, 'if they start giving out that sort of information, no-one would trust the hostels...'

'I know, I know... I didn't think. It's just, how am I supposed to start looking? I don't even know if he came to Manchester.' I cleared away the mugs. 'What about kids who don't use the hostels? Are there any places they regularly sleep out?'

'Well, we haven't got a cardboard city or anything like that. There used to be quite a lot of people under the arches, round Ardwick and down Whitworth Street in town. The council have got heavier on people sleeping rough; they don't like to admit it still goes on. There's still a bit of squatting, too, mainly in the old buildings in town – warehouses, places that are waiting demolition or re-development.'

'I suppose I'll just have to ask around. Thanks anyway. At least I didn't go making a fool of myself trying to get blood out of a stone.'

'Be careful. Visitors aren't exactly welcome. A lot of those kids have good reason for leaving home, but there's no provision for them. They're constantly hassled by the police; after all, a lot of them have to thieve or beg to get by. They might not take kindly to anyone snooping around.'

'Point taken. I'll be careful.'

Later, when Ray had put the kids to bed and we'd eaten, I wandered into the garden to clear up the toys. It was still light, though the cloudy sky threatened rain. I spent an hour staking up straggling carnations and gathering up mammoth brown slugs that had been munching their way through my bedding plants. I dropped them in the beer traps. The traps had been fairly successful but had begun to smell appalling. I'd have to clean them out and replenish them. Tomorrow. By the time I'd finished, a light rain had begun to fall along with darkness.

I climbed into a hot bath and soaked the lilac paint from my hair. The weekend stretched ahead with its pattern of chores and outings. Martin Hobbs was on hold till Monday. I wondered where he was sleeping tonight. Somewhere safe and dry, or out there in the warm wet rain?

CHAPTER FOUR

St. Matthew's was a redbrick Victorian school which had been added to, over the years, with an assortment of prefabs and a single-storey extension. Boys and girls in maroon and grey uniforms swarmed over every available inch of playground. Parking the car took some manoeuvring. Adolescents seem to move at two speeds; manic or catatonic. I made liberal use of my horn but half of them seemed to have some sort of death wish. I managed not to fulfil it.

I asked a huddle of boys on the entrance steps the way to the staff room. One of them offered to show me the way. We walked through endless corridors strewn with pupils and adorned with displays of work. En route, I let slip that I wanted to talk to Martin Hobbs' form teacher. He shrugged his shoulders.

At the staffroom door, I knocked and entered. The room was cramped. Low pvc chairs surrounded coffee tables. At the far end of the room, the smokers sat. Open shelving lined all four walls and papers spilt from every nook and cranny. Piles covered the coffee tables too. I approached the nearest group. Half-a-dozen women eating Pot Noodles, sandwiches and fruit. A couple were marking exercise books at the same time.

'Excuse me, I'm looking for Martin Hobbs' form teacher.'

'What year's he in?' one of the Pot Noodles asked me.

'Fifth, I think. He's sixteen.'

'Five Delta – Russ O'Brien – the one with the beard, in the corner.'

'Thanks.'

Russ O'Brien was a smoker. Pipe. Eyes closed, feet on the table. Stout, hairy. Looked a bit like a mountain climber.

'Mr O'Brien?'

He opened one eye, realised I wasn't a pupil and opened the other. Slid his feet from the table and sat up in his chair.

'Yes?'

'Hello.' I sat down on the chair next to him. 'I wanted a word about Martin Hobbs.'

'Yes?' He loaded the word with caution, sizing me up.

'Martin's been reported missing. His family have asked me to make a few enquiries on their behalf.'

'I see.' His eyes narrowed slightly and he re-lit his pipe.

'How long is it since Martin was in school?'

'Have you any identification? After all,' he spread his hands, 'I've only your say-so.' I blushed and fished in my jacket for one of the cards I always carry. I brushed off the fluff and crumbs and handed it over.

'Mmmm.' He wasn't impressed. I know it's only a simple photocopy job, no colours, no trendy graphics, but it states my name, number and business. He sighed and turned over the card, sighed again. I felt like I'd handed in the wrong homework.

'You can ring Mrs Hobbs if you want to confirm my identity.'

I was getting rattled by his attitude.

'It's okay,' he smiled. It wasn't much of an improvement.

'Just testing. Well, Martin's not been in for a month or so. I asked the secretary to ring home after a couple of weeks. Family said he'd left. End of story.'

'Did Martin ever say anything to you, give you any idea?...'

He laughed. 'Martin wouldn't say boo to a goose. Chronically shy.'

'Friends?'

He grimaced and sucked on his pipe. 'Not really. Bit of an oddbod, really. Tended to get left with the other spare parts, you know. Could try Barry Dixon or Max Ainsworth. He usually had to sit next to one or the other of them in his classes.'

'Where can I find 'em?'

'Barry'll be in the library – back of main building, then ask. Bright as they come and twice as loopy. Genius. No social skills, you'll see what I mean. Don't know where you'll find young Ainsworth. Hiding, no doubt. Still, that shouldn't bother you, eh? Elementary, my dear.' He gave a wheezy laugh. I smiled but I wasn't amused.

'Did Martin have any favourite subjects? Any other teachers he might have confided in?'

'Nope. He scraped through a couple of his mocks, GCSEs. Didn't shine at anything. Kept his head down. Could ask Julia over there,' he waved his pipe. 'The skinny one. Religious studies, encourages the wall-flowers, stands up for the underdog. Bit of a social worker.'

Julia wasn't much help. She confirmed Martin's shyness, described him as a loner and rued the fact that he'd never confided in her in or out of the classroom.

I made my way back to the school library. It was pretty full. Exams, I suppose. I was directed to the small cubicles at the back of the room. There I discovered Barry Dixon. When he began to talk, I realised what Russ O'Brien had been getting at. The boy's speech was spattered with asides, tangents, classical and philosophical references and quotations. He also spoke incredibly fast, like Patrick Moore on speed. He only ever broke eye-contact to blink and he broke all the rules about personal space, so I felt as though he was hemming me up against the wall of the tiny cubicle. I asked Barry if he knew where Martin had gone, if he knew why he was unhappy and if he'd ever talked of a place or people he'd like to visit. I drew three blanks in amongst the barrage of chatter.

Max Ainsworth had everything to attract the bullies. His face was raw with acne, he wore thick glasses and a brace, he was lanky and round-shouldered. He sat alone on a bench in a quieter area of the playground.

I explained why I was there and began my questions. Max thought before replying and seemed to know a great deal more about Martin than Barry Dixon had. It struck me that Barry was oblivious to other people, locked in his academic world. Max had the more common ability to hold a conversation where you take turns speaking.

'Do you know why he left home?'

'He was fed up with it. He never said much, just used to say he'd leave home soon as he was sixteen.'

'Where would he go?'

'Dunno. Try and get a job, I suppose. Not easy.'

'No. Did he ever mention other friends, places he might stay?'

'No, he was very quiet. Fishing. That was his big thing. He'd talk about that. I went with him a few times, Dean Clough, Rumworth. It was alright but I didn't have all the gear. Bit boring really. He were good at it. Won competitions and that.'

'Why was he fed up at home? What were his parents like?'

'Dunno, never went round. He came to mine a few times.'

I reckon Max was the nearest thing to a friend Martin had. I gave him one of my cards and asked him to get in touch if he thought of anything else, or if he heard from Martin.

'Like telly,' he flashed a smile. Then his voice filled with concern. 'Do you think he's alright?'

'Yes.' Reassurance came automatically. I hadn't really considered whether Martin could be in trouble, he'd not shown any leaning towards crime before... and teenage suicides don't usually leave home to escape. 'Do you?'

Max shifted on the bench. 'S'pose so, it's just...' he paused. 'There was this one time... he was getting really riled... they were giving him a hard time,' he nodded towards the kids in the playground, 'and he just went mad, lost it completely. He nearly killed this guy. Had his head, banging it against the floor, there was blood everywhere. We had to drag him off. He was in a daze, like he didn't know what he'd done. They laid off him after that. Passed it round he was a bit of a nutter.'

'Do you think he was?'

'No. It was just that once. Rest of the time he was just quiet. Scared the shit out of me, I can tell you, seeing him like that.'

'Wasn't he disciplined?'

Max shook his head. 'No-one reported it. Gibson went to hospital, his mates took him, said he'd fallen off a wall or summat like that. Martin was back the next day like it had never happened.'

I got caught in heavy traffic driving back to Manchester. I always come in through Salford, our neighbouring city, and there was only one lane open due to repair work.

The sun shone and it was hot in the car. I wound the window down and mentally crossed off my list as we edged slowly forward. It wasn't a long list. I could ask around up at Martin's old fishing haunt, though I suspected that anglers were a solitary breed. And I could wander the streets of Manchester, in search of other young runaways. See if anyone recognised Martin's photo. It was a long shot but I didn't have much option. I didn't exactly relish the prospect of trawling round town for the young homeless, so I decided to get it over and done with as soon as possible. I hadn't time to fit it in before picking the kids up but I'd do it first thing the following morning. And on Wednesday I'd go fishing...

CHAPTER FIVE

It was a June morning, just like the good old days. Not a cloud in sight, warm sun, blossom. But nobody relied on it. As I drove into town, I noticed everyone sported rolled up umbrellas. And most of the old folk were still in winter coats and hats. It was going to take more than this to convince them that summer was on its way.

I parked in a side street off Piccadilly Gardens, more of a back alley than a street. I hoped it was small enough to miss regular visits from the traffic wardens. I threaded my way through the débris that littered the alley. Rubbish from the clothing wholesalers who occupied most of the old buildings. Here and there, a pile of ripped bin-bags spilt out bones and vegetable peelings, marking the back entrance to the occasional restaurant. Tuesday must be bin-day.

I wandered through the gardens to Piccadilly Plaza. The row of shops faced the bus terminus. It was one of the busiest parts of town but had always had a seedy, run-down feel. Most of the shops were discount stores, selling tacky goods at give-away prices. Or charity shops, Oxfam and Humana. Above the parade rose the ugly Piccadilly complex; hotel, radio station, electronic billboards. It was an area I shopped in regularly (buying second-hand clothes rather than new tat) and I'd often seen youngsters begging here.

I was in luck, or so I thought at the time. A couple of lads were sitting quietly in the entrance to one of the empty shops. A cardboard sign announced they were hungry and homeless. In an old Kentucky Fried Chicken carton they'd collected a handful of coins. Hardly enough for a chicken drumstick, let alone a decent meal.

'Can I talk to you for a minute?'

The boy on the left sniggered, dug his fingers deeper into his anorak pockets.

'What about?' I judged the boy who spoke to be older, eighteen or so. He had a savage crew-cut and baby-blue eyes. 'You making a documentary or summat?'

His friend erupted into childish giggles.

'No, I'm looking for a friend of mine. He's missing. I wondered if you'd seen him?' I pulled out the photo of Martin with the carp. I'd cropped off most of the fish. Blue Eyes barely glanced at it and shook his head. He passed it to Giggler who seemed to find it hilarious.

'You got any change?' Blue Eyes nodded at the carton. With a rush of embarrassment, I realised I hadn't any money on me. I knew a cheque wouldn't be any good to them.

'I'm sorry. I came out without any money.'

'Great,' he sneered. The younger boy was beginning to roll the photo into a tube. I held out my hand and took it back.

'He went missing about a month ago. His name's Martin, Martin Hobbs. I heard he was in Manchester.'

'Big place,' said Blue Eyes aggressively.

An old woman stopped beside us and fumbled in her purse for change. She dropped some silver into the box then hurried away.

'Is there anywhere else you know I could look? Any squats you know about?' Blank stares. 'Look, there'd be a reward for useful information.'

'How much?' Blue Eyes was interested, if sceptical.

'Well, it'd depend on what it was...' I faltered.

'Fuck this. C'mon.' He scooped up the tray and leapt to his feet. Giggler followed suit.

'Twenty quid for a definite lead, if I could talk to someone who'd seen him.' Blue Eyes nodded. 'Here's my card, just ring...'

'Yeah, right... "just ring",' he mimicked my voice.

They began to walk briskly away.

'And the photo,' I screeched. People turned to look. I ran after them and thrust it towards them.

'You might need it... ' I tailed off. I felt embarrassed. I hadn't a clue whether they'd met Martin Hobbs or not, whether twenty quid was too little or too much to offer, whether they thought I was a plain-clothes police officer or a social worker. But I recognised the look of contempt on the face of the older one. He took the photo and slid it into his back pocket.

With burning cheeks, I scurried back to the car. I gathered my thoughts and reined in my emotions for a few minutes before setting off. When it came down to it, I didn't like hostility. I wanted everyone to be nice and friendly, especially to me. The people I'd just met had plenty to feel hostile about; they were hardly going to warm to a middle-class nosy-parker who hadn't even the common decency to contribute to the day's takings. My ears burned afresh. I cursed a bit. Eased my shoulders down from my ears and started the engine.

I called at Tesco's on my way back, filled a trolley and wrote out a cheque which cleared out any money I'd made on the case so far. I just had time to unpack the shopping, put on a load of washing and tidy the kitchen before collecting Maddie from Nursery School. She was tired and bad-tempered. We argued about who would fetch her coat, then about who would carry her lunch box and the letter notifying me of another outbreak of head-lice. I began to itch. I pulled her, sobbing, to the car. A couple of other parents flashed me sympathetic smiles.

It's not far to the Social Services nursery where Tom goes. The places are like gold dust, but Tom qualified as Ray is a single parent on low-income. It's a lovely place and Tom thrives on the contact with other children. He wandered out to meet me, clutching a thickly-daubed painting.

'Mrs Costello?' The woman who addressed me was new on the staff and hadn't worked out the relationships yet. Maddie sneered.

'Hello, I'm Sal Kilkenny, I share a house with Tom and his Dad.'

'Right.' She didn't let it throw her. 'We've a trip planned next week, to the museum at Castlefield, if you could fill in the slip and return it.' She handed me the form letter.

'Thanks.'

Once home, Maddie headed straight for the television. Tom followed and within seconds the squabbling started.

'Be quiet!' Maddie's voice was loud enough to wake the dead. 'I can't hear, be quiet.'

I rushed into the lounge.

'He's brumming too much,' she complained, her face pure outrage.

'Come on Tom.' I scooped up his cars and took them into the kitchen. Tom followed, dragging the battered Fisher Price garage after him. He brummed happily away. I watched him for a while. At what age do kids get labelled? When does a quiet child become chronically shy? Had Martin Hobbs played happily like Tom, absorbed in an imaginary world? Had he hated school, shrinking from other children? And what about Barry Dixon? When had he developed his strange quirks and mannerisms? Had his mother noticed? Had she encouraged his clever ways with words, or feared them? Would Tom and Maddie turn out happy, at ease with other people, leave home when the time was right, or were either of them already heading for troubled times, loneliness, rebellion?

I scoured the house with a black bin-liner, collecting rubbish. I left it by the back door and put the kettle on. I never drank the tea. Kids seem to be born with an innate instinct for knowing when you're about to start a hot drink. Since Maddie's arrival my tea-drinking had been transformed from a revitalising ritual to a series of lukewarm or clapcold disappointments.

'Mummeee!'

She was in mortal danger. I flew into the lounge.

'I've got a splinter,' she wailed.

'Where? Show me.'

'In my finger.'

'Let me see.'

'No, no.' She was hysterical.

It took ten minutes to get a look at it and a further five to reach a compromise over treatment. Cream and plaster till bedtime and if it didn't come out in the bath, then, and only then, would tweezers be used. Maddie has a great imagination and a very low pain threshold. On the way back to my cup of tea, I fell over Tom and the contents of the bin-bag. He'd laid out a neat trail of refuse from the back door, along the passage and into the kitchen.

'Dustbin man,' he beamed. I cleared up while he threw a tantrum. He stopped when I brought out the chocolate chip cookies. Bribery works.

I sat down with a fresh cup of tea when the phone rang. Maddie made no move to answer it.

'Shit.' I slammed my cup down.

'Hello.' I tried to keep the irritation from my voice.

'What's eating you?'

I'd failed. 'Diane. Oh, kids.' My old friend Diane hasn't got children but I make sure she has a fair idea of the trials of motherhood.

She laughed. 'Just checking you're still on for tonight.'

'Yes.' We were going for a drink. 'See you in there, about nine.'

My spirits were raised. There was nothing like a good natter with Diane to put things in perspective and take me out of my own little world. The kids began to argue again.

'Only two hours,' I reminded myself, 'they'll be asleep and I'll be out.'

CHAPTER SIX

Diane was ensconced in one of the cosy corner seats when I arrived at the pub. Half-way between her house in Rusholme and mine in Withington, it's one of the few locals that hasn't been done up to appeal to lager drinkers. But it's still respectable enough for husbands to bring their wives on the weekly night out. No spit and sawdust. Warm, quiet, dull if you like. I like.

After buying a pint of hand-pumped Boddington's, I slumped into the seat next to Diane and sighed theatrically.

She raised her glass. 'Cheers.'

'Cheers.' I took a long drink. 'Ah, that feels better.' I didn't just mean the alcohol. Escape. The prospect of two uninterrupted hours stretching ahead. Time to talk, to listen. Time to be me with the best company.

Diane grinned. She had a slow, lazy grin. Like a Cheshire cat. It lingered in her eyes long after it had faded from her lips.

'I like your hair.' It was a dark golden colour, shot through with streaks, cut short and asymmetrical.

'I'm going off it,' she said. It was my turn to grin. Diane changes her hairstyle every month. Perhaps it's hormonal.

'Go on,' she said, 'you first. You look like you need it.'

'Nothing dramatic. Just work, and kids. I've got a new case.'

'More matrimonials?'

'No.' I took another draught of beer. 'Missing person. Runaway boy.' I told her all about it, finishing up with my meeting with Giggler and Blue Eyes. 'I think they thought I was a plain-clothes police officer or something.'

'No chance,' Diane snorted.

'What d'you mean?'

'You're too messy.'

'What?'

'Your hair, shoes. I bet you had your trainers on, didn't you?'

'So?' I bristled.

'Even undercover, the police look neat and clean. Nice manageable hairstyles, polished shoes or perfect trainers.'

I held up my foot. The trainer was scuffed and stained. The stitching was frayed, the laces grubby.

'Well, they didn't like me.'

'So,' she stretched out her hands, 'they've no taste. Another?' She picked up her glass.

'Not yet.'

Diane walked over to the bar. She was a big, fat woman. She insisted on using that description. After twenty years of being miserable on diet after diet, she'd rebelled. Joined a group formed after the publication of *Fat Is A Feminist Issue* and had come to like her size and to flaunt it. Tonight, she sported a bright turquoise and gold knee-length tunic with gold leggings. She walked gracefully, light-footed for all her weight.

I stretched and twisted in my seat. My left shoulder ached. It's the side I carry the kids on, the side that tenses up when I drive, when I'm worried.

Diane set her drink down and tossed me a bag of

nuts.

'Well,' she pronounced, 'maybe this'll be the one that got away.'

I grimaced.

'You can't expect to solve every case, can you?' She opened her own peanuts and picked a couple out.

'But that bothers me...'

'Perfectionist.'

'No, it's not that. If I'm taking the money, I want to make it worthwhile. Get some sort of result.' I tugged at the packet of nuts. The plastic stretched but didn't tear.

'But if this lad's disappeared, doesn't want to be found, then maybe that's the result. Missing without trace or whatever they call it. Anyway, there's loads of times when people shell out money for no result.'

'Such as?' I tried using my teeth on the packet.

'Estimates for work, eye tests when nothing's changed, structural surveys; I had to fork out for three of those before I found a place that wasn't falling down.'

I grunted and made another attack on the peanuts. Shit. Salted nuts cascaded around the table and floor. I salvaged what I could.

'Anyway,' I sighed, 'there's that, and the phone isn't exactly hot with clients, plus the children were driving me...'

'Don't talk to me about children,' Diane groaned.

I bit my tongue. Our relationship has weathered the difficulties of me having a child and she choosing not to, but it hasn't always been easy. There've been times when motherhood has dominated my thoughts and feelings. When I've needed to talk about all the contradictions. But not with Diane. She's happy with an occasional update. She has a rough idea of how hard it can be and she's glad she's not a mother.

'It's Ben,' she explained. 'We had a talk.'

Ben and Diane had been going out for over a year. Their relationship had started off casually through a lonely hearts column and had gained in intensity. At New Year, Ben had suggested that they live together. Diane had declined. Since then things had been just as intense but edged with the unspoken agenda of commitment.

'He wants children?'

'He's always denied it before,' she began, 'or at least said he wasn't bothered either way. But, well, his sister's just produced one and he's all gooey-eyed about it. Wants to drag me along to the christening.'

'You don't want to go?'

'It's in Budleigh-Salterton, for Christ's sake. Can you imagine it? Hours getting there and back. Church, family. I spent years getting away from all that. Why can't he just leave things as they are?'

'Maybe he wants to know where it's going.'

'Why do we have to be going anywhere? It's a relationship, not a bloody day trip.'

'Things get stale, Diane, if there's no change on the horizon, no events looming.'

'It's been fine up till now.'

I raised my eyebrows.

'Oh, I know he was disappointed about not living together,' she retorted, 'but I thought he understood my reasons. Now he seems to be getting all broody. Not that he'll admit it.'

We carried on in this vein through another couple of rounds, till chucking out time.

I was tucked up and dreaming before midnight.

The bell kept ringing for last orders. Someone was

shouting my name. I couldn't work out who. The pub was deserted. I opened my eyes and Ray appeared round the edge of my door.

'Sal, phone.'

'What time is it?'

'Middle of the bloody night.'

Blinking in the light of the hall, I picked up the receiver.

'Hello?'

'That lad you're looking for. I found someone who met him.'

'Who is this?' My brain was still befuddled.

'You said there was twenty quid in it. Bring the dosh, I'll tell you his name.'

'Now?'

'Yeah, Chorlton Street Bus Station.' Click.

I longed to crawl back under the covers. Instead, I splashed water on my face, pulled on yesterday's clothes, left a note for Ray and went out into the night.

Once outside, a tremor of excitement enlivened me. This was more like it; the beginning of a trail. The night was cool, still. Dew on the car. Orange street-lamps lit empty roads. I passed maybe a handful of cars on the way to town. No queues, no crazy drivers, just the way I like it. I stopped at a cashpoint and got my hands on some real money.

Parking at Chorlton Street was no problem. The coach station was a glorified bus shelter, several aisles under a roof. Gloomy even on the best days. That night it looked positively menacing. Any excitement I'd had drained away. I felt the familiar clenching in my belly, buzzing in my ears. *That distorted face, spittle on his lips. My own voice, squeaky with fear, begging. The knife shaking in his hand.* I fought to regain control over my breathing, in and out, slow deep breaths.

Dragged into my mind a picture of calm and peace. The visualisation exercise that the therapist had taught me. After a couple of minutes, I was capable of getting out of the car.

Blue Eyes was sitting alone on a bench by the shuttered ticket office, a can of Pils in his hand. I sat down beside him.

'Hello.' I kept my voice steady.

'You got the dosh?'

'Yes.' I handed over two tenners. He grunted.

'Bloke called J.B. He's seen that lad.'

'Martin Hobbs?'

'Yeah. He recognised the photo. He put him up for a bit.'

'Where can I find J.B.?'

'He's squatting.' He took a swig from the can. 'One of those old warehouses off Great Ancoats, back of Piccadilly, somewhere round there.' It wasn't exactly precise information.

'How did you find him?'

'He was on the ramp, same time as me.'

'On the ramp?'

'Station approach.' He said it derisively. His blue eyes were bloodshot now. He looked pale, ill.

A sound of drunken singing carried over from the side street. Leader of the Pack. Someone was trying for harmonies.

'How'll I recognise him?'

'Lanky bloke, half-caste, wears a flat cap, got a dog.'

'How old?'

'I dunno.' He was irritated, drank from the can again. 'Twenty, twenty-one?' He stood up and drained the can, tossed it down.

'Where will you go now?' I asked.

'What's it to you?' He walked away.

'Thanks,' I said. I don't know if he heard me.

I wasn't about to start creeping round old warehouses. J.B. could wait till tomorrow. But I was pleased. At last something was moving. Someone had met Martin, might even know where he was now. As for me, there was only one place I wanted to be and it didn't take me long to get there. Bed.

CHAPTER SEVEN

On Wednesdays and Thursdays Ray is in charge of the kids: Breakfast, school run, bedtime, the lot. I lay in bed for all of ten minutes, luxuriating in that small sense of freedom. The smell of toast and clinking of pots drifted up from below. In the old days, I'd have burrowed back under the duvet till lunch-time, but Maddie had buggered up my sleep patterns for good. Ray's mum, Nana Tello (the kids shortened it from Costello), complained bitterly about waking at five o'clock and not being able to get back to sleep. I was heading for the same fate.

Maddie and Tom clattered up the stairs to yell goodbyes.

'Mummeee,' Maddie began, 'I don't want to go to school.' Her lower lip trembled.

'Well, you've got to. I'm going to work,' I slung back the covers and grabbed my dressing-gown, 'Ray's going to college and you're going to school.' To eliminate further discussion, I picked her up and thundered downstairs, Tom at my heels. She was still giggling as Ray shepherded them out the door. An improvement on most mornings.

Over breakfast, I considered whether to ring Mrs Hobbs. I'd promised to be in touch early in the week. Best to wait until I'd met J.B. Hopefully, there'd be more to report.

I got the bus to town. Parking was a nightmare and I

didn't want to tempt fate too many times by doing it illegally. From Piccadilly Gardens it was about five minutes walk to the station. The long curving ramp had nose-to-nose taxis edging up and down and a constant procession of people moving along the broad pavement. I walked up to the station concourse and back a couple of times. No luck. I hovered outside the Blood Donor Clinic for a while, scanning the steady stream of people for a lanky man, of mixed race, with a cap and a dog.

An hour had passed. Maybe I was too early. If J.B. had somewhere safe and warm to sleep, perhaps he'd stay there well into the afternoon. If yesterday had been a good day, maybe he'd not appear at all today. If I stayed where I was much longer, the Clinic people would take me for a nervous donor and come out to see if I needed a little encouragement to face the needle. I shuffled along a bit to a tool shop. Spent a while looking at the weird and wonderful machines in the window. Ray would be in seventh heaven here. Lathes, saws, chisels. A carpenter's treasure trove.

My attention was diverted for a while by a cacophony of horns from the taxis. One of the drivers had abandoned his cab, thereby preventing everyone else from moving up closer to the station, and the next fare. The horns blasted out in disharmony for a full three minutes. Passers-by grinned at the scene. It smacked of continental cities. We British rarely use our horns communally. At last, a portly man emerged from nowhere and ran towards the vacant cab. He started it up, the horns fell quiet, the queue resumed its progress up the ramp.

Another walk up to the station. Piccadilly trains run south, down to London, Oxford, Rugby. You can tell. The station's much more upmarket than Victoria, where all the trains run north, bound for the hills and borders. Piccadilly sports a Tie-Rack, a Sock-Shop, chemist, florist, newsagent, several eateries. A fresh-ground coffee shop. Wooed by the scent of coffee, I ordered an expresso and pastry. It was noon. I was bored.

I set off back for the bus. Halfway there, I came across a young girl seated in the doorway of a Pool Hall. A small, tattered sign stated she was homeless. Pale face, rats tails hair, cheap, thin clothing. She was plaiting bracelets from brightly coloured wool. The sort that are imported by Traidcraft from Third world countries.

I put a pound in her hat.

'Ta.' She glanced up and smiled faintly.

'Excuse me, have you seen J.B.?'

'Huh?' She squinted against the brightness of the sky. She looked very young.

'J.B. Got a dog, flat cap.'

'Yeah,' she bit through the wool with her teeth, 'you just missed him. He's gone for chips.'

'Where?'

'Plaza, by the buses.'

I knew the place. Open all hours, cheap take-away. I ran all the way. I got a stitch and my heart beat too hard for comfort. A couple of women waited to be served. No man, no dog.

'You just serve a bloke with a dog?' I called to the guy at the hatch.

'Don't do dogs, Miss,' he grinned, 'we do hot dogs.' He cackled at his own joke.

'Wears a cap,' I persisted.

'Dog does?' More laughter. I gritted my teeth.

He nodded. 'You just missed him.'

I dodged between buses over the road to the

Gardens. The benches were full of people lunching in the open air. Formal flower beds were ablaze with wallflowers and pansies.

He was there. The dog lay at his feet. As I approached, the man sitting next to him rolled up his newspaper, picked up his briefcase and left. Great timing. I took his place.

'J.B.?'

'What?' He swung round to face me, his eyes narrowed with suspicion.

'I'm looking for Martin Hobbs. My name's Sal Kilkenny. I'm a private investigator. Someone said you knew Martin, you put him up for a while.'

'What do you want him for?'

'He's missing. His mother came to see me. She wants to know if he's alright.'

'That it?'

'What?'

'You're not gonna try and take him back or owt?'

'No.' I was emphatic. 'All I'm interested in is finding out if Martin's okay.'

'I dunno where he is.' He threw a chip to the dog, had one himself. He was guarded, but without the hint of aggression I'd felt when talking to Blue Eyes and Giggler. J.B. had the sort of bone structure that models are made of, attractive features, clear olive skin. Black hair hung down in ringlets at the back of his head. What I could see of the sides had been shaved. He wore an old donkey jacket, white shirt, faded jeans, DM's.

'But you did meet him? When did you last see him?'

'Look,' he crumpled the chip paper into a ball, 'I've got to get back.'

'Please.' I put my hand on his sleeve. 'I really need

to find out, just give me ten minutes.'

'I dunno,' he sighed. The dog lifted its head as if concerned. He stroked it.

'Listen, anything you tell me will remain confidential. I won't pass on your name or anything that could identify you. I'm not a social worker, I've no connection with the police. I'm simply trying to find out where Martin is and if he's okay, so his mum can stop driving herself crazy with worry. Just a few minutes?'

He thought it over. Smiled, a warm, easy smile.

'Okay. C'mon, Digger.' The dog sprang up and walked to heel as we made our way across the Gardens and up one of the side streets off Piccadilly itself.

Martin hadn't been in Manchester long when J.B. had seen him begging on Market Street. He'd watched the police caution him then gone over to talk to the boy. Martin had been sleeping rough. He already looked run-down. He had no money, no sleeping bag. J.B. had offered a place in his squat for a few nights. He made it clear it was to be a temporary arrangement. 'I like to have the place to myself, now and then.' Martin was a quiet and reserved guest. He slept most of the day and went out to get money at night. He refused to get any Welfare Advice. 'He thought they'd send him back. Anyway, you get fuck-all at his age unless you're on a scheme and you can't do that without an address.'

We'd arrived at the back of old warehouses off Great Ancoats Street. J.B. moved aside a part of the wooden fencing. I followed him through the gap. The yard was piled high with débris, old pallets, a shopping trolley, mattress, the shell of a car, fridges. Weeds grew waist-high. We clambered over the lot to a set of steps leading down to a cellar door. J.B. unlocked the door and we stepped into darkness. The stench of damp

38

and mildew caught at my throat. Nobody knew I was here. Could I trust J.B? Wasn't it a little suspicious, inviting me back to his squat? Buzzing in my ears. A flush of fear burned the nape of my neck. *Please, please. Spittle on his lip.* I stumbled and yelped.

'Take my hand,' he said. His hand was soft and warm, he gripped mine firmly. The contact reassured me. I shook off my anxiety. He led me through the gloom, then up more stairs and into dim light. We crossed a massive room, pillars lying where they had fallen amidst chunks of plaster, old tea-chests and broken tables. One wall of the room was windows, row upon row, thick with grime. Broken panes gave glimpses of blue sky. Up another set of stairs and along a door-lined corridor.

'This is it.' He stopped at one of the doors and unlocked it. After the desolation of the rest of the building, I was surprised at the cleanliness and care shown in this room. It had been painted white. On the floor lay an old floral carpet and against one wall was a huge sofa with a bright green bedspread thrown over it. A guitar leant against the arm. Opposite a television, a shelf with books and mementoes. In the far corner, beyond the sofa, there was a mattress and bedding. The wall nearest to the door was broken up by windows; half-way along was a sink, Calor gas cooker, pots and pans; beyond those, a table and a couple of chairs. Everywhere I looked, pinned up on the white background were pictures, line drawings, sketches. Mostly pen and ink or charcoal; faces, street scenes, landscapes. I walked closer.

'These are brilliant. They yours?'

'Yep.' He grinned and filled a kettle.

'This is Martin.' I pointed to the portrait. Head and shoulders. The look he'd captured was one of great sadness.

'He looks lonely, sad.'

'He was.' J.B. lit the stove and came over to the wall.

'Have you studied art?'

He shook his head. 'It's a hobby.'

'You could sell these.'

'I do, now and again. But I make more on the chalkies.'

'Chalkies?'

'Pavement drawings.'

'Mickey Mouse, Madonna.'

'Yeah,' he laughed. 'Get the kids and the mums pay up.'

'These are signed P.H. So is J.B. a nickname?'

'Tell you're a detective. Yeah, short for JCB. Used to like to drive 'em away in my younger days. Sort of stuck.' He went over and made mugs of coffee. Brought them over. We sat on the sofa. He began to roll a cigarette.

'So where was Martin going when he left here?'

'Dunno.'

'Didn't he say anything?'

'Someone had set him up.'

'How d'you mean?'

He sighed. 'That second week, Martin had more money. Bought clothes. He was on the streets but it wasn't just begging any more.'

'He was a rent boy?'

'Yeah. Plenty of lads drift into it. There's a lot of demand. It's tempting. Anyway, that last night, he came in, early hours it was, said he'd found a new place, someone was going to see him right. Talked about riding round in an Aston Martin, eating out every night.'

'You mean like a sugar daddy?'

40

'Yeah,' he lit his roll-up, 'or a pimp.'

'Was he happy about it?'

'Oh, yeah. Least on the surface. Excited, like it was his big break. Martin was soft as shit. It wouldn't take much to con him. Promises of this and that, next thing he knows he's standing by the bus station every night waiting to jump into cars, giving the dosh to some guy who'd beat him up soon as look at him.'

'But it might not have been a pimp?'

'Who knows.' The dog came over and draped itself over J.B.'s feet. 'Maybe he struck lucky. And I've not seen him doing business, not on the streets. Could be working the clubs. His mum's not gonna like it much, is she?'

'No. But it could be worse, I suppose.'

He raised an eyebrow.

'Oh, God. Well, if he was on crack or something.'

'He wasn't.' His tone was sharp. The dog pricked up its ears. 'I won't have it,' he explained. 'This place is clean. I was an addict, see, but I've been clean for three years now. I won't have it around.'

'Anyway, I'm not going to tell her anything until I've checked it out. It could just be a relationship.'

'Yeah,' J.B. nodded his head, 'and I could be the President of America an' all.'

'Could you ask around a bit? See if anyone's seen him? Heard where he is?'

'Okay.'

I pulled a fiver from my bag. 'I'd like to give you something for your time.'

He looked embarrassed, a slight flush to his olive complexion.

'Oh, go on. You're the only help I've had. Get a meal or something. Treat the dog.'

'Alright,' he grinned. 'You'll like that Digger, eh?'

The dog wagged its tail.

I gave him my card and a photograph of Martin. He pinned them on the noticeboard above the sink, amongst a collage of other bits of paper. He led me back down through the gloom of the building and out into the yard. I thanked him again. As we reached the fence, it was pushed back and the young girl I'd spoken to earlier climbed through.

'Hiya.' She bent to pat the dog. His girlfriend? Or another waif he was helping out?

'Bye then, and thanks.'

Another smile. The two of them set off towards the steps and I clambered back onto the street. J.B. had given me a lot to go on. I hoped with all my heart that he'd got it wrong.

CHAPTER EIGHT

My half-painted office cried out for completion. Its pleas fell on deaf ears. I rang Mrs Hobbs instead. She wasn't in. Did she work? It was only three o'clock. Not much point in trying again till after five. I wrote out some notes about the investigation so far; added up time and expenses.

I gazed at the narrow window. A fern and a couple of sturdy dandelions cut out most of the meagre light, but they couldn't obscure the fact that it was sunny out there. The walls needed painting. My garden needed attention. No contest. Walls would keep, bedding plants wouldn't.

It was a good decision. I weeded and trimmed, staked and tidied. Dug over a bed for planting, chatted to my perennials, filled an old chimney pot with verbena, pansies and lobelia. I even changed the slug traps, gagging at the stench as I carried each one gingerly to the cellar toilet and flushed the slimy contents away. The rhythm of the work, the scent of the earth, the sun on my back left me feeling pleasantly tired and relaxed.

It was nearly six when I put the tools away and rang Mrs Hobbs.

'Mrs Hobbs, Sal Kilkenny here.'

'Yes,' she spoke quickly, 'have you found him?'

'No, I'm sorry. But I do know he came to Manchester and I've met someone who put him up for a while.

Another...' I groped for a label; homeless person, runaway, boy, young man? '...lad. He hasn't seen Martin for a couple of weeks but he's going to ask around and get back to me. So far, that's all I've been able to find out.'

Silence.

'Mrs Hobbs?'

Snuffling. 'I'm sorry. I thought, I hoped...'

I spent a couple of minutes blathering on about how hopeful I was, how lucky we were to get any lead at all, reassuring her that Martin had been fine when last seen, etc. I'd be in touch as soon as I heard anything more. All the time I was wondering how I was going to tell her the truth, if it was the truth, that Martin was alive and well and on the game, or shacked up with a sugar daddy, at best. If that ever happened to Maddie...

Now what?

I played pirates with the kids for a while and when Ray gathered them up for bed, I went and sat in the garden. Surveyed my handiwork. Ray joined me there. He handed me a glass.

'Cocktail?'

'What's this in aid of?'

'Nothing.'

I sipped it. 'Mmm. What is it?'

'Daiquiri. Rum, ice, lime, sugar.'

'Nice. So?' I turned to him.

'So?' He was a lousy dissembler. Eyes shifted like jumping beans and even his moustache couldn't hide a twitch of embarrassment round the mouth. Ray's of Italian descent but, unlike your Italian stereotype, he's not prone to extravagant displays of emotions or outbursts of generosity. Cocktails were more than a friendly gesture.

'C'mon Ray, I know you. The cocktail has a deeper

meaning. Now, as far as I'm aware you're not about to move out or have a baby or get married, so what is it?'

'It's Clive.'

'Oh, no.' I groaned theatrically.

'He's back tomorrow. We've got to sort out what we're going to say.'

'Maybe we should just give it a bit longer.'

'It's been four months and it's getting worse. The guy's a total prat.'

'We could change the locks,' I giggled. 'Oh, I don't know, he did make an effort after the last meeting.'

'Yeah, for all of twenty-four hours.'

'It's not just the practical things though, is it?' I turned to Ray.

'Nope.' He sipped his drink.

'I mean, even if he remembered to clear up after himself and keep the music down...'

'...and stop drinking all the milk, and treat the kids like human beings...'

'...and pay the rent on time,'

'He'd still be a prat,' Ray concluded.

'What is it though?' I asked. 'What defines his pratness?'

'Pseudy, unreliable, doesn't like women for starters.'

'He seemed so nice when he came round about the advert.'

'And he was the only person we'd seen,' Ray reminded me, 'and you were panicking about the rent.'

I squirmed. 'He gives me the creeps. You know, he can't talk about anyone without putting them down. It's horrible.' I drained my glass. 'What are we going to say? Sorry Clive, we want you to move out. We think you're a prat.'

'We could say we don't like his attitude,' said Ray.

'I'd rather not have to give any reasons. It could

just become a horrible slanging match. It'd be so embarrassing, Ray, and hurtful to him. We should simply ask him to leave.'

'What if he won't? I can imagine him digging his heels in.'

We carried on the conversation over dinner, bitching and worrying. The upshot was that we agreed to tackle Clive some time over the coming weekend. Give him a month's notice, be vague about reasons but, if pressed, explain we wanted someone more suited to communal living.

Ray went out that evening. Quiz night at the local. I'd gone along once to see what the attraction was. It was a dead loss for me, as nearly half the questions were about sport, an activity I loathe.

I ran a hot bath and chucked in some scented oil. My shoulder was aching and my back stiff from honest toil. I rubbed olive oil into the scar above my left breast. I'd been stabbed. My one and only murder investigation. I'd unwittingly stumbled close to solving it and the murderer had tried to silence me. The memory still panicked me. I was jumpier these days. I avoided violent plays and films. For a while, even the sight of knives in the kitchen had brought me out in a sweat.

I slipped into the steaming water, goose-pimples erupting in surprise at the heat.

After the stabbing, Diane and Ray had tried very hard to persuade me to change my job. I was tempted. Why go looking for trouble? On the other hand, I knew that if I gave it all up it would be like giving in to the threat of violence. And how many other things would I stop doing in order to feel safe? Stop going out at night, visiting new places, answering the door? In the end, I got some counselling to help with the panic and to decide on my future. It helped. I'd chosen to work even if that meant being scared some of the time. I wanted to be a survivor, not a victim.

J.B. rang as I was getting dry.

'Look, I've been asking around. Talked to a couple of the lads. Martin's not on the patch. They'd know if he was doing business round here. Then one guy I ask, he clams up. Big silence. He was scared, shit scared.'

'Why?'

'Search me. Couldn't get shut of me fast enough. Kept saying he didn't know nothing and I'd better leave it alone. Now, he's a user...'

'You think it might be something to do with drugs?'

'Possible. There's some heavy stuff going down.'

'I know.' Guns were the new addition to the so-called drugs war in the city. People had been shot. Killed. Including two little boys. Whole estates had been labelled no-go areas, to the anger of the local residents.

'I'm gonna see who's going into the clubs tonight, see if anyone's heard anything. I'll ring you tomorrow.'

'Right.' Why was J.B. being so helpful? 'You don't have to do this, you know.'

'I know,' he said, 'but you got me thinking about Martin. He couldn't look out for himself; I'd like to know he was okay. Besides, I'm curious now,' he laughed. 'Gives me summat to do.'

'Keeps you off the streets?'

'Yeah.'

'Thanks J.B.'

'See ya.'

He was a nice guy. I wanted to get him something to show my thanks. Not just money, though I'd pay him for his time; he was doing the legwork twice as effectively as I could have done. No, something personal. Of course. A sketchbook, some charcoal or maybe a drawing pen. He'd like that.

CHAPTER NINE

J.B. didn't call that Thursday. I thought it was him when the phone rang at eight-thirty in the morning. I'd got a mouthful of toast and honey. I sluiced it down with tea.

It was a new client; once he'd established that he'd got the right number, he asked for an appointment.

'There's some work I'd like you to do.' He had a local accent, a slight lisp.

'Could I have your name, please.'

'Barry Smith.'

'When would be convenient for you?'

He wanted an appointment that afternoon. It suited me. We agreed on two o'clock. I gave him the address and directions to my office.

'Da-da!' I pirouetted into the kitchen and bowed.

'You're silly,' pronounced Maddie.

'Another job,' I said to Ray. 'Two cases at once. The big time.'

'We'll need it,' he said. 'Look at this.' He passed me the phone bill.

'Jesus Christ!'

'Aw,' said Maddie, 'shouldn't say that.'

'I know. Sometimes people say things they shouldn't when they get a nasty shock.' I turned to Ray. 'It's nearly twice as much. And look at these; eight long distance calls. He'll have to pay half of it.'

Ray nodded. 'Yep. Do we tell him before or after?'

'Who?' Maddie asked.

'Clive,' I explained.

'I like Clive.' Perverse creature.

'You don't,' I said, 'you never see him.'

'I do like him.'

'Because he gives you chocolates,' said Ray.

'And lollies.'

'Coats on.' I'd had enough of this. Clive's habit of giving the kids sweets had been on the list of complaints at our last meeting with him. He thought we were being petty. I ran through the dental health arguments.

'Well, if they brush their teeth afterwards...' he said.

'They don't, not unless they're frogmarched upstairs. You buy the sweets and we have to do the frogmarching.' What irritated me most was that he gave sweets instead of time or attention.

I devoted the morning to housework, ate a salad lunch in the garden and changed into my best work clothes. Blue needlecord pants and a large blue and cream print shirt.

I was surprised to find Jackie and Grant Dobson arriving home as I reached their house.

'Skiving off?'

'No chance,' groaned Jackie, reaching into the back of the car. 'Marking.'

'Exams already?'

'Internal,' said Grant. 'GCSEs next month...'

'Then A's,' Jackie added, straightening up, her arms full of folders. 'We've not seen you about much.'

'Thing's have been pretty slow,' I said, 'but they're looking up. I've one case on the go and someone's due at two to talk about another.'

I opened the door, while they lugged in piles of

books and papers, then went down to my room. I sorted out pen, paper and diary. My watch reached two-fifteen. I picked dead leaves off the geranium on the filing cabinet. Two-thirty. I hadn't even brought anything to read. I began to sort out my files, but gave up. There wasn't enough in there to warrant serious sorting. I labelled a new folder 'Martin Hobbs' and put in the sheets of paper I'd done. Two forty-five. At three-fifteen I gave up. Thanks a bunch, Barry Smith. Presumably he'd chickened out. If he did dare to get in touch again, I'd charge him for my wasted time.

Clive didn't appear. No word. Reliable as ever. No word from J.B. either. I couldn't make any headway until I heard from him. There didn't seem much point in pursuing any other direction, like chatting to anglers up at the reservoir at Lostock. Martin was moving in rather different circles now. No. All my eggs were in J.B.'s basket. If he didn't ring me, I'd have to go and see him.

I dropped the kids at nursery and drove into town. I knew of a shop where Diane bought some of her art materials, not far from J.B.'s squat. I bought a large sketchbook, charcoal, a drawing pen and ink. It cost three times as much as I'd expected. I almost put the pen and ink back. Sod it. J.B. was a gem and he'd never be able to afford this sort of stuff.

I reached the fence surrounding the warehouse. I wasn't sure how I was going to get into the building. J.B. wasn't likely to have a bell and the windows of his room looked out the other side, across the canal to Piccadilly station. If it was locked, I'd have to leave my packages and a note.

The cellar door was ajar. I waited while my eyes adjusted to the dark, then retraced the route up the stairs and across the large room. As I reached the next door, I heard a scuffling sound. Rats? I held my breath and listened. Called out. Whining. Digger.

I pushed the door. The dog barked and bared its teeth. Startled, I stood still, began talking in a low voice.

'Easy Digger, good dog. Where's J.B.?'

The dog dropped its aggressive pose quickly enough and followed me along the corridor to J.B.'s. The door was ajar. I knocked and called out. No answer.

He lay on the sofa, on his side. Jeans and T-shirt.

'J.B.'

Digger went and lay on the floor in front of the sofa. Whining.

J.B.'s face was slack and pale, mouth open. Conker brown eyes filmed over, staring. I touched his arm and flinched at the cold. I began to shake. There was a damp patch on his jeans around the crotch. The smell of ammonia. Streaks of yellow mucus from his mouth on his lower arm. A piece of cloth tied round it. An armband.

Whimpering. The sound came from a long way away. It was swamped by the beat of blood in my ears. I looked at the dog. He wasn't whimpering. I was.

I was still clutching the packages as I ran to find a phone. I found a policeman first. I tugged at his sleeve, trying to explain through chattering teeth that he must come with me, that someone was dead. I couldn't give him an address. Getting my own name out was hard enough. He had nice eyes, crinkles at the corners. He smelt of Palmolive soap. He talked into his walkie-talkie. I don't remember getting back to J.B.'s room.

Soon it was filled with people. Two uniformed officers, the one I'd met and a woman who sat beside me on the mattress. Two others in plain-clothes. One with a tan, glasses and a moustache; the other plump and florid.

I went over everything I knew about J.B., what I was doing here, what I knew about him, first with the uniformed officer, then again with the florid plain-clothes one. He had a fine network of red and purple capillaries across his face. Answering questions helped. Gave me something to concentrate on. Every so often I blanked out, lost track of everything.

Someone arrived with a camera and took photographs with a flash. Then another man arrived with a large bag and knelt down next to the sofa. Began looking over J.B.

'I think you can go now, Miss,' said the plump detective. 'We'll need to get in touch again.' I nodded. The policewoman helped me to my feet. 'We've got a car to take you home.'

'No.' My voice echoed round the room. 'No. There's no-one there.'

'To a friend perhaps?' he suggested.

Diane. Please be in. 'Yes, yes.' I turned towards the door, then back again. 'What happened?' I was bewildered.

'Looks like an overdose, Miss. There was a syringe next to the sofa.'

'But he didn't take drugs. He told me. He'd been clean for years.'

'We'll have to wait for the post-mortem of course but it looks pretty straightforward. Now...' he held out his arm to usher me towards the door.

'You're wrong,' I protested. 'He told me...'

'Addicts often lie, I'm afraid,' the man with the tan spoke up. 'And you didn't know him particularly well, did you?'

53

'But I'm sure...'

'We'll have to wait for lab reports, to be sure,' he continued, 'but he was known to us and we're not expecting any surprises.' His tone was sharp, final.

I shook my head. 'He wouldn't...' I insisted. But I couldn't say anymore. My mouth began to stretch with tears. No-one said anything.

'This yours, Miss?' The uniformed man held out the sketchbook. I nodded.

'Can someone move this bloody dog?' the man by the sofa snapped. Digger growled as the policeman stooped to shift him.

'What'll happen to him?' I said.

'We'll take him to the morgue from here,' the florid man answered. 'The pathologist will prepare a report establishing probable cause of death...'

'No,' I interrupted and began to giggle, 'I mean the dog.' I didn't know whether I was laughing or crying. The policewoman put her hand on my arm.

'We'll take care of that,' said the man with the moustache. 'He'll go to the pound...'

'Can I take him?' I don't even like dogs much. But he'd be put down unless someone rescued him. I had to rescue something from the situation. Glances were exchanged.

'Yes, Miss.'

In the car over to Diane's, my memories of J.B., our meeting, that phone call, were intercut with the image of his corpse. I clutched the sketchbook to me. Remembered the smile he'd given me when I praised his work.

We drew up outside Diane's terraced house. Digger followed me out of the car. The policewoman guided me up to the door and rang the bell. Diane opened the door.

'Sal!' She glanced from me to the policewoman, at the dog and back to me. Concern.

'What's the matter, what on earth's happened? Are you alright?' The gentle tone of her question did it.

I dropped the packages and covered my face with my hands. Tears spilled through my fingers. I was definitely not alright.

CHAPTER TEN

'I still can't accept it, Ray. He was adamant that he didn't use drugs.'

In the four days since J.B.'s death I'd made countless phone calls to the C.I.D. to find out what was happening. I'd finally established that a post-mortem had confirmed death due to a heroin overdose and that there was no reason for any further enquiries. J.B. would be cremated by the state. He'd no relatives and had grown up in care. I'd had to ring Social Services to get the details. The funeral would be at one o'clock the following Monday at Blackley, up in North Manchester. I wanted to go and to take Digger. Were dogs allowed?

'Sal, you'd only just met the guy.'

'I can usually tell when people are lying.'

'Good judge of character?'

'I think I am.'

'What about Clive?' he said.

'You bastard.' Clive was still missing, presumed alive.

'Sorry. But the guy took an overdose. The gear was there; the post-mortem confirmed it.'

'It confirmed the cause of death. That's all.'

'What are you getting at?' Ray was getting irritated.

'Maybe someone made him take it.'

'Oh, come on. You think he was murdered? He was a known addict, wasn't he?'

'A long time ago...oh, never mind.' I sighed and began to clear the table.

'What now?' Ray asked.

'Well, I'm still looking for Martin Hobbs. I'll take over where J.B. left off. He was going to ask round the clubs. I don't know if he did that or not.'

'Sounds like a bit of a wild goose chase,' he said, as he left for college.

I also wanted to seek out the young girl I'd seen at J.B.'s. I wanted to know from her whether J.B. had lied to me. If anything had happened on that Thursday that might have sent him out looking for a fix. And if he'd any enemies.

I wasn't familiar with the club scene in Manchester, though I knew it was thriving. I bought a copy of City Life and studied the descriptions of the various night-spots. A rough guide to music, clientele, dress-sense. I tried to imagine Martin and his 'partner'. The images I came up with were sophisticated or seedy. 'Riding round in an Aston Martin, eating out every night.' J.B.'s words, Martin's originally, came back to me. There were loads of pubs and clubs that seemed possible. Too many for me to tramp round.

I rang Harry, my journalist friend. He's a mine of information; his freelance career depends on it. I explained my problem.

'Try Natterjacks. Everybody goes there now and again. It's a good mixture – some rent scene, tie and shirt brigade too. Barney's is just down the road – that's worth checking out; quite a few prostitutes use it, male and female. If you want somewhere more upmarket, try The Galaxy Club.'

I tried them all that night. I got the lay of the land and even plucked up enough courage to ask a group of teenagers at Barney's if they'd seen Martin, producing his photograph. No response. I decided I'd try them all again the following night and then consider my duty done.

Thursday night. Eleven-thirty. I'd already looked in at The Galaxy Club and driven down to Princess Street where both the other places were. After half an hour in Natterjacks, seedy but popular, I crossed the road and walked down to Barney's. Small pillars framed the doorway, which was lit by large brass carriage-lamps. Inside, it was a mix of regency stripes in red and cream and lots of long, rectangular mirrors. And it was heaving.

I ordered an expensive orange juice and, when the man behind the bar brought it over, I showed him Martin's photograph.

'I couldn't tell you dear,' he said, 'I never remember a face. But I'll tell you this,' he paused for dramatic effect and leant nearer, 'you're the second person in here flashing photos at me.'

'Same photo?'

'Don't know, as I said, I never remember a face.'

'When was it?'

'Now,' he said, 'days I'm very good at. Wednesday, last Wednesday.'

It had to be J.B.

I wandered round the place to check the dance floor, which was out of sight of the main bar, before I found a perch in a corner of the room where I could see the entrance. I tried to look occupied, as though I was expecting someone at any moment. No-one bothered me. The music in the club was loud and fast, pulsing from the dance floor at the back. By twelve-thirty, it felt as if all the air had been used up. The place was heaving, hot and noisy. The smell of expensive aftershave mingled with the pall of smoke. And I had a crashing headache. My temple pulsed with each beat of the hi-energy music. Everyone else was having a whale of a time.

I queued at the bar, trying not to gawp at the transvestites at my side. All false fingernails, cascading curls and feather boas. The Joan Collins look. I finally got served and sat nursing my orange juice, as my watch crept slowly round the dial.

Half-past one and I'd had enough. It was a relief to breathe cool fresh air. As I walked towards the car, a group came round the corner. Four men. One of them must have said something funny and there was an explosion of laughter as they reached the door. I glanced back. They were illuminated by the light from the coloured carriage lamps. The man nearest to me turned back to his companions and I caught a glimpse of his face. It was Martin Hobbs.

CHAPTER ELEVEN

The door opened and closed behind them. I ran back. Heat, smoke and noise hit me like a wall. I craned my neck, looking for Martin. I spotted him at the other side of the room. The group were squeezing into seats, while one of them set off for drinks. Martin was by far the youngest in the party. The other three men were in their fifties, I guessed. At Martin's side sat a man with craggy features; he looked like Kirk Douglas with grey hair. Next to him was a gaunt man with sunken eyes, thinning hair, a touch of Norman Tebbit. And returning from the bar with a tray of drinks was a short, stocky man with a pudding-bowl haircut and lots of jewellery. I studied them for a while, wondering which was Martin's partner, or pimp. Mind you, if they'd only just arrived it seemed unlikely that Martin was working here. Just a group of friends relaxing? Maybe. Even so, I wanted to approach Martin on his own.

I found a free high stool at one end of the bar. From there I could watch them easily enough. The conversation mainly involved the three older men. Occasionally Martin joined in, usually in short energetic bursts, waving his arms around a lot and laughing. At one point, the gaunt man leant over and slapped his arms down. It wasn't a violent act. Just as if he was restraining an unruly child. A little later, the gaunt man leant over and spoke to Martin, passed him a ten pound note. Martin nodded, got up and made his way to the bar. My heart began to putter in my chest. My head thumped in response. People were queuing two-deep at the bar, shouting conversations above the din from the disco. I slipped off my stool and edged along till I was standing next to Martin.

'Martin.'

He turned to face me, a puzzled look on his face. His eyes were bloodshot. He struggled to focus.

'I'm Sal. J.B. said I might find you here.'

'What d'you want?' he mumbled, glancing over his shoulder towards his friends.

'To talk. It might be a bit difficult in front of your friends.'

He was suspicious. 'What's it about?'

'It's a private matter. Get your drinks and I'll wait for you on the dance floor.' I moved away before he had the chance to ask any more questions.

The next ten minutes crawled by as I leant against the wall. The dance floor was bouncing like a trampoline as the bodies leapt and flailed in the harsh, flashing lights. At last, I saw him come through the narrow passageway that led from the main bar.

He was none too steady on his feet. His clothes were casual, well made. Slacks and sweat shirt.

'What's all this about?'

'I'm a private detective...'

We had to lean close and shout above the music, to be heard.

'Shit.' He glanced back towards the bar. He was about to bolt.

'Wait – just hear me out. Your mother asked me to find you; she was worried sick. When you left, she...'

'What?' Incredulity distorted his elfin features.

'She wants to know if you're alright.'

'Fuckin' 'ell.' He grimaced. Tell her to go frig

herself.'

My mouth dropped open. 'Martin, she cares about you. She's desperate.'

He began to giggle. Stopped abruptly and rounded on me. 'He put her up to it. The bastard.' He rubbed his eyes.

A steady stream of people pushed past us, coming to and from the dance floor, fracturing the conversation.

'Your father?'

He nodded.

'I don't know,' I said, 'but I told her I'd try and find out where you were. She just wants to know if you're alright.'

'She never fucking cared before.' His eyes glared with hatred. Was this the shy, withdrawn boy people had told me about?

'I got to go.' Martin wheeled away, lost his balance and slid to the floor.

'Martin.' I helped him up. He was shaking. 'What do you mean, she never cared before?'

'Why don't you ask her?' he shouted. 'She knows why I went.'

'I'm asking you.'

'I gotta go.' He pulled away from me.

'Wait.' I grabbed the back of his shirt. His arms went up around his head for protection. Astonished, I let go. He was crying. I steered Martin ahead of me and into the Ladies, which was tucked in the corner, between the main bar and the disco. I hoped we wouldn't be disturbed.

In the strip light he looked yellow; cracked lips, a bruise on his forehead. I propped him up against the pink tiled wall. Leant against the basin myself. I saw another large bruise on his neck, yellow and purple. Or was it a lovebite?

'What happened, Martin?'

He rolled his head from side to side. 'Bastard.'

'Your father?'

'Bastard.'

'What did he do?'

He covered his face with his hands. 'He... he messed about with me, didn't he.' He spoke the words quietly, softly.

'What do you mean?' Stupid question. I knew what he meant, I just didn't want to believe it. Hoped I'd got it wrong.

'He buggered me, didn't he, the fucking bastard.' His shoulders shook. I didn't want to hear this.

'Oh, Martin, I'm so sorry.' My mind ran riot with questions I wouldn't ask. 'I'm sorry.'

'I gotta go.' He lifted his head, wiped his face with his hands.

'You better wash your face,' I said. I turned, ran water into the plain white basin. Then I stood to one side while he splashed his face.

'Did your mother know?' My question came out abruptly. I felt clumsy, insensitive. But I needed to know. I pictured Mrs Hobbs; lace-trimmed hanky, sad brown eyes. Surely not?

'Yeah,' he said bitterly. He grabbed a paper towel and dabbed at his face. 'I told her. I were about ten. Fat lot of good that did.'

'She didn't do anything about it?'

'She said if I ever made up such disgusting lies again, she'd have me put away. Said I was sick in the head. Christ.' He shook his head at the memory.

'Shit,' he said, 'he'll be looking for me. What'm I gonna tell him?'

'You mean your friend with the Aston Martin?'

'How d'you know?'

'J.B. told me.'

'I'll kill him,' he said. I felt sick.

'Martin, J.B.'s dead. He died of an overdose, on...'

'What? But he didn't use...' He laughed shortly. 'That's great, that is.' He nodded as though he'd recognised some deep irony. 'Great.' Then again,'I gotta go.'

He swung out of the door with me behind him. The Norman Tebbit lookalike stood at the junction of thoroughfares, his back to us.

'Fuckin' 'ell.' Martin looked wildly around. 'Oh, Jesus Christ.'

The man turned. 'Where the hell have you been?' He spoke quietly, with great venom. Had a clipped Scottish accent.

'I got a bit dizzy,' I said. 'Your friend helped me to the Ladies. I'm much better now – think I panicked a bit.' I turned to Martin and thanked him.

The gaunt man grunted and marched off with Martin at his heels. Only then did I notice the smell of sweat from my armpits. My headache rose to a sickening peak and I returned to the Ladies and threw up.

On my way out, I glanced over at Martin's group. Nothing untoward. Outside, a light drizzle fell. The sort of gauzy rain that can run for days in Manchester. I got into the Mini.

Martin's revelation had appalled me. And I felt duped. Pictures swam in my mind. A small boy, buggered, beaten. Summoning up the courage to tell, only to be betrayed by his mother. I pictured Tom screaming, hiding, holding his secret. Christ. If Ray ever did anything like that, I'd kill him. I'd know, wouldn't I? Surely I'd know.

I wrenched my thoughts in another direction; Martin's relationship to the older man. Was he a jealous lover or a pimp? Martin was frightened of him. I'd established that Martin Hobbs was alive and I'd discovered why he'd left home. But his troubles hadn't ended there. The boy I'd met was ill, fearful and unhappy.

I was still sitting in the car when Martin's party came out of the club. Walking briskly, they rounded the corner. I wondered where they were going. Go home and sleep, my body begged. But my curiosity wouldn't hear of it. I started the car and drove slowly round the corner, in time to see a small red Aston Martin pulling away. I followed them out of town, heading south past the back of the Infirmary. Whoever was driving kept to a steady thirty-five miles an hour, which meant I could drop back now and again and hide behind other vehicles. We drove out along Kingsway, past the Tesco superstore, then towards Cheadle. Here, there was no other traffic. I hoped they wouldn't notice the battered Mini. I also hoped they weren't going far. My mouth was sour, my headache pulsing. I followed several right and left turns past large semi-detached houses, each a different design. The car pulled into a driveway. I sped past, stopping at the next junction to mark the spot on my A-Z. Then I worked out my route home.

It was after three when I got home. The birds were clamouring away. I longed for a hot bath, but didn't dare wake the household. I made a cup of tea, took two Paracetamol and got ready for bed. I sat up in bed sipping the tea and staring into the middle distance. Shattered.

As I clicked off the light and slid under the duvet, an

unmistakable wail from Maddie made my stomach lurch with anxiety and my heart seethe with resentment. I marched into her room. She sat in her bed, face creased with tears.

'C'mon Maddie.' I gathered her up and took her to my room.

'In your bed?' Her eyes were wide with surprise. I'd broken all the rules about nightmares and what we do. I simply couldn't face another half-hour getting her back to sleep in her own room.

'Yes. Now lie down, be still, don't kick and no talking. Straight to sleep.' I snapped off the light.

'Mummy.'

'Sleep.' I admonished.

'Yes. I like your bed.'

'Good. Now sleep.'

We did.

CHAPTER TWELVE

Maddie woke me with a swift elbow jab to the nose. I shouted at her. She burst into tears. I apologised, explaining how much it hurt. I wished it would bleed, to prove my point. I took her downstairs and left her with Ray and Tom.

'You look awful,' said Ray. 'Any luck?'

'Yes and no. I'll tell you later.'

I snuggled back under the duvet and shut my eyes tight. Sleep wouldn't come. I ran a hot bath, added scented oil and climbed in. Put a facecloth over my eyes. When the water cooled down, I topped it up. When the wrinkles on my fingers and toes began to look revolting, I climbed out.

At least I was clean. I had that spacey, see-through feeling that comes from too little sleep. Vulnerable. A cross word and I'd weep like a child.

I ate a huge breakfast. Digger lay in the hall, a spot he'd claimed as his own. He deserved a walk. I called him and he sprang to attention. Tail wagging, ears pricked up. I took him into the front garden first. If he was going to shit, I wanted it to happen in private, behind the tall privet hedges. The kids never played in the front. Was this how other dog owners managed? For years, I'd railed against dog dirt in the streets, the park, the playground. Now I had a dog. Thankfully, he did his business to order. I waited, squirming with embarrassment in case the next door neighbours were peering down at us. I recoiled at having to gather up the results and traipse down to the cellar toilet. Give me slug traps any day.

It was a warm, still day. Picture book clouds hung isolated in the blue sky. The scent of wallflowers and cut grass mingled as we walked the half mile to the park. I'd found an old tennis ball that Digger liked to fetch. I watched him run. He was a stereotype dog. Pointed nose and ears, brown fur, long tail. Having rescued the dog, I was now ashamed at my lack of affection for him. Was it something that grew with time, as happens with babies sometimes?

Ray had often talked of getting a dog. I'd always opposed him. All that responsibility, all that shit. It was Ray who sorted out dog food and bowls, leads and worming tablets in the first day or so while I still reeled around in shock.

Digger had quietly recognised Ray as his new master. Sitting in the cellar while Ray worked at his carpentry, emerging at his heels with a frosting of sawdust on his fur. The kids were all over him and he was tolerant of their prodding and patting, slinking away when he'd had enough.

The phone was ringing as we arrived back.

'Is Clive there?'

'No, he's not. We were expecting him back last Thursday actually, but...'

The young man on the other end sighed.

'Look, can you tell him Pete rang? Tell him the cheque bounced, will you? You don't know where he is, do you?'

'No, just said he was visiting friends.'

'Great,' he said. Didn't sound like he meant it. So we weren't the only ones having money troubles with Clive. And where the hell was he? Surely he could have rung to say he'd be away longer? I jotted the message down and left it with the pile of mail for Clive.

I made fresh coffee and debated when to ring Mrs Hobbs. Did she work? I could leave it till after tea. What if her husband answered? Did he know she'd hired me? Had he put her up to it, as Martin had suggested? I dallied around, watering plants, tidying corners, sorting newspapers and bottles for a recycling trip. Displacement activities.

'Oh, get on with it, Sal.' I spoke aloud. Checked the number in my phone book. She was in.

'Mrs Hobbs, Sal Kilkenny here. I'd like to arrange to see you.'

'Have you found him, Martin, have you found him?' Eager, hopeful.

'Yes, I've been in touch with him.'

'Is he alright? What's happened to him? How's he managing?' Her questions tumbled out, edged with relief and excitement. I was angry with her; gripped the receiver tight, spoke formally.

'He's alright. I'd rather not discuss it over the phone.'

'Oh, it's such a relief. If anything had happened... But he's alright, you say. Thank God.'

'She never cared before.' Martin's words.

I made an appointment with Mrs Hobbs for the following morning. Her effusive thanks rang in my ears as I slammed down the receiver and rubbed at the cramp in my fingers.

It obviously hadn't occurred to her that Martin might tell me about the situation at home. Or had she repressed those horrible revelations for so long that they'd ceased to exist? Denial. What did I know? Martin's leaving might have forced her to face the truth; perhaps she wanted to do all she could to make amends, even prosecute her husband.

It wasn't fair to condemn her before I'd confronted her about it. But I don't always feel fair. And I couldn't shift the image of that small boy gathering the courage to tell, waiting for the right moment, watching her face contort as she whispered her own threats and denials. Knowing it would happen again and again.

In the precious time before the school run, I worked in the garden. I cut the grass with our old roller mower, emptying the grass box on the compost heap, savouring the crisp sweet smell. I watered tubs and window boxes. I thought about J.B., re-running in my head our meeting, freezing the frame on my favourite moments. Before long those memories of him would be concentrated in one or two images. I'd forget what he actually looked like; those fine cheekbones, warm brown eyes, the olive complexion, the quality of his smile. I wondered if there was a photo or a self-portrait of him in the squat. What would happen to his pictures, his things?

I tidied up the rampant clematis round the back door. Mourned over the stumps of marigolds that the slugs had got to. The slug traps were brimming. It could have been worse. I'd killed a fair few of the buggers. There was satisfaction in that.

I hadn't told Martin about the funeral. Would he like to be there? Would he be allowed to come? He wasn't a free agent, I'd gathered that much. Though not the whys or hows of it.

I was eager to wash my hands of the whole affair. I wanted to forget about it. I'd tell Mrs Hobbs what I knew. And what I'd learned. Give her a rollicking for lying to me. Work out my bill and give her the change she was owed. Close my file on Martin Hobbs. Or so I thought. Just shows how wrong you can be.

CHAPTER THIRTEEN

Mrs Hobbs was waiting on the Dobson's doorstep when I arrived. That threw me. I'd hoped to gather my thoughts, prepare myself to tackle her.

'Sorry I'm early,' she said, 'I thought the traffic would be worse. I don't often come in on a Saturday.' She looked so respectable in her beige lightweight suit, a moss-coloured blouse with one of those old-fashioned cravat collars. Oh, I know abuse happens in every sort of family, but it still seemed incongruous that the plump, middle-aged woman who stood clutching her handbag and smiling nervously at me, had that dark secret.

'Come in.' I unlocked the door and led her downstairs. The office still smelt of paint and looked dingy and unwelcoming. I pulled up a chair for her, opposite mine.

'He's alright then? Where is he? How did you find him?' She was grinning through the questions. She had a nice smile; it reminded me of the picture of Martin with the fish. 'Oh, I was so pleased when you rang, you can't imagine...' I wasn't returning her smile. She noticed. 'Is something wrong?' Worry enlarged those brown eyes. 'I thought you said he was alright. What is it?'

'Martin's okay,' I said. 'He's found somewhere to stay in Cheadle.'

'Yes?'

My mouth was watering, a small muscle tremoring in my knee.

'Mrs Hobbs, Martin explained to me why he left home. He told me what had been going on.' I paused. Expecting some reaction. I got bewilderment.

'I'd never have agreed to take the case if you'd told me the truth. Is that why you lied to me?'

'What do you mean?' She was alarmed. 'I don't know what you're talking about.'

'Oh, come on, stop pretending.' I spoke roughly, my cheeks burning. 'Martin was abused by his father for years. When he tried to tell you about it, you threatened to send him away, called him a liar.'

'No...No...' A strangled cry. Her hand flew to her mouth.

'That's what happened. Or are you still calling him a liar?'

She began to rock, back and forth, moaning, ' Oh my God, oh my God,' over and over. She seemed genuinely shocked.

'Don't you remember? Did you really think Martin had made it up? Children don't lie about things like that. Did you even ask your husband about it?' No reply. She continued that disturbing motion. She was a long way away. She'd forgotten I was there.

'Mrs Hobbs.' I spoke sharply. She stopped rocking. Her hand still covered her mouth.

'I can't explain,' she said. 'I'm sorry.' She cried silently then. Shoulders jerking up and down. I waited for her to stop. Perhaps I'd misjudged her. Maybe she, too, had been abused by her husband. Robbed of the ability to protect herself or her child.

Finally, she looked across at me. Her face was blotchy, crumpled with defeat. My mother's face held that look once. The day my father died. Naked with pain. My stomach contracted. I swallowed hard.

'I've drawn up my account,' I said. 'This is the balance owing.'

She nodded, took the papers and put them in her bag. She stood up.

'I'm sorry,' she said. 'I didn't lie to you... you wouldn't understand... I'd better go.' I followed her as she slowly climbed the stairs. At the door, she turned to face me.

'If I'd known...' Her face squeezed shut with grief. She shook her head. 'I'm sorry.' I didn't know whether she was talking to me or Martin then. She walked away down the path.

I shut the door and leaned back against it. I felt like bawling, but my eyes were dry. My throat ached and my fists were clenched as I railed against the painful, bloody mess of it all.

I wanted to go into town and try and find the young woman I'd met at J.B.'s, but I was aware Ray had been doing the lion's share of childcare and didn't feel I could ask him to take Maddie that afternoon. I called over the road to Denise; she has a daughter at nursery with Maddie. She was happy to look after Maddie for a couple of hours.

'Fine,' she said. 'I need a break. If I have to play Princesses once more today I'll go round the bend.'

She was seated in the same doorway, plaiting her bracelets. She looked very pale, as though she'd never seen the sun. I crouched down at her side.

'Hello, I met you at J.B.'s.' I was surprised at the tremor in my voice. 'I wanted to...' I didn't get a chance to say anything else.

'You bitch,' she screamed, as she scrambled to her feet, grabbing her wool and carrier bag. 'You've got a

73

fucking cheek. 'S your fault he's dead, you know. Why can't you just leave us alone? You stupid, fucking bitch.' She was gone.

Tears started into my eyes, dribbled slowly down my cheeks and dripped off the end of my nose as I walked back to the car. What did she mean? What had I done? How could it be my fault? I'd begun to drive out of town, sniffing occasionally, when a flash of anger interrupted my self-pity. I was the one who'd found the body, for Christ's sake. I was the one who'd had to go through all the police business. I'd taken Digger. Found out about the funeral. She hadn't thought about all that.

I drove round the block and fought my way back through the traffic and over to Great Ancoats Street. I waited a few minutes for a parking space while someone loaded bags of shopping into the car and drove off.

The entrance to the warehouse was closed but not locked. In the pitch black of the basement, I waited for my eyes to adjust, then made my way up through the building to J.B.'s room. The door was shut but I sensed she was in there. I knocked.

'Hello. It's me, Sal. Can I come in?... I just want to talk.' Silence. 'I don't even know your name, but I know you were a friend of his. I don't know why you're mad at me. I didn't give him drugs; he told me he didn't touch them, that's what seemed so crazy. It was such a shock. Please open the door.' She didn't. I slid down and sat with my back to it, talking aloud, staring at the flaking plaster in the dim corridor. 'I found him you know, oh and I took Digger. The police were going to put him down; it didn't seem right. I wanted to tell you about the funeral. J.B.'s funeral. It's on Monday, one o'clock up at Blackley. I'm going. I could give you a lift if you want to come. Could you tell his friends? I don't even know who they are. Please open the door, this is ridiculous. Shit. It wasn't my bloody fault, I don't know why you think it is. I'd just met him, I...' I got to my feet. 'I'm going now. I'll leave my card here; if you want a lift, give me a ring. I still need to talk to you. I want to know what you meant. I want to know what happened. He was a good bloke.'

It'd been a lousy day and I ended up feeling guilty and depressed. The girl's accusations unsettled me. Had there been a link between my enquiries and J.B.'s death, is that what she meant? I went through the motions of cooking tea, getting the kids to bed, preoccupied by my own thoughts. There was no sense of relief at finishing the case; even the thought of a couple of hundred pounds in the bank didn't raise my spirits.

I couldn't face the thought of mooning round the house, feeling ill at ease. It was a light evening, dry and mild. I pulled on my old clothes and set out for the garden. There's a patch in the far corner that I've never done anything with, in the shade of an old elderberry. That'd do. I got down on my hands and knees and went to work, pulling out weeds, digging out brambles, forking it all over. By the time I was through, it was dark. And the events of the day had shifted into an easier perspective. In time, that little patch of ground would bloom with sweet-scented, shade-loving plants and the trials of today would be far away. Wouldn't they?

CHAPTER FOURTEEN

Sunday morning at the swimming pool. I knew Withington was closed; problems with the roof. Moss Side was open. I rang to check. Whenever staff fall ill at Gorton Tub, the city's showplace play pool, they pull replacements from the other baths, which have to close.

The swimming baths are attached to the shopping centre, a forbidding redbrick fortress. The walkway from the car park was strewn with litter, daubed with graffiti; broken glass crunched underfoot. The leisure centre was clean and well-equipped.

The water in the baby pool was deliciously warm. Tom, in his armbands and rubber ring, splashed and wriggled like a baby seal, his curls shining like black corkscrews. Maddie was going through a fearful phase, detested water on her face and rooted herself on the broad steps at the shallow end. I divided my time between the two of them, flailing around and chasing Tom to keep warm, then gently coaxing Maddie to try a little doggy paddle near the steps.

Ray had made lunch and the four of us ate together. 'Fancy a walk?' Ray asked. 'Thought I'd take Digger out for a run.' The idea appealed; it was ages since I'd sampled real fresh air, but I was itching to do more in the garden.

'I don't want to,' Maddie protested. I raised my eyes

to heaven, tried a little half-hearted encouragement. She wouldn't budge.

'Okay. Stay and help me in the garden.'

'Yuck.'

'Well, that's what I'm doing.'

'It's not fair.' She flounced out of the door, her voice rising. 'You never do what I want.'

I cleared up the kitchen. Changed into my gardening clothes. I could hear Maddie in her room, burbling away to herself. I called out to tell her where I'd be.

It was glorious out there. The honey scent of alyssum mingled with the sharp smell of warm pine baking in the sun. I hunted down slugs, winkling them out of dark, damp corners. Emptied and refilled the traps. Began some weeding. Maddie appeared at the back door. Watched me for a while.

'Phone,' she said.

'What?'

'Phone.' Through clenched teeth.

I raced inside, hoping that she hadn't left it too long before deigning to inform me.

'Hello?' Silence. 'Hello?' I heard breathing. Unsteady, shuddering. A prickle of fear stroked the back of my neck. *The knife trembled, white knuckles.* He was coming after me. The man who'd stabbed me. They'd let him out. My stomach balled like a fist. *Please, please. My voice weak, creaking.* They'd let him out and he was coming to get me.

'Who is this?'

'Please.' It was a woman's voice. 'Where is he? You didn't tell me where. I've got to see him. Please..pl..e..e.' she cried. Mrs Hobbs. Relief released my body. I trembled and sat on the chair.

'Mrs Hobbs, I don't know exactly where Martin is

and he doesn't want to see you.'

'You said he was in Cheadle. He's my son, you said he was, he's my son, you said, you said...' She was freaking out and I'd no idea how to handle it.

'He doesn't want to see you after all he's been through and...'

'Don't lie to me.' Fury spat the words. 'He's my son.'

'I don't know where he is.'

'You found him, my baby, my baby...' She repeated her song of grief. I waited. What the fuck could I say? She fell quiet. I could hear her breath, rapid, shallow. When she spoke again she sounded bright, practical.

'I'll write to him, yes. Just give me the address, I'll write. Yes, yes.'

'I'm sorry. I don't have Martin's address.'

'Liar,' she screeched. 'Liar.'

I lost my temper, shouted back. 'I don't know, for Christ's sake! All I know is it's Old Hall Lane, I followed the bloody car, Aston Martin. I didn't get the address.'

'I'll go there... Old Hall Lane. You said Cheadle. Aston Martin and Martin Hobbs. Two Martins. Martin Hobbs. That's his name now.'

'Don't go, listen.' She wasn't in a fit state to go to the post-box, let alone try tracking down Martin. 'I'll take the letter. Write and send it to me. I'll try and find the house. I'll give the letter to Martin.'

'Will you?'

'Yes, I promise.'

'He's my son.'

'Yes.'

She rang off.

Maddie was sitting at the end of the hall, clasping her doll.

'Why did you shout?'

'Oh,' I sighed and went to reassure her. 'Someone wasn't listening to me. I got cross, that's all. It's alright now.' I hugged her, craving one for myself. She squirmed away. The phone rang.

'Oh, no.' I couldn't face any more. Mrs Hobbs' distress had disturbed me, awakening memories of my own pain in the months after the stabbing.

Maddie moved towards the phone.

'No, I'll get it.'

'Aww.'

'Hello?'

'Sal? Harry.'

Phew.

'How you doing?'

'Fine.'

'Do you want to come over? Bev's gone off with the car but the rest of us are here.'

'Yeah, we'd love to. I've just got Maddie today.'

'Okay. See you soon.'

It was a relief to get out of the house and away from the phone. I cycled over to Harry and Bev's terraced house in Levenshulme. Their two boys were playing some version of goodies and baddies in the street, when we arrived. Maddie begged for my bicycle pump and ran to join them. The front door was open and I found Harry in the yard out at the back. He and Bev had transformed the small brick box into a riot of greenery, with climbers in pots, hanging baskets, even a tiny pergola complete with vine.

'Lager?' offered Harry. The deckchair creaked as he heaved himself out of it. Harry's built like a rugby player and looks like a farmhand; thatched hair and hands like hams.

'Mmm.' He fetched me a cold can and opened a sun

lounger for me. Bliss.

Harry was eager to hear how I'd got on at the clubs. I described my sorties into Manchester night-life and sketched in the unpleasant facts I'd heard from Martin.

'I felt so stupid.'

'I can imagine. So it's over?'

'Well...' I told him about the phone call from Mrs Hobbs. 'In the end I agreed to take the letter. I had to stop her barging in. She needs help.' I sighed.

'You never met the father?'

'No, thank God. So instead of it all being done and dusted, now I've got to play postman.'

'Woman.'

'Okay,' I pretended to kick him. 'Plus, there's the funeral.'

'The guy you found?'

I told Harry all about J.B., confessing my doubts about the official version of his death. He heard me out. Harry's a good listener, he's not averse to using a little imagination and I can trust him to keep confidences. When I'd finished, he sat quietly for a moment, chewing his lip. 'Who'd want to get rid of him?'

'I dunno. It's full of holes, I know. Everyone else thinks it's cut and dried.' I drained my can. 'You couldn't really attack someone with a loaded syringe, could you?'

'Not easy to find a vein. No, it's pretty unlikely. But just suppose someone did want him out the way, why choose to do it like that? There are simpler ways of killing someone.'

'That's obvious,' I replied. 'No-one would suspect foul play. Once a junkie, always a junkie. They wouldn't expect a murder enquiry; no questions, no trouble. They were right about that.'

Harry chewed his lip again.

'You think I'm wrong, don't you?'

He grimaced. 'It's a bit thin.'

I sighed. Crumpled the empty can.

I loved Harry. It wasn't physical; he was too big and beefy for my liking. But I was drawn to him and sometimes wondered what it would be like to sleep with him; whether we might have an affair if anything happened to end his relationship with Bev. Strictly fantasy. They were a happy pair. Still...

'I'm all for hunches, Sal. But that's all you've got. No motive, no evidence, nothing. You're going to have to fill in the picture a bit more to convince anyone.'

'Hang on,' I said. 'I've no intention of reopening the case or whatever they call it. I guess all I need is to hear from someone who knew J.B. well that he really was clean, that he didn't lie to me, or...'

'And if your hunch is right, if it looks less and less like an overdose, you're just going to leave it at that?' Harry was sceptical.

'What else can I do? I've no illusions about the British system of justice. Yes, if I got names and numbers, witnesses, whatever – I'd feel bound to pass that on, but it's pretty bloody unlikely.'

Harry didn't reply. Silence is consent.

I got up and shifted my lounger round, following the sun. Asked Harry about his work and lay, eyes half-closed, as he entertained me with tales of skulduggery in the world of journalism.

Maddie and I stayed for tea, enjoying a huge mixed salad, chips and veggie-burgers in the open air. It was after seven when I strapped a flagging Maddie onto the bike seat and pedalled home. She nodded off on the way. I woke her for a wee then put her to bed, grime and all.

I read the Sunday papers then ferreted out my library book. It was overdue. A crime story set on a cruise ship in the 'thirties. I couldn't concentrate. The mannered dialogue was too much effort and I found I didn't really care whodunnit or why. I scanned the television page. 'Twelve Angry Men.' I'd seen it twice but it still gripped me.

On my way to bed, I sorted out clothes for the funeral. My only black clothes were heavy winter ones and the smoke-drenched dress I'd worn to Barney's. Colour didn't matter really. It was hardly going to be a big, formal affair. I found some lightweight navy trousers and a green sweatshirt. Casual but clean.

I'd not heard from J.B.'s friend. Would I be the only mourner? I'd hardly known him. Surely, he'd have lots of friends? She would let them know, wouldn't she? He deserved that.

If they did turn up, would they talk to me? Maybe they all thought I'd been responsible for his death. But why? What had she meant?

I fell asleep defending myself against a charge of murder, not knowing what the case against me was. Only that I was innocent. Innocent.

CHAPTER FIFTEEN

'I'll give you a lift back to town?'
She hesitated. She'd be bloody daft to refuse. It was
pissing down. Her pink cotton jacket and mini skirt
were already sodden. Funeral weather. It fitted
perfectly with the miserable rite we'd both witnessed.
A few generalised platitudes from a cleric and J.B. laid
to rest in the public grave. I still called him J.B.,
though officially we'd just buried Philip Hargreaves.
Dead and gone. But not forgotten. Not yet.
   'Alright.'
I bundled Digger into the back seat. Got in the
driver's seat and opened the passenger door. She
climbed in. Her bare legs were mottled with cold.
Water dripped from the lank strands of hair onto her
shoulders. I wanted to towel her dry and put some
warm clothes on her.
   'I'm glad you came,' I said. 'Someone who knew
him.'
   'I wasn't going to,' she said. She coughed. Pulled a
squashed packet of Benson and Hedges from her
pocket. Opened it and took out a disposable lighter
and a cigarette.
   I opened my window. I didn't know which was
worse, the second-hand fag smoke or the wet dog
stench steaming off Digger.
   'Why weren't you going to come?'
She shrugged and looked away out of the window.

Her hand was trembling. I don't think it was just the cold.

'What did you mean, the other day, about it being my fault?'

'Nothing. I were just upset, right.' She was a lousy liar.

'I don't know your name.'

'Leanne.'

'I'd like to talk, Leanne.'

'What's the point?' She blew a stream of smoke straight ahead.

'Things I want to know.'

'I don't know anything.' Defensive. 'I don't know anything, right?' Wrong.

'Let's get out of here.' I started the engine. 'Find somewhere to dry off. I'll buy you a meal.'

'Not in town.'

'What?'

'Someone might see us.' She was paranoid. Perhaps with good reason. If J.B.'s overdose had not been self- administered.

'Would they know who I was?' I asked her.

'Maybe. I dunno. I can't think right when I'm hungry.'

'Better get you some food then.'

She grinned, then it was gone.

'Do you like Indian food?'

'Yeah. Anything.'

A handful of the curry houses in Rusholme open in the afternoon. The rest don't bother. Trade is slack in the daytime, brisk at night. The old Shezan was open. Empty, but open. We wouldn't be hustled to eat up and move on.

'There's a Kentucky Chicken there,' said Leanne.

'That's just a take-away. Come on.'

I held back on the questions till Leanne had got through a plateful of bhajis and samosas and well into her Prawn Dansak.

'About J.B.,' I began.

'It's over, right.' She glared at me.

'No, it isn't. I want to know what happened to him. Don't you?'

'No.' Vehemently. She set her jaw. Blinked rapidly.

'You're frightened. He didn't kill himself, did he? You know that. He told me he didn't take drugs. I don't think he lied to me. Was he in trouble?'

'Not till you poked your nose in.'

'I was trying to trace someone, a runaway...'

'Martin Hobbs. He told me. He was playing detective and all, wasn't he? Next news, he's dead.'

'When did you see him last?'

'I dunno... erm... Thursday morning.' I could see from her eyes that she was working out the right answer. She broke up pieces of naan and dropped them into the remains of her meal.

'Did he use drugs?'

She shook her head. 'No, never.'

'Why are you frightened, Leanne, what is it?' She wriggled in her seat, sighed theatrically and cast her eyes from side to side, looking for escape. She looked tired, unwell. Her skin was a pasty white, she had a cold sore and chapped lips.

'Tell me what you know.' I raised my voice and the waiter, reading his paper in the corner, glanced over. 'Please,' I said quietly. 'You were his friend, he helped you out didn't he? Whatever happened may tie up with what he was doing for me. I want to know. He'd want me to know. Don't you think you owe him that, at least?'

She poured salt onto the table, pushed it into a little heap, drew a circle in it.

'Just another dead junkie,' I said, 'that's what the police reckon, who gives a fuck? You happy with that, are you?'

'Shut up. Why you so fucking interested anyway? Fancied him, didn't you?'

How the hell did she know? My cheeks burned. It wasn't the curry.

'Don't change the subject. Stop pissing around,' I was riled now, 'and tell me.'

'Can't fucking make me.' She was all defiance, chin up, eyes hard.

I sighed. 'Please, Leanne.'

Silence. She traced shapes in the salt. At last, she began to speak, reluctantly, in a slow monotone.

J.B. had talked to her about trying to find Martin. She knew him a bit; they'd both been dossing at the squat. J.B. had hung around outside the clubs on the Wednesday night looking for people he knew. He'd got a couple of strange reactions, people overly nervous about his questions, but no information at all. On the Thursday morning everything had been as usual, though J.B. slept in after his late night. Leanne was out selling. She returned to the squat about two-thirty. She'd just entered the cellar when she heard footsteps she didn't recognise on the stairs. She hid. The man passed her and went out of the cellar door, leaving it ajar. She knew who he was, a right bastard. She went up to the flat and found J.B. He was dead. She ran away, slept out that night. Didn't return until she heard about J.B. on the grapevine.

'Why? Why on earth didn't you report it?'

'He was dead, wasn't he? What's the point?'

Defensive.

'This man?' I asked.

That look of fear. 'He's bad news. Smiley, dunno his real name. He's a right bastard. J.B. knew him, told me to keep well clear of him. He's done a lot of time in Strangeways.'

'What for?'

'You name it – drugs, porno stuff. I'm not gonna grass him up, no way.'

'But he probably did it. The police would protect you.'

'No they fucking wouldn't.' She leant forward, spoke urgently. 'They'll put me back in care, that's what they'd do, right?'

'You're not sixteen? How old? Fourteen, fifteen?'

'Thirteen, but it doesn't matter see, I'm not doing another day in care, not for you, not for anyone.' She leant back, searched for her cigarettes. Lit one. Leant forward again. 'And don't try dragging me into all this, right, 'cos I never saw anything, right? Never met you.'

'What's he look like?'

'You don't want to know.'

'Leanne...'

She shrugged. 'I dunno. Always smiling, got a scar see, he grassed on someone, they didn't like it.' She drew her finger across her face in a large crescent.

'Tall, short, black, white, how old?'

'White, getting on a bit, I dunno. I'm off.' She pushed back her chair.

'D'you need some bus-fare?'

'S'alright, I got some.'

I held out one of my cards.

'No, ta.' She handed it back.

'Just in case.'

She smiled. 'I never seen you. What would I be

doing with that?'

'I'm in the Yellow Pages,' I called, as she walked out. 'Kilkenny.'

I asked for the bill. Went and waited at the counter while the waiter added it up. Rummaged in my bag for my purse. Gone. Thirty quid. The little sod. Library tickets, Leisure Pass. Luckily, I keep my cheque book and card in a separate pocket. She'd not got that. I wondered how she'd spend the money. Clothes, food, booze, drugs? It wouldn't go far. And then she'd be back in the doorways, begging to get by. Oh, well. It was probably a fair price for what she'd told me. Only this wasn't a case; there was no client paying the expenses. If I wanted the truth, I'd have to pay for it. At that time, I'd no idea how much the whole business was going to cost me.

CHAPTER SIXTEEN

I was late getting to school. Mortal sin. I found
Maddie sitting with her teacher in the empty
classroom.

'I'm so sorry,' I gushed. 'The traffic was awful.' Mrs
Cummings looked relieved; Maddie burst into tears.
Guilt.

'Why didn't you come?' she repeated time and again
in between sobs, as we drove to collect Tom. I'd tried
to hug her but she'd shoved me away. She needed
more time to be angry, to hate me for abandoning her.
My explanations and apologies were irrelevant. The
deed had been done.

The nursery stays open till six to cater for working
parents, so my being half an hour later than usual was
neither here nor there. Tom had been on his
Castlefield Museum trip and was full of chatter about
trains with smoke coming out of them.

Maddie headed straight for the television and sought
comfort in Alvin and the Chipmunks. Tom joined her.
I took them in some biscuits and milkshake then got
myself a cup of tea.

So now I knew. J.B. hadn't been a user. Smiley had
killed him. Found some way to stick a needle in his
arm and pump him full of heroin. Oh, I was jumping
to conclusions, but it wasn't much of a jump. Now I

had a whole new crop of questions. They all began with why. Why was asking after a runaway such a threat to Smiley? After all, I'd seen Martin myself. He wasn't dead or anything.

Maybe he was mixed up with the drug cartels or starring in porno films. Interest in Martin might turn up information that jeopardised others. Worth killing to keep under wraps. But J.B. hadn't found anything out anyway, as far as I knew.

I'd have to go to the police. What's the point, as Leanne would say? All I had was hearsay. Impossible to prove without Leanne's co-operation. And running counter to the official version of events. Nevertheless, I'd have to tell them what I'd heard. There was no way I was going to pursue some nutter like Smiley. Way out of my league. Still, it wouldn't hurt to know a bit more about him. I rang Harry.

'Sal, you've saved me!'

'From?'

'Repetitive Strain Injury. I've been glued to the screen all bloody day. I forget to take breaks. They're addictive, you know.' I didn't. My funds didn't stretch to a typewriter, let alone a word-processor. It was high on my list of things I'd get when-my-boat-comes-in.

'An article?' I asked.

'Guardian. Selling off Salford – poorest city in the land. Dockland development for the rich, no-go areas for the poor.'

'I get the picture.'

'So, is this a social call?'

'No, business. I want to find out about someone, well, he's a gangster by all accounts.' Harry made a murmur of surprise.

'He was seen leaving J.B.'s flat the day he died.'

'How was the funeral?'

'Deadly.'

Harry laughed.

Maddie came out of the lounge and thrust her empty cup in my face. I nodded and pointed to the phone. She went off whining.

'I'm not up to date on the criminal fraternity,' said Harry, 'but I know a man who is. What's this bloke's name?'

'Don't know. Nickname's Smiley. Got a scar either side of his mouth. He's done time, into heavy stuff, drugs, pornography. That's all I know.'

'See what I can do. No rush, is there?'

'No. Curiosity really. I'm not about to rustle up a posse.'

'Glad to hear it.'

Bedtime was a marathon. To make amends for the day, I treated Maddie to an extra long story about space princesses with secret powers. I didn't get downstairs till half-past nine. The lounge was a tip. Littered with toys, empty cups, kids' clothes. I hadn't the energy to clear it up but I couldn't stand looking at the clutter.

I went into the kitchen and made a cup of tea. Settled into the old armchair by the big windows. Ray had been scanning the small ads; he hunts down auctions, gets tools that way. I flipped to the front page. BOLTON WOMAN BRUTAL MURDER. Photograph. Those large eyes, lit by a smile. I spilt my tea. My eyes raced over the print. I couldn't make sense of it. Oh, the facts were there; where the body was found, how she'd been killed. But the woman that stared out at me, the woman who'd cried in my office two days ago, was Janice Brookes, a single woman living alone. 'Miss Brookes leaves a mother and sister.' No son. No husband. No Mrs Hobbs.

Now what the fuck was going on?

CHAPTER SEVENTEEN

I rang the incident room number listed in the newspaper report and tried to establish whether the woman who'd been battered to death really was Janice Brookes. The man I spoke to was cagey. The police hate to answer questions. Oh, the bobby on the beat will give you the time of day or directions, but anything to do with a case is a no-no. He finally conceded that if the woman was named Janice Brookes then she must have been identified as such.

I told him that I'd recently been hired by her and emphasised that she was using an assumed name. He said he'd pass on the details to the officer in charge, who would probably contact me to arrange an interview. I tried to find out where I could contact her sister or mother, but he 'wasn't at liberty to divulge any information'.

I needed to talk to someone. Ray was out having a meal with friends, so I tried Diane. She sounded breathless when she finally answered the phone.

'Diane, it's Sal.'

'Oh, look Sal, this really isn't a good time...'

'Whoops. Sorry. Right... erm... see you tomorrow.'

'Yeah.'

What had I interrupted, a steamy session or a blazing row?

Harry was my last chance. The babysitter told me they'd gone to the pictures. Did I want to leave a message? No.

I paced around a bit then tried to tackle my confusion with pen and paper. I ended up with a list of banal questions thrown up by Mrs Hobbs' double identity and her murder. The paper went in the bin. I was hardly going to forget what was on it. I paced around a bit more.

My earlier lack of energy had been replaced by the adrenalin buzz that a shock brings. Whilst I cleared up the lounge, my mind roamed back over my meetings with Mrs Hobbs aka Janice Brookes. Several small details began to make sense. She'd never given me an address. She'd paid in cash too. No cheque, no signature. Her responses to my early questions about what clothes Martin had taken when he left had been vague. And all the lies about reporting him missing to the police and how little they did. She'd never have been to them at all.

Then there were the photos she'd given me; not school photos or holiday snaps but a newspaper cutting and two outdoor shots that could easily have been acquired by a stranger snapping from across the street. She'd said something about that, hadn't she? I struggled to remember. A fire. That's right, a fire had destroyed all the family albums. A cover story?

If she wasn't Martin's mother, why had she been pursuing him? Some weird obsession? Was she mixed up in illegal goings-on? I couldn't imagine it. Martin wasn't her runaway son, so why convince me he was? Because I'd never have taken the case if she'd told me her real reason for wanting to find him.

She'd put on a brilliant act. Tears and all. And I'd found it totally plausible. I'd swallowed it hook, line and sinker. I hated the idea that I'd been conned so completely. Hell, I'd even seen a resemblance in their faces because I expected there to be some similarity.

Perhaps she believed she was the boy's mother. You hear of people suffering from delusions, but they're usually a bit more grandiose, aren't they? Like being Jesus or Boudicca or something.

I re-read the paper. She'd been battered to death. A vicious attack. Her body had been found on rough ground off the M63 motorway, early on Monday morning, by a woman exercising (read toileting) her dog. The police had not yet determined whether there was a link between this murder and the killing of another woman, as yet unsolved, on the same stretch of motorway, the previous year. Women were advised to be vigilant when travelling alone and in the event of a breakdown, to remain in their cars and wait for police assistance. There was nothing about whether her car had been found.

I knew I wouldn't sleep well but I had to go through the motions. Wriggling away inside was a small maggot of guilt. I'd spoken to Janice Brookes on Sunday and done little to ease her distress. I'd laid into her the previous day about her betrayal of Martin, when he'd turned to her for help. But if she wasn't Mrs Hobbs, she hadn't betrayed him. Yet she'd sat there and rocked with grief. Why hadn't she denied it, told me who she really was? On Sunday, she'd been desperate to get his address. Was someone else putting pressure on her? Did she think Martin was in danger? How did she even know him?

There was one thing that I was certain of. It was no coincidence that she was dead. The M63 is a long way from Bolton. It's within spitting distance of Cheadle. She'd threatened to go after Martin. She had. And someone had killed her. Just like they had J.B. If I'd dealt more sympathetically with Sunday's phone call, she might still be alive.

It was a long time till morning.

I had a flash of inspiration as I brushed my teeth, first thing on Tuesday. Janice Brookes had a sister. Maybe they looked alike. Very alike. Like twins. Some families are like that, aren't they? The same genes coming to the fore. Janice Brookes was the victim, Mrs Hobbs would turn out to be her bereaved sister. I got very excited following this train of thought. Ignoring the strange coincidences it implied, like Mrs Hobbs' sister getting killed near Cheadle. The theory relieved me of the guilt and paranoia that had mushroomed around me. I rang Mrs Hobbs. No reply. She'd probably be busy helping with the funeral arrangements. I was clutching at straws. Sometimes, there's nothing else to clutch at.

The police knocked that one on the head straightaway. They arrived, unannounced, just as I'd got the kids into the car. It was the man with the suntan, moustache and glasses who'd sat in the background while I was questioned at J.B.'s. With him, a young sandy-haired bloke with sticky-out ears, reminiscent of Tintin. I asked them to wait a moment and fled inside to rouse Ray so he could do the school run.

The two men followed me into the kitchen. We all sat down round the oval table.

'I'm Detective Inspector Miller and this is Sergeant Boyston. You are Sal Kilkenny?'

'Yes. We met last week, actually.'

'Busy, aren't we?' Said without a trace of humour. 'Now, you contacted us regarding the murder of Miss Janice Brookes.' Tintin made notes, while Miller did the talking.

'Yes, well, if it is her.' I had an unnerving flash of déjà-vu. The last time the police had sat in my kitchen I'd just had a brick through the window, a prelude to a knife through the shoulder.

Miller looked puzzled. I dragged my brain back to the present.

'I thought it might be her sister. You see, I knew her as Mrs Hobbs. The woman I met, she looks like this one,' I pointed to the paper, 'but the wrong name. I thought if they were alike, her and her sister, then...'

The Sergeant sniggered.

'I can assure you,' said Miller, 'that they do not look alike. Perhaps if we start at the beginning.' He smiled, but his flecked brown eyes held no warmth.

I told them about Mrs Hobbs and the job she'd asked me to do. I related that I'd found Martin and that he'd wanted no contact with his family. I left out the details of his abuse; after all, that had nothing to do with Janice Brookes. I described how upset she'd been when I told her Martin didn't want to see her.

'She rang me again on Sunday.'

'What time was that?'

'About two-thirty. She wanted to go and see Martin, talk to him. I persuaded her not to. Well, I thought I had. She was going to write instead, send the letter to me to deliver.'

'Have you received it?'

'No.'

'I think she went after him,' I said. 'Where she was found, the M63, it's not far from Cheadle. You should check out the house. She could have been killed there, then moved. Was she killed where they found her?' Miller didn't acknowledge questions.

'I'd be careful about making wild accusations like that,' he said. 'After all, as I understand it, you don't know that Martin Hobbs lived there.'

'No, but...'

'Or who else lived there.'

'I know, but you must at least...'

'I'm aware of how to conduct a murder enquiry, Miss Kilkenny.' He spoke sharply. 'You have a note of the street name, Sergeant?'

'Old Hall Lane, Sir, Aston Martin, red.'

'Where were you on Sunday night?'

'Me?' My face burned with indignation. 'I was here.'

'All evening?'

'Yes.' I sounded defensive. Guilty for no good cause. 'There are children in the house.'

'And you had no further contact with Janice Brookes after that phone call?'

'No.'

'Well, I think that will do for now. We'll get in touch if we need to talk to you again.'

'Did anyone else know her as Mrs Hobbs? Was she leading a double life?'

'I can't say, Miss. We do know she had a history of mental instability.'

I wondered what you had to do to qualify for that label. Go to a therapist, as I had? Take tranquillisers? Be hospitalised? I could think of precious few people who didn't have some history of mental instability. Sergeant Boyston closed his notebook.

'I'd like to speak to her family,' I said.

'I think they've got quite enough on their plate at the moment.'

'But they might know why she was pretending to be...'

'Frankly, that's no longer any of your concern. Your client is dead. I've a murder to solve and I don't want any interference. In fact, I'd regard any further activity by you as obstruction. Is that clear?' I sent laser death rays with my glare. The two of them got to their feet.

'There's something else,' I said. 'About J.B., I mean, Philip Hargreaves.' Miller waited for me to continue. 'Someone was seen leaving his place the day he was killed.'

'Philip Hargreaves died of a self-induced drug overdose.' He was impatient, spoke with contempt.

'Well, that's what everyone thought. But this man, he's a known criminal, he was seen leaving on the Thursday afternoon. The person who saw him found J.B.'s body. He was already dead then. Twenty-four hours before I got there. But they were too scared to say anything.'

Miller stared at me until I felt uncomfortable. When he spoke it was to ridicule me.

'Philip Hargreaves was a junkie. The doctor and the coroner were both satisfied as to cause of death. There was no evidence of foul play. If this anonymous witness had seen a handful of serial killers in the vicinity, it wouldn't alter...'

'In the building. He's known as Smiley. He's got a scar...'

Miller held up his hand. 'This isn't a bloody gangster movie.' He leant towards me. 'No crime has been committed.'

'It has,' I insisted. 'Murder.'

'Wrong.' He stabbed his finger at me. 'The facts speak for themselves. There's only one murder, that of Janice Brookes.'

'But Martin's the link. They must be connected.'

'Not as far as I'm concerned. You've been under too much pressure, Miss Kilkenny.' He shook his head to and fro. 'Dealing with an accidental death and now this. Way out of your league. Can't be an easy job for a woman, anyway. We know what we're doing. We take it from here. You need a break; take the kiddies away for a few days. Help you to get things in the right perspective. This sort of hysterical reaction doesn't help anybody.' He moved towards the door. Tintin followed. 'We'll be doing our level best with the Brookes case, I can assure you of that.'

I was glad I hadn't offered the bastard a cup of tea.

Well, I'd done my duty. I'd passed on Leanne's story. If D.I. Miller thought I was going to sit back and twiddle my thumbs, he'd another think coming. Oh, they could solve the murder, I wouldn't tread on any toes there, but I would solve the mystery. I had to know why Janice Brookes was willing to spend a grand tracing a runaway schoolboy. And if I hadn't easy access to the Brookes family, then I'd start with the other side of the family. With the real Mrs Hobbs.

CHAPTER EIGHTEEN

The rain came down like stair rods as I drove over to Bolton. Traffic was bad, with road-works along the M61. I made it to St. Matthew's just before the end of lunch break.

After a few enquiries, I found Max Ainsworth in the Chemistry Lab. The smell of sulphur took me straight back to interminable Friday afternoons, perched on a high wooden stool, listening to Miss Jackson drone on. We'd given her hell. Turning on unlit Bunsen burners in attempts to gas the class out of existence, competing with each other to see how many test-tubes could be broken during one experiment. At fourteen, we dropped chemistry like a shot.

'Max, can I have a quick word?' He followed me out into the corridor.

''S it about Martin?' He looked concerned.

'Yeah. He's okay. I managed to find him. He's living in Manchester. The thing is, I never got his parents' address, only the phone number, and the damn thing's out of order.'

'It's Glover Street, twenty-three, I think, twenty-three or twenty-five. 'S got one of them clipped hedges, shaped like a bird, you know.'

'Thanks. You never went there?'

'Just to call for him once, when we went fishing, like.'

'You ever meet his parents?'

He thought about it, frowning through his thick glasses.

'Nope.'

'Martin say anything about them?'

'No. He wasn't one for talking. Why?'

'That's why he left, his parents.'

'Oh.' He reddened slightly. 'So he's alright then?'

'Well, he's alive, he's got somewhere to stay, that's about all I know.'

'Better go,' Max grinned. 'Here comes Tiny.' A huge man with a small, bald head was steaming towards us down the corridor. I thanked Max and left him to his potions.

It wasn't far to Glover Street, according to the A-Z, but I wasn't exactly raring to get there. Lunch first. I don't know Bolton and didn't fancy tackling the one-way system in the town centre, so I drove around the outskirts till I found a corner cafe.

That was a mistake. It was a genuine greasy spoon. I don't eat meat and the only vegetarian options were fried egg on toast or beans on toast. Beans seemed a safer bet. There's not much you can do to render a bean inedible. Not much, but whatever there was, they'd done it. Mushy, overcooked, crusty round the edges. The colour of the tea matched the beans. Coated my mouth instantly with orange fuzz. In my student days, I'd survived on meals like that, even enjoyed them. Long time ago.

The house on Glover Street was a large 'thirties semi. The ridiculous privet chicken marked it out from the rest. The garage was shut, no car in the driveway. There was no response to the bell. I peered through the frosted glass, trying to detect any movement.

Then I crouched down and peered through the letter-box.

'Can I help, dear?' Startled, I jumped to my feet and whirled round. The woman on the pavement had a small terrier on a lead.

'I was looking for Mrs Hobbs.' I walked down the path. 'There doesn't seem to be anyone in.'

'They're away, dear. Back tonight. Malta. They go twice a year. I keep an eye on the place. I'm next door.' She nodded her head to the left. I sensed she required some sort of explanation.

'I'm a friend of Martin's.' Her face creased with concern. She moved nearer and lowered her voice. 'A terrible business.

It put years on Sheila. Is there any improvement?' The dog snuffled around my ankles.

'No, I don't think so,' I said carefully.

'These things take time, don't they? So young.' She shook her head and sighed too. The dog made interested grunting sounds. I kept quiet, hoping desperately for a clue. 'Still, they can do a lot these days, can't they? Not like it used to be. I knew a lady worked up at Prestwich – the stories she used to tell. Poor things stuck in strait-jackets, given electric shocks.' She touched my arm. 'If you ask me, people got better in spite of all that, not because of it.'

'Yes.' I smiled and nodded. The dog mounted my right leg and made disconcerting movements. I tried to edge away.

'Well, I'd better be going,' I said. 'I'll call some other time.'

'Okey-dokey. Come on, Millie.' She tugged the terrier away. It nearly choked, straining to return to my feet.

So, the neighbours had been told that Martin was in a mental institution. A funny sort of explanation for his sudden disappearance. Would admitting he'd run away be more embarrassing? Possibly. People would've expected them to be making every effort to find him, enquiring about their efforts. This way, the issue could be avoided. A simple 'no improvement' would solicit sympathy and a change of conversation.

'But that's awful,' Diane said.

I shrugged. 'Stops people asking too many questions.'

'Do you think they knew this woman, then?'

'No idea. She could have been a friend of the family, but that doesn't really tell me why she was so keen to find Martin.'

We were on our second pint and I'd taken Diane through the whole caboodle, eliciting just the right exclamations as I related seeing the photo in the paper, Leanne's story, the attitude of the police.

'You look tired, Sal.'

'Don't you start. I'm always tired anyway, comes with motherhood, you know.'

'It's not just that,' said Diane. 'This job, it's such a mess. No-one's paying you any more. Why bother?'

'I want to know who she was, why she was after him.'

'Why?' Diane was pushing me. I didn't like it.

'Curiosity, loose ends.' I took a long drink. Diane started to speak, then thought better of it.

'What?' I demanded.

'Nothing.'

'What?'

She sighed. 'Curiosity killed the cat.'

'Diane! That's pathetic. Anyway, I'm not a cat.'

'Sorry. I just worry about you. There has been a

murder after all... after last year...'

'Don't,' I interrupted. Diane had been my confidante throughout the case which had ended with me getting knifed. She also knew how close I'd come to falling apart in the months afterwards. I thought she'd understood my decision to carry on in my line of work. How it was all tied up with wanting to be strong again, asserting my right to earn my living this way, not wanting to spend the rest of my life ruled by fears of what might happen. Maybe she just thought I was being pig-headed.

'That was different. You know, I'd think twice about taking on anything dodgy. It started off as a missing person, remember. I'm not trying to solve the murder, am I? I just want to know who she was.'

She shot me her sceptical look. 'The two things aren't connected?'

'How the hell do I know?' I retorted.

She sighed and drained her glass.

'I'll be careful, I am careful.' I said. 'Another?'

When I returned from the bar, I changed the conversation, asking Diane what I'd interrupted the previous evening.

'Printing. I'd had this brilliant idea for a silk screen. I was in the middle of putting the first colour on.'

I burst out laughing. 'I thought you were in the middle of a session with Ben. You were all out of breath.'

'I get like that when the muse is on me.'

'And Ben?'

'Not artistic at all.'

'Diane!'

'State of truce. He's going to the christening, I'm not. We're having a weekend away in Barcelona.' She made it sound like a trip to the dentist. Ben was paying for the whole thing, which made her uncomfortable. Diane's a proud pauper, scraping a subsistence living from her artwork. And she feared that being thrown together would bring to a head all the tensions in the relationship.

'Think of the culture, though,' I said.

'I know, Gaudi, cafe society, music...'

'Construction sites for the Olympics,' I cut in. She jabbed me in the ribs. 'Send me a postcard, bring me some vino back.'

Cycling home, I got a puncture. It was still raining. I felt deflated too. Diane's words rankled. I'd been defensive about wanting to establish what Janice Brookes had been playing at. Cars swished past me, spraying me with water. I wanted to sleep. Diane was right, I was tired. Work usually gave me energy, a sense of purpose, achievement. But I'd had too many shocks to the system and no time to settle myself.

I fantasised about all the treats I could do with; a weekend away, a massage, even just a few days with the garden and the kids. Just what the Detective Inspector ordered. Sod it. A few more days and I'd have the answer to the mystery, and if I didn't I'd jack it in anyway.

Wheeling up the street, I saw that the house was ablaze with lights. My heart kicked. Something was wrong. Maddie. Tom. I dropped the bike on the drive and raced in. Into the kitchen. The smell of take-away. Wrappers strewn across the table. Lager cans. An overflowing ashtray.

Clive was back.

I put my bike away, then turned out the lights and crept upstairs to the bathroom. I had a pee, washed my hands and face and brushed my teeth as quietly as possible. I couldn't face him now. Crawled into bed. The bass on his hi-fi thumped steadily above me. Turn it down, turn it down. It seemed to go on for ever. I lay tense and angry, close to tears. It's not fair, I whispered, it's just not fair.

CHAPTER NINETEEN

Day-break. I was cold. No matter how I pulled the duvet round me, my insides were shivering. My mouth began to water. I reached the toilet just in time, retched until my stomach was empty. My skin felt raw all over as though I'd been peeled.

I filled a hot water bottle. Went and made a cup of peppermint tea. It was six-thirty. The rain had stopped. Clouds gone. The morning sun streamed into the kitchen. I put the cans and take-away wrappers in the bin, gagging at the smells. Settled in the armchair. Digger came and lay at my feet. I was honoured.

What did I really have to do? Visit the Hobbs'. It could wait a day. At seven, Ray and the kids emerged. Maddie and Tom were amused at us both being there so early. I sat huddled in the chair while they had a lively breakfast. Once they'd left for school, I topped up my water bottle and went back to bed.

I was woken by the doorbell. Ringing persistently. I fumbled for my dressing gown, struggled into it then discovered it was inside out. It'd have to do. I fell down the last stair – my body didn't work on automatic anymore – and cracked my funny bone on the banister.

When I opened the front door, the light made me wince. Jackie Dobson was on the doorstep.

'Sal, you look awful.'

'Bug.'

'This came yesterday.' She waved a white envelope.
'I meant to drop it in, then Jessica fell off the bunks
and I forgot all about it till tea-time. Then, what with
swimming lessons and...' The fact that Jackie could
deal with a full-time job plus four daughters and still
manage to forward a letter, was nothing short of a
miracle as far as I was concerned.

''S alright. Thanks. I was in bed.'

'You get back there,' she said. 'There's a lot of it
about at the moment.'

I made myself another herb tea. My belly rumbled,
but I wasn't going to throw any food at it. I slit open
the envelope. There was a second one inside,
addressed to Martin Hobbs, and a note. 'Please take
this to Martin.' No name, no signature. I knew who it
was from. A dead woman. I couldn't deal with it. I
foraged for my pocket and stuffed it all in there.

'Lady of leisure,' Clive brayed. I started and spilt
my tea. I hadn't heard him come downstairs.

'It's flu, actually. I'm going back to bed.'

'I've heard that one before. Fancy a day off, did we?'

'Excuse me.' I squeezed past him.

'Hey, Sal,' he bellowed up the stairs after me,
'what's the dog doing here?'

'He lives here. He's called Digger. I'll explain later.'

I slept the day away, waking a couple of times from
feverish dreams. Disturbing images melted away
before I could grasp them. I surfaced briefly at six
o'clock, to make more herb tea and wish the children
good night. Ten minutes on my feet and I was ready
to collapse. Back to bed, clasping my hot water bottle.
I slept the clock round. It was only a twenty-four hour
bug. I felt weak, a bit spaced-out, the following day,
but well enough to eat. Ready, if not eager, to visit Mr

and Mrs Hobbs. I scraped the burnt edges off the toast before Maddie spotted them. Mr Hobbs may well be at work but it'd probably be easier to talk to Martin's mother alone. The neighbour hadn't said anything about her working.

'I don't want to go to school, Mummy.'

'You've got to, love, everyone goes to school.'

'But I feel sick.'

'I feel sick,' Tom chimed in, beaming.

'You ate three lots of Krispies, Maddie, no wonder you feel sick.' Malingering or not? I never knew with Maddie. She tried it on every now and then. The last time I'd kept her off school, she'd bounced round the house like Tigger all day. She didn't look pale. I felt her forehead. No temperature.

'Ray'll tell Mrs Cummings to keep an eye on you. Now get your coat.'

'Aww.'

'Come on, Maddie.' Ray guided her out.

I rang the Coroner's Court to see if they had any information on the inquest for Janice Brookes. They had. It was scheduled for eleven o'clock Friday, the following morning, Court number one. I'd be there. So would the family. A chance to make contact.

Before I could get back upstairs, the phone rang. It was Pete, Clive's friend, though he didn't sound all that chummy. Clive hadn't been in touch about the money he owed him. Was he back? Yes. Had I passed on the message? Yes. I began to feel I was to blame. I promised Pete I'd make sure that Clive knew he'd rung. I dutifully wrote a note and left it by the phone.

I felt unclean after my sojourn in bed. I stripped the sheets and made it afresh. Thick, cotton sheets that I'd bought in the old days of regular income. I gathered up towels, sheets, face-flannels, my dressing-

gown. Crackle in the pocket. The letter. I prickled
with apprehension. The letter to Martin. From a dead
woman. A love letter? A warning? The rantings of an
obsessed stranger? I'd no way of knowing. Unless I
opened it. But I couldn't do that. It was probably the
last thing she'd written. She'd trusted me to deliver it.
I would if I could.

I put the letter in my bag, put the load in the
washer, put myself in the bath.

Something was worrying me as I lay there. I ticked
off in my mind all the things that I knew were
worrying me: J.B.'s death; Janice Brookes' murder;
having to visit Martin's parents; having to deliver the
letter; money – no-one was paying me any, would
have to apply for Family Credit again. Still something
else. I fished around. Diane? Maddie? Ray? Clive. Yes,
it was Clive.

'You're pathetic,' I told myself, as I pulled the plug.
But there it was. An unpleasant task waiting to be
tackled. And all the worse because it didn't belong to
the big, bad world out there. I couldn't face it, then
come home, safe, and shut the door on it. It was here,
in my home. I hated that.

I got ready to leave for Bolton, ignoring the
enquiring glances from the dog. Walk? No chance.
The phone rang. Maddie had been sick. Would I go
and fetch her. Shit. Guilt.

On the way there, I worked out the options. There
were two. Stay home with Maddie and put my visit to
Bolton off another day, or ask Nana Tello, Ray's mum,
to mind Maddie for a couple of hours. I'd psyched
myself up to visit Mr and Mrs Hobbs, but it was hardly
urgent. Was it worth grovelling to Nana Tello, who I
usually reserved for dire emergencies? She always
sent me double messages about minding the kids.

She'd hum and haw when asked and complain about their behaviour afterwards, then throw a fit if she heard we'd asked anyone else to mind them.

'Why don't you ask me? I'm a grandmother. I never see them.'

I collected Maddie, her face paper-white, dressed in ill-matched spare clothes. Made my apologies. The smell of vomit and disinfectant still lingered in the air. Poor kid.

On the way home, she solemnly related the saga. She'd thrown up three times, in the home corner, by the paints and in the toilet. Now she was tired.

I rang Nana Tello to sound her out. She wasn't home. Hah! Probably at the bookie's. She had a passion for the horses and a little flutter made her day. She'd spend hours pouring over the odds and selecting the winners.

Maddie's not the easiest invalid in the world. Petulant and full of self-pity. Still, I summoned up loads of patience and nursed her through the day. Got plenty of water down her. Resisted her tears when I forbade any biscuits. I heard Clive stirring in the early afternoon. Clattering round the kitchen. Maddie was asleep. I sat quietly in the lounge beside her. The door slammed. He'd left. I wondered whether Ray had said anything to him about the bills, his rent or having a meeting. I doubted it, somehow. I'd have to take the initiative. Later.

CHAPTER TWENTY

The inquest was adjourned, pending further enquiries by the police. It was Detective Inspector Miller who made the formal request that the body be held over. The coroner established that a murder enquiry was in progress and explained to the rest of us that he would not be releasing the body for burial.

There were only a handful of us in the Coroner's Court. An elderly woman, Janice's mother, sat with a younger black woman; a social worker, perhaps, or a neighbour. No sign of her sister. There were a couple of reporters, notebooks in hand, and Sergeant Boyston hovering at the back.

Miller flashed me a look of impatience. I pretended not to notice. He was impeccably dressed, crisp striped shirt and tie, navy gabardine. Looked more like an executive than a policeman.

The old-fashioned court, with its heavy oak pews and benches, and green and white tiled walls, lurked in the depths of the Old Fire Station on London Road, opposite Piccadilly Station ramp. It created just the right atmosphere for judging sudden and suspicious death.

We were instructed to rise and the Coroner left the court. People filed out. I hung back. I wanted to speak to Mrs Brookes, but not in the court. If I could find out where she lived... As I stepped through the door into bright sunshine, a hand on my arm made me jump.

'Miss Kilkenny.' It was Miller. I jerked my arm

away. 'I understood you were taking a break from all this.'

'I am, it's just, I wanted...' Out of the corner of my eye, I watched Mrs Brookes and her companion cross the road to the central reservation, towards the stairs leading up to the train station.

'We don't take kindly to interference in police matters.' He stared through his tinted designer specs. 'I thought I made that plain.'

'I'm not interfering.' The two women disappeared up the stairwell.

'I hope not. There are charges we can bring; obstruction, for example.'

'I've just come for the inquest, that's all. There's no law against that, is there?'

'As long as we understand each other.' He moved away abruptly, followed by Boyston. Once they'd turned the corner, I hurried over the road and climbed the steep steps, two at a time. Had Mrs Brookes come by train? I hoped not. I could end up in Milton Keynes for all I knew. At least if they were driving, I could turn back if it looked like a long distance.

I emerged onto the top of the ramp and looked around. There they were, black hair and white hair, walking slowly towards the car park. Bingo. I was also parked there. I fumbled with the locks on the Mini while I watched to see which was their car. Should I go over now? Introduce myself? Just then, I saw Mrs Brookes raise her hands to her face and start to cry. The younger woman put her arms round her. I couldn't barge in on that. The women parted and got into the black Datsun. I started my engine and followed them out of the car park. The young woman drove quickly. Easy enough to trail through town, but would I lose her later? She led me through Salford, along the M61, and off onto the A666, the road to Bolton.

Road-works slowed the traffic and it was easy to keep the Datsun in view. We left the motorway and took the dual carriageway into Bolton town centre. Round the maze of the one-way system, then out along an arterial road. Farms and moorland in-between the villages.

We entered the next one-street village and the Datsun drew up in front of the terraced row on the left. A little way ahead was a row of shops. I parked outside the chippie and watched in my rear-view mirror as the driver helped Mrs Brookes from the car and supported her up the steep steps into the terrace house. Red gate. I walked back along the road and noted the number. Thought about knocking on the door. The woman had just been to her daughter's inquest. I'd return another day to ask my questions.

I bought fish and chips in the little shop, wrapped in newspaper (I'm not a real vegetarian – it's just meat I won't eat). Found Chorley cakes and a milkshake in the newsagents next door. I drove up the road onto the tops and found a place to stop. It was windy. A clump of thorn bushes grew sideways, showing which way the wind blew. I was on the ridge between two valleys. Behind me lay the town, rows of redbrick terraces, sections of wasteland where they'd been cleared, new industrial estates, old mill chimneys. I could just make out Le Mans Crescent with its ornate public buildings sand-blasted to their former glory.

In the valley ahead nestled a few farms, scattered villages and the moors. I gazed at them while I ate my lunch. The fish and chips were classic: crisp batter, moist flakes of cod, large chips freshly fried. The Chorley cake, all sweet spicy fruit and oily pastry, needed washing down with the milkshake. My blood sugar level and no doubt my cholesterol level soared. I felt sleepy. But I had work to do. I was in the area. I had no excuse. I consulted the A-Z and worked out my route to twenty-three Glover Street.

He opened the door. Dark hair dashed with grey; holiday tan. A pleasant face, square jaw, laughter lines. Marks and Sparks cardigan and slacks.

'Mr Hobbs.'

'Yes?'

'Sal Kilkenny. Can I come in a minute? I'd like to have a word with you and your wife.'

'What's it about?' His smile faded.

'If we could talk inside?'

'Well, I...'

'Who is it, Keith?' She came through from the kitchen, peeling off rubber gloves. She was the real sun-seeker in the family. Her skin a rich ambre-solaire brown, set off nicely by the cream and blue shirt-dress. The tan would last about a week in this climate. She had streaked, permed hair, a small, pointed face, restrained make-up.

'Wants to talk to us.' Mr Hobbs said.

'Market research?' she asked.

'No, it's personal, actually.'

'You'd better come in,' she said, 'in the lounge. I'll just put these in the kitchen.' She waved the yellow gloves.

Mr Hobbs sat on one of the winged armchairs, I on the other. Mrs Hobbs settled herself on the sofa. The room was old-fashioned, comfortable, cream and green, muted patterns. Begonias and bizzy-lizzies on the window-sills and the piano.

'Well, what is it? Don't keep us in suspense,' said Mr Hobbs, forcing a laugh.

'I'm a private detective,' I said. I fished for the

picture of Janice Brookes in my bag. 'Do either of you know this woman?' Mr Hobbs studied the clipping, shook his head, passed it to his wife.

'No,' she said. She handed it back to me. 'Should we?'

'I thought you might,' I began. 'She came to me recently. She wanted me to trace a missing person. You're sure you've never met her, seen her locally perhaps?'

'No,' they spoke in unison.

'Why did you think we'd know her?' asked Mr Hobbs.

I took a breath. 'She wanted me to find Martin, your son.' Mrs Hobbs gasped, glanced at her husband. He sat very still.

'I'm afraid Martin isn't here,' he said. He fiddled with the buckle on his watch strap. 'He's in hospital. You see, he's... erm, he's been diagnosed as schizophrenic.' He spoke calmly, with just the right impression of restrained grief.

'No, he isn't,' I said. 'Martin left home. He's living in Manchester.'

'Rubbish,' Mr Hobbs blurted out. He'd gone very pale. His wife blinked rapidly.

'I talked to him last week.'

'How is he?' Mrs Hobbs said. I turned to answer her. She lowered her gaze, as if ashamed of asking.

'Hard to tell...'

Mr Hobbs interrupted. His voice under control, reasonable. 'We don't know who this woman is, so we can't really help you, I'm afraid.' He began to rise.

'What puzzles me,' I said, 'is why she was looking for Martin? If she's not a relative, a family friend?'

'Why don't you ask her?' he said.

'I would. But she's dead, you see. She was murdered

last week. Janice Brookes, her name was. It was in all the papers.'

'Oh God.' Mrs Hobbs pressed her knuckles to her mouth. I couldn't tell whether my bald announcement of the murder had provoked that, or whether the name meant something to her.

'We were away,' he said.

'Does the name mean anything to you?' I addressed my question to Mrs Brookes. She didn't respond.

'My wife's upset. I think you'd better go.' A muscle in his jaw twitched repeatedly.

'I know why Martin left home,' I said.

Mr Hobbs gave a wan smile. 'Do you now? That's more than either of us know.' He looked over at Mrs Hobbs. She sat staring at the carpet.

'Sexual abuse,' I said baldly. 'You were abusing him.' He gave me a look of incredulity.

'What?' He looked appalled.

'You heard.'

'Of all the...! The boy's a congenital liar, always was. Living in cloud bloody cuckoo-land. You can't believe a thing he says. It's attention-seeking, that's all. If you believe that claptrap...'

'Oh, I believe it.' I looked him in the eye. He sat back in his chair. Shook his head in disbelief.

'Get out,' he said. 'Get out of my house.'

I stood up. 'Goodbye, Mrs Hobbs.' She didn't respond. I left her frozen in position, her eyes unfocused, knuckles pressed tight against her mouth. If she didn't react to or acknowledge the situation, maybe it wasn't happening. Like someone in shock.

I was shaking. Took a few deep breaths in the car. My palms were clammy, my shoulder ached. I'd half-expected the outright denial I'd got. What was odd was that they didn't seem to have an inkling of curiosity about why Janice Brookes was looking for Martin. Was that just indifference, not wanting to have anything to do with Martin, or did they know something I didn't? I was pretty sure they were genuine about not recognising the photograph, but what about the name? Maybe Martin had talked about her, perhaps she'd rung the house.

I called at Tesco's on the way to collect Maddie from school. I'd not made a list, but I knew we needed virtually everything. I couldn't shake the picture of Mrs Hobbs from my mind, as I loaded the trolley. Beans, tomatoes, kidney beans. She was his mother. She instinctively asked how he was. She loved him. Vermicelli, pizza bases, rice. Yet she thought him a liar, all those years ago, when he'd tried to tell her what Dad was doing to him. Weetabix, Krispies. Then I come crashing in, a stranger, and I believe Martin. Was she still sitting there now, petrified? Was he talking her round, swearing to his innocence?

If Maddie told me Ray was messing with her, how would I react? Disbelief, yes, because I wouldn't want it to be true. But I'd try to hide that from Maddie. I'd heard enough about abuse to know that children rarely lie about it. And I would act on what she'd told me.

I was still brooding as I waited for Maddie at school. One in ten is the conservative estimate. Three kids in Maddie's class. I watched them as their names were called and they trotted out, laden with lunch-boxes and art-work. Some of them were tired and maungy, others greeted their parents with smiles and questions. Maddie was maungy. I bent to take her lunch-box and she launched a tantrum. Mouth stretched wide, tears coursing. God knows why. I didn't attempt to find out. It'd only make her worse. We collected Tom. Drove home. I unloaded the shopping. Made a cuppa. Started cooking. The phone rang. It was Harry.

'Sal, that information you wanted... Smiley?'

'Yes.'

'My guy knew of him. He went away back in the 'seventies, part of a vice bust. Seems they were into a bit of everything – porn, drugs. There was a big undercover operation. The police did very well. Now, your bloke only did two years. Co-operated with the police, as they say.'

'That's why he got cut up?'

'That's right. Word is he's a bit of a fixer. Someone wants something, he puts them in touch with the right people. He's not been back inside since then. Tends to work on his own. The criminal fraternity don't exactly trust him.'

'Anything more specific; what he might be involved in at the moment?'

'No, I did ask. The man reckons it can't be anything big or he'd have heard about him. You can rule him out of the main drug cartels, anything like that. But he's likely to be dealing in that sort of area; prostitution, drugs. He hasn't taken up art-theft or cat-burglary, or so my source tells me.' Harry dramatised his use of words. I laughed.

'Any use?' he asked.

'Not really. Still, thanks anyway.'

'Pleasure. Now, I must go. The kids are beating shit out of each other.'

'Thanks, Harry.' Nice man.

CHAPTER TWENTY ONE

Martin's letter was still in my bag. A letter from a dead woman. I wanted rid. Saturday seemed as good a day as any to deliver it. It was with some foreboding that I set off to the house in Cheadle. After all, it could have been the scene of a murder. But, presumably, the police would have made their enquiries by now. Found out whether Janice Brookes had called there the previous Sunday. Whether she'd left there alive. If anyone was a likely suspect.

Like Martin. Maybe her connection with him was a threat to his new life. Or maybe she was part of it. Whatever 'it' was. Max had talked about Martin losing control, that time in the playground. Dragged away before he beat the guy to death. It made my skin crawl. If not Martin, there was his 'friend'. The man who'd come looking for him at Barney's. He'd struck me as cold, domineering – but a killer?

There hadn't been anything in the paper about it. No small paragraph stating that a man was helping police with their enquiries. That helped a bit.

I recognised the place from its position on the winding road. These were big, expensive houses. No two alike. Most, like this one, were well hidden from the road. I parked in front of the beech hedge and made my way up the drive. Rhododendron bushes and lawns on either side. A graceful weeping willow. The house was built to impress. Small pillars framed the doorway. Two storeys with plenty of large windows. To the left of the building, a double garage and, at the other side, a glass conservatory. Gravel crunched underfoot. The neighbouring house to the left was completely screened by tall conifers. I could see the roof of the one on the right and a small stairway window between a pair of sycamores.

The red car was parked in front of the doorway. Someone was home. I rang the bell. The man who looked like Norman Tebbit, gaunt face and receding hair, answered.

'Hello,' I said brightly, 'is Martin in?'

'Martin?' He looked puzzled.

'Martin Hobbs.'

'There's nobody of that name here,' he said, in his precise clipped Scottish accent. He began to close the door.

'But he said he was staying here,' I bluffed. 'I just want to give him a message.'

'You're mistaken.'

'Wait.' I pulled a copy of the angling photograph from my bag. 'This is him.'

He gave it a cursory glance. 'Sorry. I can't help you. I've never seen the boy before.' He shut the door. I had to step back to keep my balance.

I walked back down the drive; turned back to look at the house. The man stood in one of the upstairs windows, watching me. He made no attempt to disguise the fact. Gave me the creeps.

Although the Mini couldn't be seen from the house, I wanted to give the impression, if anyone was interested, that I'd gone. I got in and drove round the corner a quarter of a mile and parked on one of the side roads. I took off my red jacket, put on an outsized baseball cap of Tom's and walked back to the neighbour's house. If there'd been a corner shop, I could have flashed Martin's photo around, but this wasn't corner shop country. Strictly residential.

The neighbour's house was Spanish ranch style. A wooden verandah ran round the base, balconies jutting out above. There was plenty of black and white wrought-iron and shutters all over the place. Pampas grass grew in the garden, along with spiky cordylines. A series of terracotta urns spilt a riot of pink and orange geraniums and fuchsias against the white plaster walls.

I couldn't find a bell, just a huge door-knocker shaped like a horseshoe. I banged. Frenzied barking erupted within. A woman's voice silenced the dog. I heard chains and locks being drawn back. The door opened. The woman who stood there was in her late thirties. She wore a loose flowing housecoat, in colours to match the floral display outside. A bandanna round her tawny hair. Sun-glasses.

'Yes?' she snapped.

'I wonder if I could talk to you?'

'What are you selling?' She had a transatlantic twang, a rude delivery.

'Nothing.'

'So, what do you want to talk to me about?' She stressed the me.

'Your neighbours.'

She rolled her eyes. 'Tell me more.' She waved me through into a huge living room that ran from the front of the house through to the back. All in white. Splashes of colour provided by scatter-cushions and large abstract paintings. I prayed my shoes were clean.

I sank into a creaking white leather Chesterfield. She settled in a white reclining chair.

'I'm a private detective,' I began. 'I've been trying to

123

find a missing boy, sixteen years old. I heard he was staying next door,' I pointed the direction, 'but when I asked there, I didn't get much co-operation.'

'Fraser's a pain in the ass,' she replied. 'I thought the English were snotty, but God, he makes it into an art-form.'

'Do you know him?'

'Barely. I think we've met three times in as many years. Usually if the mail gets dropped in the wrong box. He's always made it plain that he values his privacy.'

'Does Mr Fraser live on his own?'

She laughed. 'Not Mr Fraser. Fraser's his first name; Fraser Mackinlay. Yeah, he's on his own.'

'What does he do for a living?'

'Business. Communications, computers, video, that sort of thing. Jack managed to embarrass him into coming over for drinks, when we first moved in. They talked business. All evening. Fascinating.' She stretched the word out, dripping with sarcasm. 'Fraser couldn't wait to get away, but Jack's not too hot reading the old body language.'

'Do you remember the name of his company?'

'Nope. Jack may. Say, isn't this rather un-English, prying into folks' affairs...?'

I must have looked worried.

She grinned. 'No problem. I love it. Drink?' She opened a white wicker cabinet and removed a bottle.

'No thanks.'

'Too early? I hope you're not the moralising type. Jack hates to see me drink before noon. Not that he does, he's hardly ever here.' She clunked ice-cubes into a glass, pointed the bottle at me. 'Never marry an entrepreneur. They fly home every couple of months to get the dry-cleaning done, then off they go. Money's no problem,' she nodded at the room, 'but the company stinks.' She poured her drink and took a good swig.

'What did you say your name was?'

'Sal, Sal Kilkenny.'

'Irish. I like the Irish. I have a quarter Irish blood, you know, most of it Bushmills.' She laughed and raised her glass in a salute. 'I'm Zaleski, Nina. Jack's Polish stock. So, you guess Fraser's seen this boy?'

I told her about following the car the night I'd found Martin at Barney's, and Fraser's outright denial.

'So, Fraser's telling lies.' She drained her glass. 'Tut, tut. Maybe he's something to hide. Like a penchant for sixteen year old boys. That's illegal here, isn't it? Good enough reason to fib a little.'

'That did occur to me,' I said, 'but all I want is to get in touch with Martin. I'm not going to feed what I find to the tabloids.'

I showed her Martin's photo. Asked if she'd seen him around.

'No, but these places aren't exactly built for talking over the garden fence.'

'I don't even know if he is living there; he could have just gone back that one night. It's none of my business what the relationship is, but I need to find out where Martin is; that's the job I've been hired to do.'

'Miss Kilkenny! Are you asking me to spy on my neighbour?'

'No, not at...'

''Cos I'd just love to. Life is dull. A little project like that might add some interest. If I keep my beady little eye on all the comings and goings, I'll see your Martin, sooner or later. That is, if he is staying there.'

'I don't know. If Fraser wants to keep Martin a secret, if he thought you were spying on him...'

'I'll be the soul of discretion.' She put her hand on

her heart. 'I have some excellent binoculars and a pair of ghastly net curtains. When in Rome... I shall also develop a sudden interest in walking Fang.'

I raised my eyebrows.

'The dog,' she explained. 'And I'll create a new flower garden at the bottom of the drive. Fraser knows I have a fondness for the bottle and that I'm an American. My eccentric behaviour will confirm his prejudices.' She winked. 'I can't wait to get started.'

I had acquired a mole. I left her my card and strict instructions to be careful. I returned home with Martin's letter still in my bag. Address to be confirmed.

CHAPTER TWENTY TWO

'Sal, it's Jackie. I think you'd better come over. We've had a break-in in the cellar. I'm afraid your office is in a right mess.'

I arrived at the Dobson's at the same time as the young policewoman. No-one I recognised. Jackie showed us the side door, which had been forced open, the wood shattered, the frame split. The door had been locked and bolted but the intruders had simply battered their way in.

'Didn't you hear anything?' I asked.

'We were all out. Once in a blue moon. The twins had a party, Grant and I went to the pictures, the other two were in town. We got back just after eleven and went straight to bed. We didn't even check the door – stupid, I know, but it'd been locked when we left and everything was the same as usual. I noticed the smell of paint, though.' Jackie led us along the hall to the door leading down to the cellar. 'I thought you'd had a sudden burst of DIY again,' she added. 'Sal, it's a bit of a mess.'

Mess. It was an abomination. Paint had been poured and daubed over everything; my desk, telephone, the carpet, filing cabinets. Pictures from the wall, my dead geranium in its pot, had been smashed and mixed in. The two old dining chairs had been broken and scattered around.

I drew breath in sharply and clutched Jackie's arm.

The memories again. *Knife glinting, spittle on his lips, wetting my pants with fear.*

'Oh, God.'

'Bit of a mess,' ventured the W.P.C. 'Can you tell if anything's missing?' Her mundane practicality brought me back to the present.

'I don't think so, I didn't have much here. Nothing valuable.'

'Looks like kids,' she said. 'We've had a lot of this recently.'

'Come on upstairs,' said Jackie.

While Jackie provided cups of tea, the young policewoman listened to me speculating about whether it was a random break-in or whether I was the target of something more sinister. I explained that the woman I'd been working for had been murdered. Could it have been to keep her quiet? Maybe they thought she'd told me something I shouldn't know. I could tell I sounded paranoid. She didn't even bother to make notes. She asked if I was still working on the case. I denied it. After all, so my silent rationalisations went, no-one was paying me, I wasn't trying to solve Janice Brookes' murder or even J.B.'s overdose. I was simply trying to deliver a letter and find out a bit more about a woman who'd hired me under false pretences. Besides, I didn't want Detective Inspector Miller hearing that I was still nosing around. I shut up when the tea arrived.

She repeated her assertion that it looked like the work of kids, that there'd been a lot of mindless destruction of property over the last few months and advised Jackie to think about fitting an alarm and an outside sensor light. Jackie saw her out and returned to the kitchen.

'God, Jackie, I'm sorry. The mess and...'

'Don't worry about that.'

'But it's your home.'

'My cellar.' She laughed. 'Sal, our school gets this sort of treatment every month. She's right. There's a lot of it about. I don't let it get to me anymore. I'd go loopy. At least they didn't touch the rest of the place and nothing seems to have been stolen. And they didn't leave a calling card.'

'What?'

'They often have a shit for good measure.'

'Oh, no.'

'What was all that about it being a message for you? What's going on? Can you talk about it?' Bless her cotton socks. It was just what I needed. I swore her to secrecy.

'It's a bit confusing. I started off with a woman called Mrs Hobbs. She wanted me to find her son, Martin. I find him and he wants nothing to do with her. Two weeks later this woman is murdered and it turns out she's not Mrs Hobbs at all. Not Mrs anything. She's Janice Brookes and I haven't got a clue why she wanted me to find Martin. The man who gives Martin a lift home denies ever having seen him and a friend of Martin's who never touches drugs is found dead from a heroin overdose. Meanwhile, the real Mrs Hobbs does exist, she has got a son called Martin and he has left home. But the family are putting it about that he's in hospital, a schizophrenic.'

'What?'

'Plenty of deception, eh?'

'So the dead Mrs Hobbs is the impostor?'

'Yes, really Miss Brookes. She did a hell of a job acting the distressed mother. I fell for it. Right from the word go.'

I told Jackie the lot, starting with that first visit from the nervous 'Mrs Hobbs', right up to calling on Fraser

Mackinlay. Then I talked myself out of breath about whether the attack was just a random crime or a warning to me.

'It's a bit oblique, as far as warnings go,' said Jackie.

'Yeah. You think they'd have made it plain. Slogans on the wall or a wreath in the mail.'

'What?'

'They send people wreaths or hearses,' I said. 'I read it in a book.' Suddenly the idea struck me as funny and I had a fit of the giggles. 'I suppose headstones are too expensive,' I spluttered, 'and coffins would be a bugger to wrap.'

When I'd calmed down, Jackie asked me what I was going to do.

'Oh, I don't know. Clean up. I can't afford to replace anything. I never renewed the insurance.'

'Oh, Sal.' She shook her head at me, got up and began to get potatoes from the veg rack.

'Don't say it. It hardly seemed worth it and I never had the money to spare. I only took it out for the first year 'cos I thought the Enterprise Allowance people might check.'

'Well, if there's anything in the other cellar you can use, feel free. But what are you going to do about these loose ends, as you put it?'

'I don't know. Sleep on it. Work out whether I'm being paranoid or stupid.'

'I think that policewoman was right, you know.' She began to scrape the potatoes. 'It did look like kids messing about.'

'Coincidences do happen,' I sighed. 'I'm going to have another look.'

As I stood in the doorway and surveyed the mayhem, I began to wonder whether it was really worth replacing anything. My work paid the bills if I was lucky and frugal. There were aspects of it I relished: No two days the same; out and about; no boss peering over my shoulder; following people; checking things out; adding them up; the challenge of unravelling each trail. I loved the look on people's faces when they asked what I did. The whole seedy romance of being a private eye.

And then there was the rest. The long wait in between jobs, red herrings and false starts, the isolation, the potential for nasty situations. I was starting to get maudlin.

How the hell had I come to this? After the stabbing, I'd sworn to myself I'd only take safe work. Checking on erring spouses, watching light-fingered employees, tracing missing persons. No murders, no violent crime, no security stuff.

Martin Hobbs had started out as a missing person. It'd all seemed so straightforward. Cast about a bit, see if anything bites. If not, no loss. Since then, J.B. had gone looking and he was dead. Janice Brookes had gone looking and she was dead too. I'd gone looking and some prat had sloshed lilac emulsion all over my office.

The bathos made me smile. Sod it. Time enough for big decisions. Time to go home. I'd take the kids to the park, wear them out. And once they were in bed, I'd get well and truly drunk.

I walked into the kitchen to find Ray mopping the floor.

'Oh, shit, your mother's coming. Sorry, I didn't mean it like that. I forgot all about it. My office is a right mess, paint everywhere. The police reckon it's the local youth. Where are the kids?'

'Out doing over someone's house.' Ray straightened

up and brushed his dark hair back. His forehead was gleaming and he was breathless.

'Good exercise, floor mopping, you ought to do it more often.'

He ignored me. 'Clive's taken them to the park; Digger too.'

'Clive has!' Clive had never taken the kids anywhere.

'He's got a woman with him. I think he's trying to impress her with his caring male persona.'

'Bloody typical.'

'Have you said anything to him?' Ray asked.

'No, I haven't had a chance.' It came out defensively. 'Can't you do it? Just tell him we want a meeting.'

Our conversation was interrupted by the party's arrival back from the park. Clive disappeared upstairs with his friend. I entertained the kids while Ray cooked. The smell of real minestrone began to permeate the house.

The doorbell rang. The kids ran to get it, chanting 'Nana Tello, Nana Tello.' I gritted my teeth. We always seemed to rub each other up the wrong way.

She bustled in, chiding Maddie for shouting and stooping to rub Tom's face with her hanky.

'Sal,' she said, 'you look tired. You getting enough iron? Liver. You need liver for the blood. When Raymond was little, I ate liver twice a week. You should try it. Now, where is that boy?' She sailed past me into the kitchen. I trailed after her like a sulky teenager. The woman infuriated me. She was bossy, brusque, insensitive, manipulative. And I felt guilty for feeling so unsisterly.

She regarded me as the major obstacle to Ray settling down with a nice Catholic girl. I don't think she believed our relationship was platonic. Once in a while, I made a renewed effort to call a truce with her, to find some common ground, to talk to her like I would any other woman. But we always ended up behaving like stereotypes, overbearing mother and bolshie daughter.

I survived the meal without rising to any of the jibes that came my way. I drank lots of red wine. Ray drove her home. I got the kids to bed and opened another bottle of wine. Ray came in and flung himself on the sofa.

'Mothers,' I said. 'More wine? Do you think Tom and Maddie will feel like this about us one day? I'm regarding you as a surrogate mother for the purpose of the discussion.'

'Don't they already?'

The phone rang. I heaved myself out of the chair to answer it. It was Mrs Hobbs. The real Mrs Hobbs. She wanted to see me. I had an unnerving flash of déjà-vu. I'd been here before. And I didn't fancy a re-run.

CHAPTER TWENTY THREE

'Why did you want to see me?' My question jerked her attention away from the cup of coffee she was stirring. She darted a glance up at me, blinked rapidly and ducked again. We were sitting in the cafe at the Royal Exchange Theatre. It was all very civilised. We'd already been through the banalities of queuing for coffee, choosing a table, settling in.

'Martin,' she said quietly. 'You said you'd spoken to him. Was he really alright?'

I cut her off. 'Why?'

'What?' Her brow creased.

'Why do you want to know?'

'He's my son. I...' Her eyes filled up. She pressed her mouth shut. Fought to keep control.

'Martin doesn't want any contact with you.'

She let her breath out in a shudder. 'The things you said,' she faltered. 'This is very hard for me... I can't believe... Keith would never. There must have been some terrible misunderstanding.'

'You still don't believe Martin.'

She didn't reply.

'Whose idea was it to tell the neighbours Martin was ill?'

'There'd been a terrible scene. I wasn't there, but Martin, he'd... he'd threatened Keith with a knife. He'd always been a bit moody, shy... but never violent. Keith was very angry, very, very angry. He's got heart trouble... it could've...' She shook her head at the thought. 'Martin had stormed off. Said he was never coming back. Keith said it was best to leave it be. No point in dragging the police into it all. It was difficult to know what to say to people...'

'It could have been rather awkward for your husband if the police had been involved. After all, Martin might have spilled the beans. I think that's why your husband was so keen on the hospital story.'

She shook her head. I wasn't giving her the reassurance she wanted. 'Please, just tell me he's alright. I've been out of my mind with worry. Is he living in Manchester?'

'I don't know. I saw him briefly. He was upset, angry. I didn't find out where he was living.'

'Did he say anything about me?' she asked.

I stalled, wondering what to say.

'What did he say? Tell me. What did he say?'

I took a breath. 'He thought you'd hired me to find him. He said you'd never cared before.'

'That's just not...' She pressed her lips tight together, but the tears still coursed down her cheeks. 'It's not...' Her voice rose in pitch, then she broke off.

'Mrs Hobbs, I have to ask you this. The woman I talked about – Janice Brookes...' But she'd already lurched to her feet, rocking the table, spilling the coffee. I let her go. I could hardly force her to stay, to talk. She pushed her way through the crowd. I lost sight of her.

I felt lousy. Perhaps I shouldn't have told her what Martin had said. It was pretty brutal, after all. But then maybe it would help her to believe Martin's version of events. Ignoring the curious glances of other patrons, I shook coffee off my jacket, rubbed my trousers with a hanky, stuffed it in my pocket and left.

I walked back to Victoria train station where I'd left

the car. The day hadn't started too well. I ran through the possibilities for the rest of it. Go home and be domestic? Plenty to do, but then Clive might be hanging around. I wanted Ray to be the one to tell Clive we needed to meet. Not just because I shrank from the task, but also because I was sick of being the one to initiate that sort of thing. It was time for Ray to take his turn. Not home then. What else? I could tire myself out, window-shopping in town. Gaze at all the lovely summer clothes that Maddie and I would have to manage without. Yeah, great. End up exhausted and envious.

I got in the Mini and took the road down to Strangeways, past Boddingtons brewery near the prison and through Salford, to join the motorway to Bolton. Might as well be hung for a sheep as a lamb. I'd already shattered one mother's day and this would be even trickier. I had a whole heap of questions for Mrs Brookes, Janice's mother, but the main one concerned Martin. Why had Janice wanted to find him?

Sheila Hobbs had lost her son. Mrs Brookes had lost her daughter. Martin Hobbs had run away. Janice Brookes had run after him. And been killed.

Why? I hadn't the faintest idea.

The hamlet outside Bolton was shrouded in an unseasonal mist. The sky was grey and leaden. No point in stopping to admire the view. The black Datsun was still there. The woman who'd driven it was probably a neighbour, then.

I mounted the steep steps, in-between walls spilling aubretia and alyssum. I rang the bell.

The black woman who'd accompanied Mrs Brookes to the inquest opened the door. Whoops. Was this her house? Did Mrs Brookes live next door? Up close, she was younger than I'd thought. She wore her hair pulled tightly into a top-knot. Sloppy T-shirt, cycling shorts.

'Hello, I'm looking for Mrs Brookes.'

She frowned. Suspicion in her eyes. 'Who?'

'Mrs Brookes. Janice's mother.'

I caught a flash of anger. 'You from the papers?' She moved towards me, blocking the door.

'No, no. I knew Janice. I wanted to talk to her mother, if she's in.'

'She doesn't live here.' She was very cagey. I felt as though I was making a right fool of myself. Admit it.

'I'm sorry,' I said. 'I must have made a stupid mistake. If you could just give me the right address?' She stared.

'Or her sister,' I carried on. 'Do you know where she lives?'

'I'm her sister.'

'Oh. God.' That threw me completely. 'Look, I'm sorry... about Janice. I didn't realise...'

The look in her eyes told me that she'd been here countless times before. Watching people grapple with the surprise; black woman, white woman – sisters.

'Half-sister,' she said. 'You were at the inquest, weren't you? What's this all about? How did you know Janice?'

'I was working for her before she died.'

'Working for her?' It was her turn to be surprised.

'Yes.' I decided to be bold. 'Can I come in and explain?'

She moved aside, by way of reply, and led me along the narrow hallway into the small back room. A young boy lounged on a bean bag, gazing at Sesame Street.

'Alex,' the woman said. 'Upstairs.'

'But Mama...'

'Now.' She didn't need to raise her voice. He knew she meant it and disappeared.

We sat either side of the table below the window. Through the nets I could see the backyard, neat and tidy, and beyond, the sweep of hills.

'What d'you mean, you were working for Janice?'

I explained. I didn't go into much detail. I wanted to see what her reaction was. She didn't give much away. There was a slight frown creasing her forehead, but her deep brown eyes were sharp. Regarding me steadily.

'And that's it,' I finished. 'I've spoken to the police, told them there may be a connection between Janice's murder and her search for Martin Hobbs. But I've no idea why she wanted to find the boy. Why she pretended to be his mother.'

'What did the police say?'

'Not a lot.' I shrugged. ' Said they'd look into it. Thought I had a lively imagination. They also said...' I hesitated. She tilted her head to one side, waiting. I didn't want to offend her. 'Well, they said Janice had been ill, mentally ill. That could have been why she acted like she was someone else.'

'She did get ill, but she never forgot who she was.'

'Did she ever talk to you about Martin? Did you know him?'

'No.' She got up from the table and went into the tiny kitchen, filled the kettle. Came back and leant on the door jamb. 'But then I wouldn't. Janice had left home by the time I was seven. She came back a couple of times. When things got really bad. But we were never close. Tea, coffee?'

'Tea, please. Was she ever in trouble with the police, with drugs or anything like that?'

'Janice! Bloody hell, no. You met her, didn't you?' I

nodded. She was right. It was hard to imagine. 'She couldn't even tell lies, Janice.'

'She lied to me.'

'Yeah, well.' She came through with the drinks.

'So you're not called Brookes?' I checked.

'Nope. Mitchell. Natalie Mitchell. I'm married now. Was Williams. That was my dad's name.'

He was dead then. 'And your mother's?'

'Yeah.'

'So,' she took a sip of coffee, 'you reckon this Martin Hobbs might have killed Janice?'

'No, no...' I lowered my mug with a clunk. 'It's just...' Just what? I had thought of the possibility. But I didn't like it. The Martin I'd met was messed up, vulnerable, frightened but he wasn't a murderer, was he? He had been violent though. The time in the playground that Max had told me about. And he'd gone for his father with a knife. If Janice had some hold over Martin, if she posed some threat...

'Look, I don't know. I just think there could be a link. When she spoke to me, she was all for chasing after him. The next morning, the place she was found, it's not far from where he was staying...' I sighed. Took a drink. 'Had you seen Janice recently?'

'Not since Christmas. We all met up at Mum's. That's the only time we ever saw each other.' There was a trace of regret in her voice.

'I would like to talk to your mother, if you could give me her address.'

'She might not want to see you. She's still very upset. She's had the police round, and the papers. I'd have to ask her first.'

'Okay.' I was hoping she might ring there and then but made no move. 'When will you be able to let me know?'

'I'll ring her tonight. See what she says.' She stood up. I fished out a card and gave it to her.

'Did she owe you any money?'

The question startled me. Then I blushed. 'No. We settled it the last time she called.'

'I just don't want Mum worried with stuff like that.' She led me out of the room and into the hallway.

'I don't work like that,' I said, angry that she suspected me of chasing unpaid bills. 'No-one's paying me to do this – I just want to know what was going on.'

'Yeah. So do I.'

It was like a game of May-I. There I was getting fairy steps, when what I really needed was a couple of giant leaps. Least I seemed to be heading in the right direction. Away from deception and towards the truth. I'd traced Janice's sister – someone who actually knew her, though she'd not been much help in solving the mystery.

It was over three weeks since her half-sister had sat in my office, asking me to look for her runaway child. June had rolled into July. Janice Brookes hadn't made it that far. I hoped her mother would agree to talk to me.

At home, the post was on the table. Top of the pile, a bill for me, a prancing logo, final reminder from British Telecom. Shit. I'd just slammed it down, when Clive strolled in.

'Greetings.'

'Clive, have you seen this bill? Final reminder. We've got to pay it now.' I tried to keep my voice level and practical.

'Aahh,' Clive said. 'I should be getting some cash next week.'

140

'They'll have cut us off by then.'

He tutted. 'How much is it? My share, I mean.'

'Yours is the lion's share.'

'How come?'

'Long distance calls, eight of them. You owe about sixty quid.'

'Sixty! I can't pay that.'

'Well, you should have thought of that before you made the calls.' I was beginning to sound frayed.

'I didn't make those calls.' I could see the lie in the set of his mouth.

'Oh, come on.'

'I didn't, really Sal.' He was blinking a lot. Did he think that implied honesty or something? 'They've made a mistake. You should ring them up and tell them.'

'You ring them up. And what about when you called your father in Milan and that friend in Washington?'

'That's only two. I never made eight calls. Maybe it's the kids, messing with it.' I wanted to brain him.

'Why the hell should I pay your bills? You already owe the rent and the gas, which we've had to pay. I've got an overdraft too, you know. I don't earn much more then you.'

'God,' he sneered, 'you're so materialistic. It's all you care about, isn't it, money?' And he bounded upstairs.

Someone would have to pay the bill. Re-connection charges were punitive and the thought of being cut off made me anxious. It was the phone that had alerted people when I'd been attacked here. I hadn't answered it. He wouldn't let me. And that had caused enough alarm to bring help.

I'd pay the bill.

I wrote the cheque then and there, knowing I'd be well overdrawn once it was cleared. I could post it first thing.

I'd tackled Clive over that – one credit to me. So Ray could set up the meeting with Clive. It was his turn. Materialistic indeed!

CHAPTER TWENTY FOUR

I didn't hear from Natalie Mitchell till late the following day. I thought it was her when the phone rang mid-morning. I was wrong. But it was work. The sort of straight-forward request that puts food on the table or helps pay the phone bill. Another erring spouse. A woman this time. The husband asked if I'd furnish proof. He wanted photos. I was happy to snap the odd shot of people meeting, people in public, but I made it clear I wouldn't be peering through keyholes or bursting into bedrooms. I don't mind seedy but I draw the line at sordid.

The woman claimed to be going to aerobics that evening, then on for a drink with the girls. My client suspected otherwise. I got the details I needed and arranged to call with any evidence the following morning. I drew up a few doors down from their new-built semi, at the appointed time.

Within an hour, I'd established that she was indeed lying to him and, to prove it, I'd taken several shots of her getting into the white Fiesta.

Back home, I rang Nina Zaleski. Had there been any sign of Martin? Nothing. She would keep on looking. I wondered how I'd get the letter to him if he'd left Manchester altogether.

I pottered round the garden. It had been a true summer's day and even now the air was warm and still. It was nine o'clock and the sun was only just dipping behind the roofs of the houses at the back.

Scent from next door's mock orange blossom hung in the air and mingled with the smell of pine and earth that rose as I watered tubs and borders. We hadn't had rain for a week and the heavy clay soil was starting to crack and split apart, fired hard by the hot sun of the day.

I made myself a glass of fresh orange juice and took the paper outside. I automatically flicked through, looking for any news about the murder of Janice Brookes. There was nothing there. But a photograph in the Business section caught my eye. There was a page full of posed photographs, showing people handing over giant-sized cheques to various good causes. One of the faces looked familiar. I peered closer. It was one of the men I'd seen with Martin at Barney's nightclub. The one I'd likened to Kirk Douglas; deep cleft chin and craggy features.

I took it into the kitchen where the light was better. The man was called Bruce Sharrocks. He was pictured with Mrs Nancy Sharrocks, receiving a generous donation from local businessman Stanley Gleaver (and Mrs Gleaver) on behalf of the Dandelion Trust, an organisation for children in need. Mr Sharrocks was a director of the Trust.

I was sure I'd heard of the Dandelion Trust but I wasn't sure exactly what it did. I looked it up in the local Thomson's directory. It was listed. An address in Chorlton-cum-Hardy. It was too late to ring now, but I could try in the morning. Do a little digging around, make use of Harry's press card and try to interview Mr Sharrocks. I wondered how he knew Fraser Mackinlay. Was he another generous benefactor? After all, someone who drives an Aston Martin isn't exactly strapped for cash. Would Bruce Sharrocks deny knowing Martin Hobbs, like Fraser had?

The shrilling phone made me jump. It was Natalie Mitchell. Her mother had agreed to talk to me. She passed on the phone number. I didn't recognise the code. Where was it? Lancaster, she said. I groaned inwardly. An hour and a half up the motorway, an hour and a half back. A tankful of petrol. C'est la vie. I could hardly conduct the interview over the phone. After all, it wasn't market research. I was going to talk to a woman whose daughter had been beaten to death a few hours after I'd spoken to her. Lancaster it would be.

In the early morning post was a card from the local Victim Support scheme, offering a sympathetic ear should I wish to talk to anyone about my recent experience. I didn't take them up on it, but I liked the thought that there was someone out there for those of us on the receiving end.

Ray set off for school with the kids and I cycled round to the one-hour photo-processing shop. Back home, I rang Mrs Williams. Having seen her at the inquest, I'd formed an image of a frail, elderly woman but the voice on the other end of the line was firm and clear, edged with a twangy Liverpool accent. Mrs Williams made it clear that she was as eager to talk to me as I was to talk to her.

'I want to know what happened to Janice,' she said.

I hoped she wouldn't expect me to have all the answers.

I told her I was free to travel up then and there, if she'd no other arrangements. That suited her. She gave me the address.

'Don't ask me for directions,' she said. 'I don't drive. But once you get into town, I'm near the hospital – it's the road at the back.'

Before leaving home, I gathered together my library

books. I would dutifully call and return them and report the loss of my ticket.

I collected the incriminating photos, woman with white Fiesta, and delivered them to my client. He paid in cash.

The library was shut. A notice informed me that, due to cut-backs, it would be closed every Wednesday. Wonderful. I was tempted to leave the books in the doorway with a note attached: 'Sorry, can't look after them any longer, besides the fine's mounting up.' I didn't.

Preston's about halfway to Lancaster and, beyond Preston, I got the impression of leaving behind all the great northern cities: Leeds, Liverpool, Manchester. This was the rural north. All signs led to Carlisle, The Lakes and The North.

Lancaster, with its wide river, castle and creamy stone buildings, had all the neat bustle of a market town. No dusty red-brick backstreets here. I missed all the signs for the hospital, asked directions several times and eventually drew up outside the house, an Edwardian terrace. Mrs Williams had the ground floor flat.

'I'm Sal Kilkenny.'

'Eleanor Williams.' She shook my hand. Up close, she was attractive, broad cheekbones, a generous mouth. Her white hair was thick, styled simply like Doris Day, no perm. There wasn't much resemblance to Janice except for the eyes, large and brown. Mrs Williams wore spectacles on a chain round her neck, a navy leisure suit. When she smiled, she had dimples in her cheeks.

'Tea?'

'Yes, please. No sugar. Could I use the toilet?'

'Through there.' She pointed with the teaspoon. 'Second right.'

The bathroom had a simple feel to it. Plain, painted walls, pink and green mats and towels, a huge loofah, an ancient set of scales, no frills. I washed my hands and examined myself in the mirror. I realised I was holding my breath. My shoulder ached and a taste of acetate rose in my mouth. I took a couple of deep breaths and went back.

We sat on the cottage suite in the living room. Tea in mugs. Framed photographs covered the top of a small sideboard. Three oil paintings hung on the cream walls. A ship, a dockside scene, a woman holding an umbrella. Mrs Williams saw me looking at them.

'Martin did them, my second husband. He loved to paint.'

'That was Natalie's father?'

'Yes,' she nodded. Leant forward and removed her glasses, placed them and her mug on the coffee table. I followed suit. It was time to talk.

'I'm sorry about Janice,' I began. 'As I said on the phone, I was working for her, that's how I met her. She asked me to trace a teenager, a boy who'd run away from home.' I looked across at her. Did this sound bizarre? How much had Natalie told her? I couldn't read anything in her face.

'He was called Martin Hobbs,' I said. 'The strange thing is, Janice claimed to be his mother – I knew her as Mrs Hobbs. I thought I was looking for her son. I did trace him eventually. He didn't want anything to do with his family; he claimed his father had abused him.'

Mrs Williams regarded me steadily; only a slight

147

nod indicated that I should continue.

'Well, I told Janice, Mrs Hobbs as I thought she was, what I'd found out. End of case. She was very upset.' I sighed. 'That was the Saturday. On the Sunday she rang me. She was very distressed, not making sense really, except it was clear she wanted to see Martin.' My chest tightened as I remembered the phone call. When I spoke again, I couldn't keep the tremor from my voice. 'I didn't know the address. I knew which street Martin was staying in and I knew what sort of car to look out for. That came out during the phone call. I shouldn't have said anything, but I gave enough away... I didn't think she should pursue him. She said she'd write, and would I deliver a letter? I agreed to that, mainly to keep her away...'

But it hadn't worked. I swallowed saliva. Mrs Williams still said nothing.

I spoke again. 'The place where they found her, it's not far from where Martin was staying. I think she went there. I don't know if that's why she was killed, or whether that was some awful coincidence. And I still don't know why she wanted to find Martin, how she knew him, why she pretended that he was her son.'

'He was.'

I only just caught the words. 'But he can't be. I've met his real mother and...'

'Janice was his real mother. She gave him up for adoption when he was born. He was her son.'

CHAPTER TWENTY FIVE

'I even offered to raise the child myself, but Janice wasn't having it. Social worker didn't like the idea either...' She stopped, caught by a memory, then just as suddenly resumed her story. 'I never knew whether she made the right choice. All I could do was stand by her. It wasn't easy for her, but it was the child she was thinking of. She said it wouldn't be fair on the baby if she got ill again. And she couldn't bear the thought of growing close and then losing the child.'

'But surely with treatment, with support...?' I protested.

'I don't know.' She ran her hands through the thick white hair. 'Janice had plenty of treatment. Never seemed to make much difference. She was in hospital again within the year. That was her third time. Who can say whether it would have been the same if she'd kept him? I really don't know. She was hurt, over the adoption.' She sighed. 'There's no easy way to lose a child.' Her mouth pulled and I remembered her own loss. She rummaged in her pocket and drew out a large white hanky. Wiped her eyes and blew her nose.

'I still keep forgetting,' she said, smiling gently, 'that she's gone. You'd think it would have sunk in by now.'

'When did she first trace Martin?'

'Way back. He was five. She'd thought about it a lot. Reckoned it'd be easier to trace him once he was registered at school. She used a private investigator then. Didn't let on to me till it was all done.'

'Did she think you'd disapprove?'

She nodded. 'Raking up the past. I thought it'd hurt her even more. She'd given up all claim on him. That's what adoption is. Was then, anyway. He had a new family, a new name. Anyway, this bloke knew what he was doing; followed up birth certificates and this and that and came back to Janice with two possibilities. He'd got photos. One of them was Martin.'

'How could you be sure?'

'He was the spitting image of Janice at that age. To a 't'. She was over the moon. She went and watched him going to school one day. It was then that she told me about it.'

'And after that?' I asked.

'She was happy enough to know where he was. Now and then, she'd drop by the school or pass by his house. Few times a year. She never said much about it – just that she'd seen Martin. I used to worry that it'd stir things up, you know, open up old wounds, but she coped alright. In the end, I suppose I thought it was harmless enough. Then, this last couple of years she starts worrying about when he leaves home; how she'll know where he is, which college will he go to? Janice was always bright, you see; she'd have gone a long way if it hadn't have been for her troubles. More brains than the rest of us put together.' She grinned and I saw again the smile of Janice in the paper, the smile of Martin with his fish. 'Anyway,' she paused for a moment as if searching for the best way to tell me something awkward, 'she began to talk about making contact. Martin was nearly sixteen, she reckoned he'd a right to know.' She sighed with exasperation. 'We argued about it. I thought it was wrong. He might not even know he was adopted. When she gave him up, she gave up all those rights.' She cut the air with her hands to emphasise the point.

'I couldn't get her to see sense, but she never mentioned it again. I hoped she'd given up on the idea.'

'She didn't tell you about coming to me?'

'No.' She leant across and retrieved her glasses, wove the chain between her fingers as she talked. 'She told me Martin had left home. She rang up in a right state. She'd not seen him at school, so she'd gone to the house and watched there. In the end, she rang the house; pretended to be some careers advisor or some such thing. Mrs Hobbs tells her Martin's in hospital, that he's had a breakdown. Well, you can imagine what that did to Janice.'

'Oh, God.'

'I persuaded her to come and stay here for a couple of nights. She was worrying herself sick. Which hospital was he in, had he been sectioned? She wouldn't let up. In the end, we rang all the hospitals. No trace of him. We didn't know what on earth was going on.'

'When was this?'

'Towards the end of May. Knowing he wasn't in hospital calmed her down. We began to think there'd been some strange mix-up. Anyway, I let her go home. Next thing I know, she's on the phone, terribly agitated, talking about Martin being,' she struggled with the word, pulling the spectacle chain taut across her palm, 'well, being abused, you know, by his father.'

She leant forward, clasping the glasses in her lap, looking at them as she spoke. ' I thought she'd flipped. That she was getting it all mixed up... losing touch. If I'd only realised...'

I kept quiet, sensing there was more to come.

'It was bad enough her hearing that Martin had got ill,

but then that...' Her breathing came fast and shallow. 'To find out... just the same... the same.'

The penny dropped. Janice Brookes had been a victim of abuse too. Mrs Williams still bent forward, her face obscured by the cap of white hair falling over it.

I had to break the silence; acknowledge what I'd heard.

'Was it her father?' I asked. My voice sounded thin and reedy.

She nodded her head. 'Bastard.' She whispered the curse, but there was anguish in her quiet delivery of the words. 'She was only a kid. I had no idea.' She looked up at me now, hiding nothing of the pain in her brown eyes and the tremors that shook her lips. 'I've never forgiven myself. How could I not know, in my own house? When you can't even protect your own...' Her Scouse accent was more pronounced now. 'I threw him out sharp enough once I found out, but it was too late, too late for Janice. That's what made her ill. I'm sure of it.'

In the silence that followed, I heard the sing-song of a siren approaching the hospital and the shrieks and calls of children playing in some nearby school.

And I thought of Janice, whose childhood had been stolen; of Martin. I felt the pain of the white-haired woman opposite me and thought of my own daughter, of the passion that bound me to her. I could never bear for her to suffer in the ways that Janice had. How could any mother bear it? My throat ached and tears started in my own eyes.

'I don't know about you,' Mrs Williams said huskily, tears coursing down her cheeks, her nose reddening, 'but I'm ready for another cuppa.'

'Yes,' I smiled, 'that'd be great.'

I'd managed to regain my composure by the time she

returned. I concentrated on filling in the factual gaps in Janice's story. Janice hadn't been in touch again after the Saturday. Mrs Williams knew of no reason for her daughter, who lived in Bolton, to be in South Manchester. Janice had been working part-time in a sandwich bar. She gave me the address. She'd been friendly with staff there and also with her next door neighbour. No other friends her mother knew about. She hadn't been involved with anyone romantically.

The police hadn't been back in touch with Mrs Williams since their initial interview. At that time, she'd had no reason to connect Martin with her daughter's sudden death. Natalie had never known about her half-sister's child. She'd only been nine when Martin was born.

I asked her whether she knew who the father was.

'Yes. Edward Mullins.' She screwed her face up into a grimace. 'Right waste of space, he was. Janice was working in his shop. He flattered her – he could turn on the charm. She caught first time. She never told him. Tell me about Martin.'

The question took me by surprise. Though he was her grandson... I described the shy schoolboy, with his love of fishing, and the distraught young man I'd talked to at the nightclub. It wasn't a particularly rosy portrait. I showed her the pictures that Janice had left with me.

'She never showed me these; probably thought I wouldn't approve,' she said regretfully. 'He's got a look of her, in the smile.'

'Why didn't she tell me what her real relationship to Martin was?' I asked. 'Why all the pretence? After all, she'd used a private eye to trace him before.'

'I don't know,' she shrugged. 'Maybe the fact that she wanted to make contact this time. It is illegal, isn't it?'

'No, not really.'

'Janice probably thought it was. You still have the letter she wrote him?'

'Yes,' I said. 'I'm trying to find out if Martin is still staying in Cheadle. If he is, I'll try and deliver it. The man who owns the house denies ever having met him.'

'If Janice told Martin who she really was, if he was upset anyway... you say he had these outbursts...'

The question, though unspoken, was clear. 'I don't know. He wasn't a violent boy; there's only been the odd occasion. It's not...'

'It would explain why he's missing,' she insisted.

I didn't reply. She needed to consider the worst possible version of events, a sort of protection policy. Nothing could be worse, could it, than discovering that Martin had murdered his mother?

'You'll ask him, won't you, if you find him?'

'The police have made it clear I'm not...'

'I don't give a damn about the police.' She reined in her anger, keeping her voice low, but her eyes flashed. 'My daughter's dead and there's some sort of connection with Martin Hobbs. He must know something. Even if she never got to the house, that tells us something...'

I wasn't going to start asking about Janice's murder. I just wanted to find Martin and give him the letter. Finish. Anything else was beyond me.

'I've told the police most of this; they'll have interviewed anyone...'

'I'm not asking the police' – she was exasperated with me, stood up and marched over to the fireplace – 'I'm asking you. If it's a question of money, I'll pay whatever it takes.'

'It's not, it's not money...' What could I say? I'm scared. I'm a coward. Someone killed your daughter and they might do the same to me. I sighed and looked over at Mrs Williams. She stood, head up, waiting for my answer. It was a foregone conclusion.

'Alright, if I find Martin and if I get the chance, I'll see whether he knows anything about Janice. And if other information comes my way, I'll let you know; but that's it. I haven't the resources or the authority to take it as far as the police can. And if they hear about this – you've employed me. It wasn't my idea.'

'Fair enough.' I saw her shoulders relax. The clock on the mantelpiece had traced the afternoon round. I had to go. She saw me to the door.

'When you find him...'

'If I find him.'

'Yes, if it's alright, if you don't think he's...' – she paused, searching for a word other than guilty – '...involved, will you tell him I'm here, if he ever needs anybody, if he wants to know about her?'

I nodded, struggling again with sudden tears, impressed by her dignity and generosity.

Mrs Williams stood on the doorstep, watching, while I got in the car. She waved once and disappeared into the house.

I started back for Manchester.

I'd agreed to do more than I wanted and that promise sat like a stone in my stomach. Why couldn't I have said no? Admitted my fears and inadequacies? Just said no.

Because you feel guilty, you feel responsible for Janice and you feel you owe her mother.

I sighed and hit the accelerator. I just wanted to get home.

CHAPTER TWENTY SIX

I walked in on mayhem. Maddie, her face red with rage, was screaming at Ray, who was on his knees trying to mop up a pool of stuff that looked like cooking oil. Tom was standing on a chair at the kitchen table doing something creative with salt, ketchup and milk.

I'd hoped for a little attention myself when I got back. Some idiot had cut straight across me, where the motorways merged, on the way back into Salford and Manchester. One of those get-in-lane-quick spots. I'd practically done an emergency stop to avoid him. If there'd been anyone close behind me... I say 'him'; I was too busy watching my life pass before my eyes to take note of the driver, or even the make of car, but I assume it was a man. I've never yet been in a car with a woman who drives like a maniac.

By the time I reached home, the shakes had subsided and I'd run through my gamut of revenge fantasies. It looked like tea and sympathy was off.

'For Christ's sake, Maddie, shut up or go somewhere else and make that noise. I've had enough.' Ray's outburst was heartfelt. And harsh enough to make me wince and Maddie draw breath. For a split second, I wanted to defend her, criticise Ray for his lousy handling of the situation. The moment passed. I'd been there myself, many times, at the end of my tether, running out of tactics and lashing out with my tongue. But I felt dispirited all the same. Why was it so hard to

be the parents we wanted to be? Humane, mature –
giving our children respect and dignity. Wasn't the
verbal slap, the belittling comment, part of the same
continuum that also dished out beatings and child
rape?

I moved over and disengaged Tom from his collage,
hoisted him onto my hip, took Maddie by the hand.

'Come on, you two, let's go to the shop.'

'Can we get sweets?' Maddie's voice rose in hope.
Ray shot me a look.

'No. We're going to get a drink for Ray and then
we'll come back and help clean up.'

'Shoes,' demanded Tom.

'Doesn't matter,' I said. I carried him piggy-back and
took Maddie's hand. Mr Mohammad at the corner shop
knew us well enough to make a joke about the grimy,
tear-stained faces of the kids. I bought cheap white
wine and lager from the fridge and a bag of Hula-hoops
each for them. If it didn't have sugar in it, it wasn't
really a bribe.

As I waited for my change, a ripple of fatigue
washed through me, tangible enough to make me
steady myself on the counter. My back ached, not just
from the drive or carrying Tom, but my period was
due. Self-pity. I went with the flow. Saw myself
throwing in the towel, giving in to the pressures.
Walking out of the shop, leaving the children there,
leaving Ray to his floor, giving up on the case,
crawling to my bed. I reined in the fantasy, disturbed
at how shaky I felt. The revelations of the afternoon
had upset me more than I'd realised and I was
shattered. I picked up the shopping, pulled myself
together and carried on coping.

I helped myself to beans on toast and tea. Ray had
calmed down a lot, but there was still an edge to his

voice as he took the children up to get ready for bed. I fought the impulse to make a martyr of myself and offer to do bedtime. I wandered out to the garden, watered the tubs and the window-boxes. Digger was out there, sprawled under the table. He raised an eyelid in answer to my greeting, then lowered it again.

When I could tell the children were out of the bath, I went up to say goodnight and then retreated to the bath myself. I ran it up to the overflow, covered my face with a flannel and steeped. Fragments of the afternoon came and went; Mrs Williams' face, attractive, mobile, listening, smiling, crumpling with grief. I didn't want to think about it. I wanted to go to bed.

It was nine-thirty when I padded into the kitchen. Ray had started the wine but I made cocoa. I could hear the television on in the lounge and went through to say goodnight to Ray.

'I've fixed up a meeting with Clive,' he announced. 'Friday, after the kids are in bed.'

My heart sank.

It took us another hour to sort out our line for the meeting. We kept getting waylaid by exchanging gossip and bits of news about our lives. Ray was furious about rumours that the council were going to start charging for nursery places.

'They can't,' I protested. 'People only get those places if they really need it. People couldn't possibly afford to pay...'

He shrugged. 'It'll be means-tested, but even so...'

'But the principle, as well; free childcare, provision for under-fives...' We rumbled on about that for a while, too.

In bed, I nestled round the slow groping pains of my period and soon sank into a thick, heavy sleep.

There was a child crying. It was my fault. I'd locked her in the coffin and there wasn't enough air. She'd die. It was a mistake. I lurched awake and placed the crying. Tom. I went through to him. In the dim light, his face was shiny with tears. His hair formed damp whorls on his forehead.

I lifted him up, murmuring reassurance. He burrowed into my neck, sharp little breaths jolting his body. I walked round the room, patting him on the bottom and whispering lullabies. Longing for him to settle. When I felt his body slacken, I did a couple more circuits, then lowered him gently down, trying not to tense myself and so alert him to the change.

I stole back to my room. So heavy, so tired. Craving sleep. Tom was bawling again. My stomach lurched with dismay. Anger and resentment surged through me. I need to sleep, I need to fucking sleep. Stop it. Be quiet. Leave me alone. I reached their bedroom door, ready to seize him too swiftly, stalk round batting his bottom a little too hard, the ache of frustration ringing my throat. I checked myself, knocked on Ray's door. 'Tom's awake, I've put him down once but he won't settle.'

'Shit!'

I escaped, dived back to my dreamless sleep.

The next day I felt spacey. Pains came and went, blood seeped. I felt fizzy with fatigue. Over breakfast, I speculated how civilised it would be if I could withdraw from the world for the duration. Go off and commune with myself, while other people cared for the kids and cleaned the house. Fat chance.

I'd lain in bed till the kids had gone and I was trying to cut through the fog in my brain, to sort out what I was meant to be doing. I couldn't focus on anything. I wanted to go in the garden and play with the plants. I made another cup of tea.

Maybe I'd do better at the office. Aw, shit. The office. I'd managed to forget about the office over the last three days. Sigh. I hated to think what the Dobsons would be saying about me if I didn't sort it out soon. Oh, well, maybe sorting it out would have a knock-on effect on my thought processes. Let a little light into my clouded mind.

I gathered together cleaning stuff, bin-bags, rubber gloves and a stanley knife to cut up the carpet. Made a flask and a sandwich.

The Dobsons were all out at school. I went down the cellar stairs, bracing myself for the shock. I got a surprise. Someone had cleared up. More than that, they'd sorted the room out. The carpet had gone, a faded but serviceable patterned rug in its place. All the walls and the ceiling had been painted white, faintly pink, one of those hint-of-a-touch numbers. Two collapsible garden chairs and a small plain desk had been set to one side of the room. Opposite, stood my filing cabinet, still streaked with lilac splashes. Beside it on the floor, two stacks of files, one lot smothered in paint, the other relatively unscathed.

Gratitude and guilt fought for the upper hand. There was a note on the desk next to the (clean) phone.

'Sal – raided the attic, plus car-boot sale. You owe us a tenner! Girls displayed cringe-making propensity for nest-building. Jackie.'

I laughed. Jackie was terrified that her four daughters would all opt for marriage and children at an early age and rebel against her hopes that they would go on to further education and economic independence.

Now I had no excuse. I fished out some paper from the clean files and sat with pen poised. My head still buzzed with nothing. In the end, I resorted to talking aloud and making a list of things I needed to do. I still needed to establish whether Martin was at Fraser Mackinlay's and, to do that, I needed to see whether Nina Zaleski had seen him.

RING NINA.

If he was there, I needed to find a time when Fraser was out, in order to see him. After my last visit, I knew Fraser wouldn't let me see Martin and I wouldn't trust him with the letter.

CLEAR COAST? DELIVER LETTER. I knew now that it was from his birth mother. How the hell was I to tell him she was dead, worse, murdered? I'm not a fucking social worker.

Plus, I'd promised Mrs Williams that I'd ask if Martin knew anything about Janice; if she had visited the house. There was something obscene about it. Shit, it was heavy enough going to see the lad and revealing that he was adopted. Then what would I say? 'Oh and, by the way, your mother was murdered. Could even have happened here; she was headed this way. Ring any bells?'

I got to my feet, appalled at the scenes running through my head. I just couldn't do this.

Who was Martin Hobbs? I was chasing a chimera. First, I'm looking for a runaway who doesn't want finding. I find him and he turns into an incest survivor. Next thing I know, he's a foundling, a precious child given up, a chosen child betrayed. Now he's an orphan, maybe even a matricide. And I have a letter, with his name on, a message to Martin...

I walked back over to the desk. Looked down at my list. Concentrate on the job, I told myself. Don't think about how he might or might not react. Just do it. I rang Nina Zaleski, but there was no reply. My

161

frustration was tinged with relief.

I ate lunch, then decided to fish around a bit after Bruce Sharrocks, the man who'd accompanied Martin and Fraser to Barney's; the leading light of the Dandelion Trust. A perky voice answered. When I asked to speak to Mr Sharrocks, she told me he wasn't in the office. Could she help? I trotted out my cover story; I was doing a feature on local children's charities, and the people behind them, for City Life. I wanted to interview Mr Sharrocks. The prospect of publicity did the trick. She explained that he worked elsewhere but she was sure I could contact him there. It was a Town Hall number, Social Services department.

I rang my friend and ex-lodger, Chris, and asked her if she could find anything out about Bruce Sharrocks; if she knew anyone in Social Services. I persuaded her I was just after general impressions – nothing dodgy about the request. She said she'd see what she could do, but I could tell that she didn't really like being asked.

I sorted through the pile of paint-free files and put them back in the filing cabinet. The file on Martin wasn't among them. My stomach tightened. If it wasn't here, if it had been removed, then I couldn't really go on acting as though the paint-job was just the work of local youths. I began to prise apart the files that were congealed with paint. It was there, drenched with lilac vinyl silk like the rest of them. I made sure the skeletal notes I'd had were actually inside, if illegible, and sighed with relief. Then I chucked the whole stack.

I drafted a small ad for the local weekly free-sheet, advertising my services. If I was back in business, it was about time I generated some. Discreet service, reasonable rates.

On my way to deliver it, I called at the library. The newly-introduced computer system informed me that I owed three pounds and ninety-five pence, and charged me another fifty pence for a replacement ticket. I restricted myself to two books. A Loren D. Estleman crime thriller and the latest in the Sue Grafton Alphabet series. Least they were still buying books.

I cycled round to the Reporter office and dropped in my advert. A week on Saturday, they'd be beating a path to my door. I lived in hope.

CHAPTER TWENTY SEVEN

Things were hotting up. Temperatures were in the eighties. Trouble in the air. The evening paper was full of it. 'Heatwave – Crimewave,' screamed the headline. 'Brutal Violence Erupts In Night Of Terror.' There'd been riots in Salford. Youths circling the police station, setting fire to the flats and shops. In Cheetham Hill, two teenagers had died in a gunfight and, further south, a young black man had been fished from the Mersey. Police were treating both these cases as part of the on-going drugs war, with rival teenage gangs competing for a share of the lucrative and expanding crack market.

I folded up the paper and chucked it on the grass. It was hot, wonderfully hot, though I didn't think three days really rated as a heatwave. I relished every sweaty moment, every airless night. It couldn't last.

Tom sat in the paddling pool, chortling and gasping for air, as Maddie doused him with buckets of water. I closed my eyes, seeing amber through my eyelids. Thoughts drifted past. What did Sharrocks, a married man and doer of good works, have in common with Fraser Mackinlay, who could afford an Aston Martin and had taken up with a homeless sixteen year old working as a rent boy? Did Fraser hand cash out to the Dandelion Trust? If Sharrocks was working to help children in need, wouldn't the relationship between the wealthy Mackinlay and the poor teenager trouble his scruples just a little? Was I completely misreading it? Perhaps Fraser was a philanthropist, giving Martin the shelter he needed. But why deny knowing him, when I'd shown the photo? And if they were simply lovers, what about Martin's fearful reaction at the nightclub?

Had Martin ever been told he was adopted? Did he know now? Had Janice reached him before death reached her? Maybe Fraser had shut her out, as he had me? She'd driven off; there'd been some trouble with the car, or something made her pull over on the motorway. The killer had struck. Any victim would do. But what if Martin had answered the door? Janice, distraught, had blurted out her story. My baby, my baby, I'm here now... Frightened, Martin had pushed her. She'd fallen...

Ray called me in to the phone. It was Nina Zaleski.

'I just saw him, in the car.'

My guts clenched. This was it – back on the scent. He did exist. 'Coming or going?'

'Going. Fraser got back maybe an hour ago. I had to go collect something from the dry-cleaners, I was driving back and they went past.' She was all excited, too.

'You're sure it was him?'

'Small, young, dark hair. I'm looking at the photo now. If it ain't him, it's his brother.'

'So, he is still staying there,' I said.

'Well hidden. That boy has not been out of that house all week, not that I've seen. Fraser's off to work every morning, then nothing. By the way, I asked Jack what Fraser's company was called. I didn't tell him why, of course. I told him we'd had some junk mail about computers and I wondered if it was the same set-up? Anyway, Jack says it's M.K. Communications or M.K.C. Now.,' she ran on, while I jotted the name down, 'Jack and I are out to dinner tonight, so I won't be able to keep an eye out here.'

'Don't worry. At least he's still around. Now, I need to know the next time Fraser goes out. Ring me tomorrow when he leaves for work. Then I can get to see Martin on his own.'

'Sure. Least you'll be able to reassure his mom,' she said.

'Oh, yeah.' I'd forgotten that Nina only knew an edited version of events. 'Yeah, she'll be, er, really pleased. Of course, I do need to actually see him myself.'

'Okay.' She was brisk, energised. 'So I'll call when he leaves for work tomorrow. He usually leaves about eight-thirty.' I thanked her again.

'Hey,' she said before she hung up, 'ain't it just like Cagney and Lacey?'

At last. Confirmation that Martin was there, and a lead on Fraser. I was on the right track.

As soon as I got the dialling tone, I rang Harry's. Bev answered. I felt a tinge of disappointment. He was out.

'Down in Salford,' she said. 'He's practically living there since the trouble. The Guardian Weekend want something from him and The Observer are making encouraging noises.'

We chatted about the children for a while and I agreed to call round on Saturday, anyway, with Maddie and Tom. Bev said she'd tell Harry I called.

Ray had made an assortment of salads. It was too hot to eat anything else. We ate in the garden, wafting the occasional wasp off the plates. I described to Ray the refurbishment job the Dobsons had done on my office, garden chairs and all.

'I could make you a couple of nice chairs,' he said, squinting into the sun.

'For a price. Look, I can probably pick up something

at a car-boot if I decide the white vinyl's too...'

'Frivolous?'

'Yeah – as long as it's wooden...'

'No taste,' he protested.

'No money.'

'Speaking of which, or whom, Clive gave me a cheque towards the rent.'

I widened my eyes. 'How much?'

'Ooh, you're so mercenary.'

'Ray! Anyway, it was materialistic, not mercenary.'

'Two hundred,' he said.

I groaned. It was a quarter of what was owing.

'Better than nothing.'

'We're not the only ones he owes, you know. There's this guy been ringing...'

'Pete?'

'Yes. It's so embarrassing – he probably thinks we're not passing messages on or we're sheltering him, or something.'

Ray nodded. 'Tom!' His tone halted Tom in mid-swipe. The rake was inches from Maddie's head. 'Away, in the shed, you know you're not to play with those.'

As the kids fought about who would put them away, I thought about Mrs Hobbs. How many times had she averted an accident, kissed Martin better, put a plaster on his knee? Protected him? The little boy she'd adopted. But when he suffered most, she couldn't face it, too monstrous to accept. The phone bleated as I carried Maddie into the house. I put her down to answer it and she screeched hysterically. It was Diane. I said I'd ring her back.

It was an hour and a half later that I remembered.

'Diane, how was it? When did you get back?'

'Dreadful. Oh, Sal it was awful. We got back

yesterday.'

'Oh, no. So what's, what about Ben and...'

'It's over,' she said, 'very definitely.' She was speaking with clenched teeth.

'Do you want me to come round?' I prayed she'd say no. It was nearly ten.

'No, I'm going to bed.'

'Tomorrow?' I offered.

'Yeah.'

'Your place or the pub?'

'Here,' she said. 'I've got some duty-free. I'll dig out my old Leonard Cohen.'

'Oh, Diane. Oh, shit!' I remembered the meeting with Clive. 'Look, can we make it Saturday, or daytime tomorrow? I'm really sorry, but Ray's set up the showdown with Clive.'

She was working Friday, away visiting her mum over the weekend. The first opportunity was going to be Monday night. We agreed on that.

In the fridge, there were still a couple of glasses of wine in the bottle that Ray had opened the previous night. I poured myself one and took it outside, along with the book by Loren D. Estleman. Detroit crime and low-life was comfortably distant from that of Manchester. Across the way, a Strimmer was screaming across someone's lawn and someone was having fun with a high-speed drill. I drifted into my book. Next time I surfaced, the power tools had been turned off. There were a couple of minutes' peace, then someone down the street flung wide their windows and treated the whole neighbourhood to repeat plays of their latest acquisition, with the bass turned up – 'Let's Talk about Sex, Baby'. Subtle. I read on. The words faded to dusk on the page. I stretched and drained my glass. All I could hear now was the spatting and caterwauling of a couple of cats, occasional traffic and a siren howling in the distance.

The sky was glowing, fiery, peach and mandarin, a single violet cloud. A sign of good weather to come. Or maybe Salford going up. Summer in the city.

CHAPTER TWENTY EIGHT

Friday. Waiting for word from Nina. I paced the office.
Sorted half-heartedly through my files. Time and again
I ran the scene in my head.

I go to the house, Martin answers the door. He's
taken aback at first, reluctant to let me in, but I win him
over. I tell him I have a letter for him, but that first I
need to ask a few questions. He's happy to co-operate.
He's already been through this with the police. Janice
never called here on that Sunday night. Relief. Gently, I
explain that Janice was his birth mother, that it was she
who employed me to find him; the letter I have is from
her. I tell him I'm sorry. He nods, understanding. I
leave him both Mrs Williams' phone number and mine.
Time to go. I walk away sadder, wiser. Cleansed of
responsibility.

Nina didn't ring. By the time it got to twelve-thirty, I
rang her myself.

'The car's still there,' she said. 'Looks like he's
staying home today. I guess it'll be Monday before
you can be sure he's not just gone to fetch the papers
and stuff. Jack's not flying out till Sunday night,
anyhow, so I'm not going to be able to do that much
till then anyway.'

I paced around a bit more. Going nowhere. I could
forget taking the letter till Monday, but I needed to do
something. I decided to visit the sandwich bar where
Janice had worked. I just had time to fit that in before

school. Make absolutely sure that Janice didn't have friends in the Cheadle area.

I'd reached the Dobson's front door when I heard my office phone. I raced back downstairs. This was it. Fraser had gone out; Martin was alone. I missed my footing on the last stair, trod heavily into air and wrenched my foot on its side. Shit. I took a couple of steps to the phone, singing with pain.

"'S that Sal?'

I didn't recognise her voice, young, Mancunian accent.

'Yes, who's that?'

'Leanne.'

I was blank for a beat or two. Then I remembered. Leanne of the dripping, ratty hair. J.B.'s friend. Leanne who'd been scared to tell me what she knew. Leanne of the light fingers.

'I thought you better know,' she said. 'That bloke Smiley, he's been asking about you, wanting to know if you've been round here again, asking questions and all that. I'd watch it if I were you.'

'But why would...?' I heard the click and the dialling tone. The little swine. Had it been a warning or a threat? Had Leanne rung me out of the goodness of her heart or was she working for Smiley? Why did she have to hang up on me? Sod Leanne. She wasn't going to get away with it. I wanted to know exactly what Smiley had said; when, where, the lot.

I got to my feet, ready to drive into town, and gasped with the pain. My skin went clammy. I sat back down and examined my ankle. It was swollen already. There was a large, white lump beneath my ankle bone. The skin around it was puffed up. Well and truly sprained. Brilliant. I wouldn't be driving anywhere.

Feeling slightly foolish, I crawled up the stairs and

hopped along the road and round the corner home. Digger jumped up to greet me. I shoved him down. 'Get out of the way, you stupid, bloody dog.' He slunk off. I found a crepe bandage in the drawer where the odd things live. I drenched some lint with witch hazel and wrapped the bandage round, drenched that too.

I couldn't collect the kids.

Ray was at college but I had a number to leave messages. I used it. If Ray could get Tom on his way home, then I could ask Denise over the road to pick up Maddie when she went for her own daughter. I limped over there. The pain made me feel sick. She apologised; Jade was at home poorly, they wouldn't be going to the school.

Maybe Clive could do it. I'd never asked before. It was only a twenty minute job. Was he in or out? I rang the front doorbell several times but he didn't appear. Well, Ray would just have to get both of them.

I lowered myself onto the sofa and sat with my feet up. I wanted to sleep. I could feel the weariness lapping up my spine, dissolving my bones. My head jerked. I lurched awake. It was nearly three and no word from Ray. I phoned a taxi, seething. The cost, the hassle, the injustice. I collected both children and got them home.

Maddie raced to answer the phone. I remembered Leanne's call and shouted out to stop her, but she was already reciting the number.

'It's Chris,' she said.

I hopped into the hall.

'Hello.'

'Bruce Sharrocks,' she said. 'He's one of the principal officers involved in residential care. Bit of an innovator, well-liked, done a lot of work in the field himself, not just a bureaucrat. Workaholic. He set up the Dandelion Trust practically single-handed. That's about it.'

I don't know what I'd expected, but it wasn't that. I felt deflated. It didn't make the connection between Sharrocks and Fraser Mackinlay any clearer.

'Is he gay?'

'What?'

'Do you know if he's gay?'

'Why the hell do you need to know that?'

I felt crass and my ears got hot.

'Well... it's just that I saw him with this missing teenager I was tracing. I've heard the boy's been working as a rent boy.'

'Oh, yes?' she said. 'And if Sharrocks is gay, he's bound to use boys, isn't he?'

My heart sank. Chris was a lesbian herself and quick to spot oppressive behaviour. I'd blundered again.

'No. But it might be relevant,' I protested.

'People say that a lot,' she countered. 'They usually mean they want information that's none of their business. What if he is gay? That make it easier to see him as a potential criminal? After all, that's often how we're seen, isn't it? Deviants, perverts.'

'Oh, come on Chris...'

'Sal, I don't like it. You're asking for personal information, sensitive stuff. I've no idea how you're going to use it.'

Maybe she was right. Did I really need to know? Search me. In investigative work, it's only later that you can see what's relevant and what's not.

There was an uncomfortable silence. As it stretched out, I tried to think about what I'd said and what I'd been accused of. I was the first to speak.

'I'm sorry.' It was pretty lame but it was all I could come up with in the circumstances. I wasn't clear enough in my own mind whether I was making unfair assumptions, pigeon-holing people. There could well be some truth in Chris's view of how I'd been leaping to conclusions.

'Yeah, well. I'd prefer it if you didn't ask me about people at work again. It puts me in a terrible position.'

'Okay. See you soon.' I rang off.

I had a hot little stone of shame in my belly, souring my saliva. Guilt. Neither use nor ornament. But maybe I could learn from my mistakes.

I rang up and ordered pizzas to be delivered. No way was I going to cook. We'd just finished eating when Ray arrived.

'Sal's broke her leg,' Tom announced.

'She can't even walk,' added Maddie.

Ray raised his eyebrows at me.

'Sprained, not broken,' I said.

He moved to the kettle. 'Does it hurt?'

Stupid question. 'Yeah. I left a message at college. I couldn't drive, I couldn't pick up the kids.'

'I didn't get any message.' He bristled defensively.

'I know you didn't get it.' I hated the carping edge in my voice. 'I had to get a taxi in the end.'

'So it's my fault.' Ray turned to face me, hands on hips. He ducked his head as he spoke. It reminded me of a goat butting its horns.

'I didn't say that. But it's not much of a system, is it? Suppose something really bad had happened...?'

'It didn't did it. Jesus!' He turned back to throw tea bags in the pot. The set of his shoulders said everything.

'I'll find out why it wasn't passed on. Okay?'

No, not okay. Not at all okay. My ankle hurt, Chris was pissed off with me, Ray didn't care, a thug called Smiley was asking about me.

'I'm going to lie down for a bit,' I said. I shuffled out of the room.

'Don't forget we're meeting Clive,' Ray called after me.

Shit. 'I won't,' I said. I had.

So had Clive. Least that's what he claimed on Sunday when he finally reappeared. Friday night, Ray and I had sat waiting for him to show. At ten o' clock we put the tele on. The Maltese Falcon was just starting. When it finished an hour and a half later, there was still no Clive.

Ray stood up and stretched. He still wore the navy bermuda shorts and white T-shirt he'd arrived home in. His legs were covered in long, straight, black hairs, unlike the curls on his head. He yawned, smoothed his moustache. I tried to recall what sort of hairs Harry had on his legs, caught myself at it and for an awful moment wondered if I'd said anything aloud.

'So now what?' I asked.

'Rearrange it.' Ray yawned again. 'Your turn.'

Groan. I lay back and watched two flies buzz in and out of the lampshade.

'Digger.' Ray whistled and the dog appeared. 'Walk.' Ray had taken to walking him last thing at night.

'Where do you take him?' I asked.

'Park and back.'

'Ray, I don't want him fouling the park.'

'He doesn't. He's a good boy, aren't you Digger?' He fondled the dog's ears. 'He still goes in the front; I clear it up.'

'I should never have brought him home.'

'He's fine,' Ray protested. 'I like him, the kids like him.'

'But I can't be bothered with it all, the feeding and the walking...'

'I've noticed. Let's just say he's my dog now – I'll look after him – no longer a shared responsibility.'

'You sure?' I stared at the dog. I didn't feel any affection for it at all. Just a tinge of guilt. 'We could always send it to a home or whatever.'

'Bloody won't.'

There was real urgency in his voice. I propped myself up on my elbows to look at him. 'You really like that dog, don't you?'

'We're not all cold and unfeeling.'

They left. I watched the flies a bit longer, then left myself.

CHAPTER TWENTY NINE

The swelling on my ankle had gone down quite a bit by morning, though it was still very tender. I was itching to call on Leanne. The warning, friendly or otherwise, lingered like a hangover, making me uneasy. But I needed to rest my ankle so it'd heal quicker. And I wanted time with Maddie.

The two of us spent most of the day in the garden. Ray took Tom off to Nana Tello's. We played make-believe. I had speaking parts only. The baddie, the judge, the teacher, the daddy. In between, Maddie messed in the sand-pit and dragged armfuls of toys from the house out into the garden. Maddie chattered away, a stream of consciousness, scolding, informing, protesting. I loved to watch her play. The intensity of it all, the fluidity of her movements; hunkering down to rearrange her teddy, then up in a flowing sequence.

'Maddie.'

'And you be the policeman.'

'Maddie, I want to tell you something.'

'What?' She frowned, straightened up and stared.

'You know your body is yours, don't you?'

''Course it is,' she retorted, as though I'd said something incredibly stupid.

'And no-one's allowed to touch you if you don't want them to.'

'I hate washing my hair.'

'I don't mean that. I mean your private bits, like

your fanny or your bottom. You can say no, 'cos it's your body.'

'I know.' She was impatient, didn't want to hear me.

'And if anyone, anyone at all, ever hurts you, or touches you when you don't want them to, or if they make you touch their body, you tell me.' I sounded like some health promotion leaflet. 'I promise I won't be cross...'

'Yeah. You be the policeman.'

'Do you understand?'

'Yes,' she shouted. 'Now play. You be the policeman.'

I sighed. Had any of it got through? Should I have given her more graphic examples and risked frightening her?

'I'll be a policewoman instead.'

'No, a man. You've got to be a man.'

'Why?'

''Cos there isn't a policewoman in this game.'

On Sunday, my ankle was strong enough to put a bit of weight on it so I drove over to Bev and Harry's with Tom and Maddie. Harry looked exhausted; there was a grey tinge to his complexion, purple hammocks under his eyes. Bev was brittle and prickly. Of course, the kids were on their worst behaviour.

After a strained lunch, I dried the dishes while Harry washed. I asked him if he'd any way of checking up on a business I was investigating.

'I can access data on corporations, holding companies, directors, that sort of stuff. What you after?'

'I don't know, anything at all.'

'That specific, huh?'

'I don't even know that there is anything.'

'But it would be nice?' He grinned.

I followed him through to the front room and stood behind him as he sat at the console.

'Okay, what's the name?'

'M.K.C. or M.K. Communications.'

He punched it in. Lists scrolled up the screen.

'There we are.' He pointed to the initials. 'So it does exist. Directors...' He keyed in some more commands and a list of names appeared. The only one I recognised was Fraser Mackinlay.

'Anything?' Harry asked.

'Nothing unexpected.'

'Okay – sister companies.' Another list. M.K. Software, M.K. Distribution, Kincoma Products, M.K.C. International.

'I'm sorry,' I said, 'it doesn't mean anything. It's a waste of time.'

''S fine. Leave it with me. I'll print these out for you, run a list of directors for this lot. Leave it at that.'

''Erm.' I wasn't sure it was worth the trouble.

'Won't take a minute.'

'Go on then.'

In the back room, Bev had persuaded the kids to set up the clockwork train set.

'Tom's ruining it,' screamed Maddie. He was trying to run the train over the half-finished track.

'Wait Tom, wait till it's finished.'

'Let's go out the back,' said Bev. It was hot, but cloudy and close. Storm coming.

'You look tired,' I said, once we'd settled.

'I am. Work's awful; all this talk of the hospital closing, merging with Wythenshawe. We just don't know what's going to happen.'

'But what about the campaign? It's so popular...'

She shrugged. 'It is. But whether it'll actually stop them closing us down in the long run... We'll be the

179

last to find out. On top of all that, Harry's driving himself into the ground with the Salford stuff – he's hardly here and when he is, he's plugged into that bloody machine. I'm sorry Sal. I just hate living like this. It was never part of the plan.' She smiled ruefully.

I'd heard a lot about the plan. Bev and Harry had wanted to raise their children jointly. They'd both taken part-time work; Bev at the lab at Withington Hospital and Harry with his free-lancing. They'd been poorer as a result and hadn't been able to go up the career structure like full-timers. But, from the outside, it seemed to have worked, till now.

'I hate having to do all the childcare,' said Bev. 'I don't understand how single parents cope. How did you manage before Ray moved in?'

'I don't know. You just do, you have to. You're always, always knackered. But worse than that, there's no-one to talk to, no adult company. And you're skint all the time so you can't go to nice places with your child.' I shuddered at the memory.

'Sal' – Harry sounded surprised – 'look at this.' He came out clutching a printout. 'These names here,' he pointed. 'Recognise any of them?'

'Only Mackinlay. Why?'

'Kenton, Eddie Kenton. It has to be the same guy. You remember Operation Sadie?'

I shook my head.

'Four, maybe five years back. Big police operation uncovered a pornography network: Holland, Germany and here. Eddie Kenton was the brains behind the Manchester end of things. He was arrested, along with a few others. Lived out in the sticks, Mottram way, built himself a big house up there. He ran a production company; educational films, training and that; did very well out of it. But he also used it to front the porn movies. Eddie's case never got to court; police had taken short cuts with the warrants that were used. They couldn't touch him. Of course, he had to clean his act up, lay low for a bit. They probably still keep an eye on him.'

'What's he doing on the list?'

'He's a director for one of Mackinlay's firms, Kincoma Products.'

So, maybe Fraser Mackinlay and Martin Hobbs were mixed up with this Kenton character, producing porn movies? It would explain Fraser's reluctance to talk or let me see Martin. And if J.B. had discovered that when he'd been asking round the clubs...

'Here,' said Harry. 'Trading out of an industrial unit in Longsight – might be worth a visit.'

'What do they do?'

'Ring 'em up and see,' Harry smiled. 'Tell 'em Sadie sent you.'

I was scrubbing new potatoes when Clive made his appearance. Only two days late. He poked around in the fridge. I don't know why. He hadn't put any food in it for over a week. I was quietly pleased that it was empty – I'd just chopped up everything that was left-over, for Sunday tea.

'What a weekend,' he groaned. 'Started at a rave and then this house party last night – talk about gross! This girl whose house it was...'

'Woman.'

'Yeah, well, she'd got this awful music, really naff. And she thought she could dance... God,' he snorted with derision.

'Clive, we were supposed to have a meeting on Friday.'

'This Friday?'

I didn't believe that incredulous tone for one moment. I nodded.

'God. Sorry. You have to remind me of these things. Head like a sieve.' He foraged in the bread bin. Took out the end of the loaf and began slicing it up.

'So let's have it tomorrow,' I said.

He hummed. Spread jam on the bread. Took a mouthful. Chewed it over.

'Or Tuesday?' I persisted.

'Mmm.' He nodded. 'Tuesday's better. Yeah, Tuesday.' He turned to go.

'Clive, can you go and get some bread? – we need it for the kids' sandwiches.'

'Oh. Trouble is, 'fraid I haven't any cash... erm...' He batted his pockets. Grimaced inanely.

I bit the side of my cheek, walked slowly to my bag and fished a pound coin from my purse. Handed it to him. He winked and wheeled away. I wanted to slap him.

The weather broke during the night. The clouds opened. I woke in the early hours to the steady beat of heavy rain. In the distance, cars whooshed like irregular waves. So that was summer done and dusted.

CHAPTER THIRTY

Wrong. Morning brought deep blue skies and enough sun to dry up the pavements before I got out of the house. More like the continent than England. The world smelt glorious, clean and fragrant.

When I got back from school, I cautiously removed my crepe bandage. The swelling had gone completely. The air felt cool round my ankle and I still favoured my other foot, but I no longer needed the bandage.

I rang Nina Zaleski. I needed to know if the coast was clear so I could deliver Janice Brookes' letter. I let it breep twenty-five times. No reply. Having waited this long, there was no point in going over there on the off-chance that Fraser was out and Martin was in. I'd wait for word from Nina. Was she out or just out for the count? If Jack had flown out the previous evening she may well have celebrated. I got the impression she had to restrain her boozing when he was home.

If I couldn't get to Martin, I'd go after Leanne. Tell her it was bad manners to hang up on someone. If I could find her.

It wasn't difficult. She was asleep in the squat.

I picked my way through the tall weeds, sending puffs of seed-heads floating through the air. I went down the dark steps and turned the door handle. It wasn't locked. In the sudden darkness I had a flash of déjà-vu; felt again the ripple of fear I'd had here, the dry warmth of J.B.'s hand taking hold of mine. It faded. I reached the massive room with its crumbling pillars. Walked with my head tilted, straining to hear. Quiet. The room was baking, dry as tinder. Sunbeams spilt through the broken windows and a host of dust motes whirled and pranced.

Up the final stairs to the dim corridor. The stairs cracked and squeaked as I climbed them.

It took a while to rouse her. Plenty of banging produced an irritated 'Alright!' from within.

She'd bleached her hair, cut it too. Before, it'd hung limp and mousy; now it was dried-out, a peculiar colour like egg-yolk. Seeing me, she made a swift movement to shut the door. I shoved back.

'I just want to talk, Leanne.'

'You're off your fucking head coming here.' We were both still straining away at the door. I could tell I was stronger but I didn't want to use force to get in.

'Oh, come on,' I said.

''S your funeral.' She let go suddenly and moved back. I lurched forward but regained my balance. Caught a smirk on her face. She wore an outsize black T-shirt, proclaiming something was Naff-naff. She looked tired, older than her thirteen years.

The room stank of dustbin. It was a tip. The green cover had gone from the sofa, revealing tan plastic. Someone had slashed it and gouts of foam stuck out like fungus. Beer cans, take-away trays and papers, cigarette ends littered the carpet and formed little heaps at either end of the sofa and over round the sink. Several of J.B.'s pictures had fallen off the wall and lay curling on the floor.

On the mattress in the far corner, I could see someone sleeping. A crown of brown hair above the sleeping bag.

'Oh,' I said. 'Should we talk somewhere else?'

'Nah. They won't be up for hours yet.'

Now she'd said it, I could see there were two people, but just one head visible.

'Are they friends of...?'

'Can't keep your fucking nose out, can you? What've you come here for?'

I moved over to the table by the windows, pulled out a chair and sat down. I didn't want a stand-up fight. Leanne leant against the sink.

'What did Smiley say?' I asked.

'I told you, right; he just wanted to know if you'd been round asking questions and that.' She crossed to the sofa, rummaged in a bag and came back with her cigarettes. She pulled one out and lit it.

'Did he know my name?'

'Dunno.' She inhaled deeply.

'Well, think about it. When he asked about me, did he describe me or what?'

She sighed and shifted her weight.

'It's important to me – I don't know how much he knows about me. How he found out about me, anything.'

'He didn't say your name; just summat like, has anyone been round asking questions, a bird, let him know.'

'What did you say?'

'Well, I'm not going to tell him to piss off, am I? Said I'd let him know, if you came.'

A bluebottle landed on the table and began stroking away at a blob of congealed tomato sauce.

'You going to tell him I came today?'

She shrugged, sucked on her cigarette and cleared her throat.

'Depends,' she coughed. 'If I think he'll find out, I'd

best tell him anyway. I've got to watch out for myself, right.'

'Did he tell you to ring me?'

'What?'

'Why did you ring me? Did he tell you to do that too?'

'No, he fucking didn't.' Realisation dawned on her face. 'You thought I was doing it for him, to frighten you off? I don't work for him, you know, right. Well clear. I stay well clear. He wants me to – and I'm not talking about telephone work, neither.' Leanne stopped abruptly; she'd said more than she'd wanted to.

'I had to find out whether it was you warning me, or him threatening.'

'Same difference, isn't it, really?' She dropped the cigarette into a styrofoam cup. It hissed. The bluebottle flew a lazy circle back to its breakfast.

'Is Smiley dealing drugs?'

Her face closed in on itself, pinched.

'I dunno. I don't know anything about him.' Wary now.

'Cut the crap, Leanne. We both know he's a pimp, we both know he's done time, that he got carved up for grassing on his mates. You know if he's involved in any other business?'

'I mind my own; you ought to, an' all. He's bad news.'

'Where can I find him?'

'What?' She was aghast.

'If I can't find out any other way, I'll have to go straight to him.'

'Yer cracked. He'd kill you. You haven't got a clue, have you?'

'Why are you protecting him?'

186

'I'm not. I'm looking out for myself, right.' She leant forward, yelling at me. 'J.B.'s dead, Derek's dead; you think I'm going to have a slack mouth?'

'Who's Derek?'

She averted her face, stared at the windows. There was no view out there; they were encrusted with decades of grime.

'Just a mate of mine.'

'He knew Smiley?'

She nodded, addressed the windows as she talked. 'He did a bit of running around for him, got paid in kind. He couldn't see it was doing his head in. Said it made him feel good. There's not much makes you feel good round here.'

My eyes flicked to her bare arms; no sign of tracks, bruises. She noticed.

'People smoke it nowadays. Don't you watch the documentaries on tele?' She gave a short laugh.

'What happened to Derek?'

'They fished him out of the Mersey, didn't they...'

'This last week? The paper said it was to do with the drug gangs.'

'Don't know what they said that for. Load of crap.'

'What do you think happened?'

'How should I know? He was a good mate, Derek. We was in care together. He always...' Emotion got the better of her and her mouth formed a small o shape. She breathed slowly. I watched the bluebottle for a minute or so.

Leanne lit another cigarette.

'Do you think Smiley had anything to do with it?' She shrugged. Feigned indifference. 'He kept giving him the stuff. It was just a matter of time.'

I sensed she was hiding again. From me, or the truth that she feared?

One of the bodies stirred and turned, pulling the cover from the other. A young boy; grubby T-shirt and shorts. Leanne's age or maybe a bit older. And this was home. Did his mother know where he was?

Leanne walked over and tugged the cover over him again.

'You better go.' She flashed me a look of defiance. 'You shouldn't have come, anyway.'

I got the message. Stood up and pulled a tenner from my purse. Handed it over. She took it with the same sullen look. I kept my other hand firmly on my purse.

'I found out where Martin's staying,' I said.

'I don't want to know.'

At the door, I turned back. 'Leanne, thanks for the warning.' I glanced at the room, the rubbish. 'If there's anything I can do...'

Her shrug said it all.

As I picked my way back through chunks of plaster and broken furniture, I thought back to when I was thirteen. I longed to be sixteen and grown up. I could never get enough to eat. I played in the school netball team. My friend and I whispered about periods, neither of us having experienced them yet, and both had a crush on our history teacher. We had uncontrollable giggling fits and invented our own secret code.

What had changed? Were there kids like Leanne around back then, surviving on the edge, underage and worldly-wise? Or were they a new breed, emerging from the weakened Welfare State at a time when hope and help were measured in terms of cost-effectiveness?

I paused at the fence. Peeped through to make sure all was quiet, before swinging aside the loose section and clambering through. Leanne might tell Smiley;

she might not. At least I could be vigilant.

CHAPTER THIRTY ONE

What was Smiley worried about? That I knew something about his involvement in J.B.'s 'overdose'? J.B. was dead and buried. Three weeks had passed since his death. Without witnesses, evidence or even a motive, I wasn't in any position to pursue it, even if I wanted to.

Perhaps he thought that J.B. had passed on information to me before he'd been silenced and Smiley was anxious to know if I was acting on it. Something to do with drugs? But what? Surely it'd be common knowledge on the streets that Smiley was supplying? How did Martin Hobbs fit into the picture? Had the two things got mixed up? Whilst looking for leads on Martin, had J.B. stumbled on something else?

I kept coming back to the missing hours between J.B.'s phone call, when he'd sounded chirpy and relaxed, about to go off asking round the clubs, and the following afternoon, when Leanne had seen Smiley hurrying away from the squat and had found J.B. dead. In those few hours he'd found out something serious enough to invite murder. Maybe I needed to retrace his footsteps – go round the clubs asking about him. I shuddered. Who wants to step into dead men's shoes?

On the way to the car, I used a call-box to ring Nina Zaleski. Still no reply. My mole had gone AWOL.

My stomach was growling. It knew it was lunchtime.

I queued in a town centre sandwich bar and bought a cheese and chutney barmcake and a piece of flapjack. I ate in the car. The barmcake was middle-of-the-road but the flapjack was wicked; hundred per cent syrup, tacky as toffee. Great exercise for the old jaw muscles.

It took only ten minutes to get to Longsight. The industrial estate I wanted crouched behind the back of a large redbrick mill, surrounded by waste-ground. Some attempt at landscaping had been made, with mounds of grass here and there and the odd sickly sapling in its little cage. There were ten identical units – breeze block and corrugated iron. Unit 9 was Kincoma Products. I sat in the car for a few minutes. Somebody was in; the mesh security screen was ajar, though there were no other cars parked in front.

I rang the bell. The woman who answered was in her mid-twenties. She had a neat, triangular face and permed hair. She wore a tan cotton-knit short-sleeved top and an orange mini skirt with orange slingbacks. She had a gold cross round her neck.

'Is it about the heating?' She had a rich Irish accent.

'No,' I said. 'Market Research.'

'You want to talk to me?' She raised her eyebrows.

'Whoever's here.'

'I'm on my own right now, but if I'll do...' She didn't ask for identification. I followed her. Her heels made a slapping sound on the concrete floor. 'I thought you was the heating. It's frigging perishing in here. I rang 'em first thing.'

She was right. Inside, there was no hint of the warm weather. We were in a vast corrugated box. Dexion shelving supported racks of cardboard boxes. A narrow aisle ran down the centre of the building. The plastic corrugated skylights let in some daylight, but not enough to lift the gloom. She led me to a partitioned room, reception-cum-kitchen.

'Sit down.' She nodded at a scuffed bucket seat. 'You'll have a drink?'

'Tea, please.'

She filled an electric kettle, spooned instant tea into matching red mugs. 'I've had to have the oven on, try and thaw out a bit. It's not just me. The stock needs to be kept at a reasonable temperature. Doesn't like extremes, apparently.'

'What sort of thing?'

'Tapes, computer software, video training programmes. All high tech. Moderate temperatures, keep the dust down. Sugar?'

I shook my head. She handed me a mug, sat on another of the plastic seats – red to match the mugs, no doubt – and cradled her own drink. I got out my notepad and pen.

'What's this research, then?'

'I'm doing a profile of small businesses; work patterns, effects of the recession, that sort of thing.' Pretty vague, but she didn't seem bothered.

'Fire away.'

'You deal in videos?'

'A little bit. They're training things, most of 'em. But that's only a little part, really. I'd say ninety per cent of the business was the computer software stuff.'

'And how many staff work here?'

'Well, just me.'

I marked my paper. 'What sort of market are you catering for?'

She screwed up her nose. 'I don't know, really.'

'Entertainment, adults only, educational?'

She burst out laughing. 'They're not that sort of video – good God, I wish they were. Give us something to watch when it's slack. Look, I'll show you.'

She went out of a door at the end of the long narrow kitchen and re-emerged with a couple of magazines. Computer magazines. She pointed out a couple of the small ads for training packages and software. The titles didn't even use words I'd heard of. They certainly weren't the porno movies I'd been expecting. That didn't mean that everything here was all it seemed but, judging by her mirth, I reckoned this was all she knew about the business.

'It's mail order, see.' She pointed to the advert. 'I get these in and send the stock out by post. Everything's entered on a computer and it tells me when to re-order stuff.'

'So how about the recession; have there been any lay-offs, redundancies, short-time?'

'Hell, no. There's only me here, anyway.'

'But it's not your business?'

She snorted and kicked up her feet. 'You kidding, or what? The boss comes in most days to check things out. He deals with the suppliers, any changes to the ads and that. I'm just the office girl. If he sacked me, he'd have to do all the work himself and I don't think he'd be over the moon about that.'

Sounds at the front door interrupted our cosy chat. 'Now, maybe that's the heating.' She flip-flopped briskly out to see.

There wasn't much point in pursuing my 'research'. It all seemed above-board. Anything that wasn't was well hidden. If Kincoma Products was being used as a cover for some porn merchandising, the evidence could be anywhere in those huge stacks of boxes.

I put my pen and paper away as I heard her coming back from the main door. She came into the room, followed by a man. A man I'd seen before. Short, thickset, hair cut like a pudding bowl. The man I'd seen with the others at Barney's. The third man. My heart kick-started. 'Now, here's the one you want to talk to,' trilled the woman. 'The man himself. It's market research she's doing. I didn't get your name...? This is Mr Kenton.'

He made a slight bowing motion. My mouth went dry and my palms clammy.

'Janice,' I heard myself saying. Why pick that? Of all the stupid bloody... 'Smith,' I added.

If he'd any inkling, his rounded eyes didn't betray it. But his fingers clutched his car keys so hard that the flesh strained white.

'And who are you doing this research for, Janice?' He had the husky voice of a heavy smoker. He'd brought the peppery smell of nicotine, mingled with some sweet aftershave, into the room.

'Myself, really.' I laughed and shifted in the chair. 'For college – it's part of my course. Business studies; we're doing marketing and research. We have to go round and talk to small businesses.'

'And what brings you to this neck of the woods?' He adjusted his pristine shirt cuffs as I began to answer. Even on a summer's day like today, he wore a business suit. An expensive one. The gold chunks on his fingers and the sickly aftershave undermined the effect a bit.

'Chance,' I said. 'It was the first industrial estate I passed. Thought I'd start here.' I smiled. I was damned if I was going to give away my real interest.

'Tea, Eddie?' the woman asked, blissfully unaware of the prickly atmosphere between us. He gave a faint nod in response.

'Bit risky isn't it? Sending students off on their own like that? Could get into some nasty situations, couldn't you, Janice?' It was a threat delivered in a tone of concern.

I said nothing. If he knew I was an impostor, there wasn't much point in carrying on the charade. And if he didn't, he was behaving like a shit and I wanted out.

I stood up, clasped my bag in front of me.

'I'll see Miss Smith out, Moya.'

I walked quickly ahead of him to the front door, turned the Yale and stepped out. The brilliant sunshine was blinding. I fumbled for my car keys. I sensed he was right behind me. I stooped to unlock the car door.

'I don't know what you're playing at, girlie,' he murmured, 'but you're gonna land yourself in big trouble.'

The key finally turned. I slid in and shoved it into the ignition. The plastic seat burnt the back of my legs. There was a weight pressing on my chest, buzzing in my ears; it was hard to get my breath.

I reversed out of my parking space and swung the Mini round. I allowed myself a brief revenge fantasy – ploughing into the white Mercedes that Eddie Kenton stood next to. As I drove off, I saw him in my rearview mirror. Summer suit and crisp, white shirt; that boyish haircut. He was smiling. Least I think that's what it was.

I got home with reeking armpits and a knot the size of an apple in my shoulder. I stripped off and stood under the shower, letting the water smooth away the worst of the tension and rinse away all of that sharp smell.

Eddie Kenton had sussed out I wasn't a student, but did he know who I was? Was there any reason he should? He'd not seen me at Barney's and, although I'd called on his friend Fraser Mackinlay, I hadn't given my name or my profession away. As far as I knew, Fraser thought I was a friend of Martin's, so it was hardly likely he'd mention me to Kenton. The more I dwelt on it, the more certain I became that Kenton couldn't know who I was and that his hostility was more general; he was suspicious of my research story. He'd probably notched me up as an investigative journalist or a media hack – someone in the know about his past record, digging for dirt.

I pulled on a pair of shorts and a T-shirt and set off early enough to walk to school. Do my bit for the planet. Maddie was churlish at the prospect of walking, but soon brightened up as we played don't-step-on-the-cracks. Once we'd collected Tom, we made a detour to the shops for ice-creams. There was still a shadow of anxiety in my stomach but playing happy families helped to take my mind off it.

I was aware that I still hadn't heard from Nina, but there was little point in ringing her now. It was too late to go round there and, even if Fraser had been at work, he'd be heading back for his tea anytime. I'd ring Nina tomorrow.

I was washing up when Ray arrived back from his Mum's. He'd been helping her put up some new kitchen units.

'I see they've got someone for that murder, then,' he said.

'What? Which murder?'

'The woman that came to you – Janice Brookes. Haven't you seen the paper? Front page. Here.'

I grabbed a tea-towel and swept at the suds on my arm. My head swam a little as I walked over to the table. He was just spreading the paper out so I could see. Janice. Who'd killed Janice? I didn't want to know. Held my breath as I read, still clutching the tea-towel. My eyes stumbled over words as I searched for the names I half expected. Martin wasn't there, nor Fraser.

No. The man that police now 'strongly linked to the brutal slaying of Janice Brookes,' the man that the police were now awaiting forensic reports on, was an eighteen year old black kid called Derek. Five days ago they'd pulled him from the Mersey, a victim of drug related violence; today, the victim was a murderer, near as damn it, and no comment was being made about whether Derek jumped or whether he was pushed.

I breathed out and sat down. I kept going over the article but it still made little sense. I wanted it all to feel neat and tidy. Leanne had talked about this young man as she leant against the sink; a good mate, she'd said. She'd had to stop to swallow tears. Doing his head in, she'd said that as well.

It wasn't neat, or tidy. There was no sense of justice in it. And there was one big question that wouldn't stop echoing in my mind. Why? Why? And behind that lurked the realisation that I'd probably never know that; no-one would.

'Cos dead boys can't talk.

CHAPTER THIRTY TWO

I rang Mrs Williams. I needed to talk to someone who was involved – to share my sense of shock and the sadness that lurked behind it, now that a picture of Janice's murder was emerging.

She sounded fine. I told her I'd seen the news in the paper; that it'd been a complete surprise. I asked whether the police had given her any idea how long it would be for the forensics.

There was a pause at the other end of the line.

'What news?' Dread in her voice.

I felt my cheeks tighten with embarrassment. 'Oh, I'm so sorry. I thought the police would have been in touch before they talked to the press.' The bastards. 'They think they've got a suspect, a young man. He was found dead himself, in the river, last week. It doesn't say much more than that, really; just that they are awaiting forensic reports before they can make a definite statement.'

'Who's this man?'

'He's called Derek Carlton. He's eighteen.' I told her what I knew about Derek; it didn't take long. She asked me to read out the article. When I'd finished, she was quiet for a moment.

When she did speak, the fury tumbled out. 'Why didn't they ring me? It's only common decency. It's my daughter they're talking about. The whole of Manchester is reading it and I didn't even know...' Rage choked her words. I bristled in sympathy.

'Ring Miller,' I said. 'It's out of order, it's atrocious.' She was all for it. I wouldn't have relished being on the receiving end of that call.

We talked a bit more, about the details in the paper, about the implications if Derek was guilty.

'They'll be able to release the body now,' she said. 'It's been awful waiting for that, not being able to bury her – like she's not really gone.'

Before ringing off, I checked that she'd someone to call on if she needed company. Asked her to let me know what Miller said.

Later, as I sorted through a jumble of clean clothes that were stiff from drying in the sun, I began to explore the new picture for myself. If Derek had killed Janice, a pretty good bet, given the way it was splashed all over the front page, then Fraser and Martin were off the hook. All my disturbing fantasies about it happening at that Cheadle house were just the product of an overactive imagination. I could forget it all, bar the letter.

I carried a heap of Tom's clothes upstairs and put them on his shelves. Across in my room, I got the long white envelope out of my bag. Inside was the letter Janice had left to me in trust for her son. I imagined steaming it open but it was pure fantasy. I was nervous about what might be inside, how it might move me. Besides, I felt guilty enough about Janice's death, without adding to the burden. I slipped it back into my bag and made my way downstairs for the next armful, wondering what had happened to the clothes basket.

What was the situation if the suspected murderer was dead? Would there be a trial or would it be covered in Janice's inquest? Who would have to be convinced of Derek's guilt? Or did his death mean that no hearing about his crime could be held?

What of his death? The paper said preliminary autopsy reports showed that Derek had drowned and that a substantial level of crack cocaine had been found in his bloodstream. It read like suicide or accidental death. No mention anymore of the drug war.

I carried Maddie's pile upstairs. What would forensics be looking for? Samples of his skin under Janice's fingernails, hairs in her car? Had there been any sexual assault? The details began to chill me. I pushed that line of thought away.

Okay. Suppose Derek did it, say all the evidence led to Derek Carlton... Why didn't it make me feel any better? Just 'cos it hadn't matched up with my own pet theories, was that why? I'd thought Janice's death and Martin's new life were bound up together – she was found near Cheadle, he lived there; must be him or Fraser or a crony. Wrong. It was coincidence, not connection. I said it aloud.

I still wasn't convinced. Too many loose threads went wandering across, making it impossible to pull Derek and Janice out of the basket without tugging on lots of others. Leanne... she knew J.B., now dead; Derek, now dead; Martin... and Smiley had known them all. I was getting tangled.

Fingering Derek for the murder released a swarm of questions. One buzzed louder than the rest, making me shake my head. Why? Over and over again, why? Why would Derek batter Janice Brookes to death?

'You stupid fucking bitch.' The words spat hoarsely down the phone were so unexpected, that for a split second I thought I'd misheard.

'It won't be paint next time, bitch.' What on earth did he mean? Was this some crank? Paint what?

'It'll be blood. Yours, maybe the kiddies'.' I saw my office, lilac emulsion, crimson splashes. Outrage rose like bile in my throat. How dare he!

'Now look here...'

'Shut it,' he rapped, 'and keep your fucking nose out, you got that? Keep your fucking nose out, cunt.'

'Out of what?' I screamed into the receiver, but already I could hear the drone of the dialling tone. I put the phone down and sat on the bottom step. My right knee was trembling, a spasm I had no control over. My face was burning. I sat and rocked a little, took ten deep breaths, let them out slowly. Then cramps sent me racing for the toilet.

I found Ray in the cellar. He was carving lengths of wood with some new moulding tools that left fancy edges behind. I sat on the high stool and fingered the curls of wood shavings. Ray looked up.

'I just got a threatening phone call.' I told him the gist of it. He blanched, then dull spots of colour rose in his cheeks.

'Jesus Christ.' He put down the piece of wood he held and moved round the work-bench to me.

'Are you okay?'

'Yes.' By the time the word was out, I was bawling like a toddler. Ray pulled my head to his chest, hugged me. I could smell the gingery scent of his sweat, feel the grains of sawdust pitting my cheek. I was glad he was there even though there was that stiffness in his embrace, the embarrassment of bodily contact. I was glad he was there but I really wanted someone else to be holding me tight. As the realisation dawned, it set me off afresh. I wanted my Mum.

So Leanne had told Smiley. Willingly? Eagerly, even? Had she gone trotting off as soon as I'd left or had Smiley come asking again, sensed she was keeping something back, shaken it out of her?

Tea in hand, face washed and nose blown, I sat opposite Ray at the kitchen table. He was lecturing me, insisting I cease whatever I was doing to warrant the heavy phone call. What did he think I was going to do, go looking for trouble? Did he really think me that stupid – or that brave?

'Of course I'll pack it in – I'm not going to put the kids at risk, Ray! For Christ's sake, it's over.' No more visits to Leanne, not even to ask if she blew the whistle, no more questions about J.B. Finito. 'I just wish I could let the bastard know. Total surrender. Maybe I should put an ad in the paper, send it out on Piccadilly: SMILEY – I QUIT. LOVE SAL.'

'You could drape a white sheet out the window.'

'Yeah,' I sighed. 'Bit rude though, issuing an ultimatum like that and not waiting for an answer.'

I was pulling on clean, if crinkled, clothes, getting ready to go round to Diane's, when the phone rang again. My stomach corkscrewed. I didn't want to answer it. Ray was downstairs and he called up, 'For you, Sal.'

He held out the receiver and whispered, 'A woman – American, I think.'

'Hello, Nina?'

'Sal.' Her voice was gravel-thick.

'Are you okay? You sound awful.'

'I'm sorry, oh...' The words were slurred.

'Nina, what's wrong? What's the matter?'

She moaned, then there was a clatter as the phone

was dropped. I couldn't get an answer from her. Shit.

I raced back into my room and pulled a sweatshirt on over my jeans and T-shirt. Ray was in the shower. I called out to him that I had to go out, work, I'd leave the address downstairs. I scrawled the Zaleski's address on the back of an envelope with a wax crayon.

'It's not anything to do with that nutter, is it?' he called from the top of the stairs.

'No way, Ray.'

CHAPTER THIRTY THREE

There were no lights on at Nina's. The drive had taken
me fifteen minutes, during which time I'd imagined
every horror under the sun to account for the aborted
phone call. I parked in front of the verandah. I looked
about before getting out of the car but the twilight
played games with the shapes and shadows.

As I stepped up onto the verandah steps, an intruder
light snapped on, flooding the porch and beyond with
glaring sodium light. I fought the impulse to flee and
knocked loudly with the lion's paw. Somewhere in the
back of the house, the dog Fang set up a rhythmic
barking. I knocked again and again. In between the
steady woofs, I listened, ears cocked for any other
sounds. I heard a car on the road slowing down, slow
enough to turn into the drive. I skipped down from the
door and listened in the dark. The car was nearby but
not coming up Nina's drive. I heard the rattle of gravel,
next door's perhaps.

I jumped back into the limelight and made my way
round the side of the house. I'd hoped to peer in
through windows but elaborate shutters covered them
all, except for a small frosted glass rectangle towards
the back of the house, on the right-hand side.

I hesitated for a few seconds. Would it be better to
go and find a phone box, try rousing Nina that way?
But I was too worried to delay any longer. Nina had
been distressed; she could be lying in there, bleeding

to death. There were a couple of hideous wrought-iron sculptures at either side of the verandah steps. I picked one up and carried it round to the glass window. Fang was quiet.

I raised the twisted iron and brought it down hard against the window. The glass buckled rather than shattered, reinforced in some way. No bells or sirens. Fang went apeshit. He was nearby, but not in the room itself. Mixed with his deep-throated barking was the clatter of claws scrabbling against a door.

I had to hit the glass several times to break it up, like smashing toffee. I pushed lumps of it into the room with the edge of the sculpture. When I'd made a clear hole, I heaved myself up and lunged over the sill head first. It was dark and, when I was half-way in, I realised I'd no idea how far I was going to drop. I could only go forward but I didn't relish breaking my neck. I put out my hands and flailed around, felt canvas and metal, a tent, leaning against the wall beneath me. I carried on wriggling forward, wincing at the pain as my hip-bones caught on the edge of the window frame. I was aiming to slither down the tent, to buffet my fall. My weight shifted suddenly, I pulled my hands round my head for protection and tumbled onto the carpeted floor only inches below. I felt my way across the carpet till I found the skirting board. Followed that round to the door-jamb. Felt up both edges till I got the light switch. Bingo.

A storeroom. The tent that had eased my entrance was actually a bag of golf clubs. Other leisure accessories were neatly arranged round the room; skis, a beautiful wooden toboggan, rucksacks, a massive lime green and pink snow-suit hanging up like a day-glo Michelin Man. I felt like climbing into it for protection. Instead, I selected a golf club and put my ear to the door. Fang's barking was close but not too close. I inched the door open. No movement in the hall.

I established that Fang was behind the kitchen door to my left. He was becoming hoarse with fury. I switched on the hall light and walked along to the white lounge at the front of the house. It was disarrayed but only with the débris of ordinary life; magazines, a newspaper, empty mugs and discarded shoes. I called Nina's name out a couple of times as I prowled. Checked behind the huge white Chesterfield. Went upstairs. Half-way up, I heard another car and froze as I listened. Again, I heard the vehicle slow and the telltale rasp of gravel. I went on up and looked out of the landing window, the one that overlooked Fraser Mackinlay's. His porch, columns and all, was illuminated by the same sort of ghastly light. It spilled out and swept an arc over the gravel. I could see a couple of cars there. A figure was silhouetted at the door. Anonymous. The door opened, he entered. Darkness fell. Plenty of callers for a Monday night.

Nina was in the main bedroom, which ran above the lounge at the front of the house. The room was big enough to split into a boudoir and a lounging area, all done out in red and black. I saw her from the doorway, on the floor next to a chaise-longue, the phone beside her. I moved closer, my pulse speeding up in dread. I gulped in a powerful, sweet stench. Alcohol, lots of it, mingled with the acrid notes of vomit and shit.

She'd been sick where she lay, her cheek rested in it. There were patches on the crimson housecoat she wore. Her face was the colour of putty, with the same oily sheen. Eyes closed. I felt for a pulse, ignoring the frantic pace of my own. There was one. Weak but discernible. As I touched her cheek, she drew a shallow breath. I

206

followed first-aid procedure with the narrow-minded clarity that accompanies shock; checked her mouth for obstructions; put her in the recovery position; shuffled her away from the pool of sick. As I settled her head, a thin trickle of dark bile leaked from the corner of her mouth.

I punched 999 into the handset and gritted my teeth while I answered the pro-forma questions that had to be answered before the ambulance would be dispatched. I turned back to Nina. Was she breathing, still? Oh, God. I placed my hand on her sternum and felt the slight rise and fall. That reassured me. I kept it there.

Surveying the room, I wondered who had chosen the decor, the wrought-iron headboard, the wall lights with their crown of thorns brackets, the fluffy orange carpet with its black fleur-de-lys motif. Jack or Nina? Maybe an interior designer had come up with the concept; sort of barbed wire and shag pile. Whoever it was would be better off designing the inside of aerosol cans.

I heard the ambulance approach at the same time as its headlights swept across the ceiling. I ran down to open the door.

The man at the door was young and bearded. He followed me upstairs, knelt by Nina, took her pulse, raised an eyelid and went back down to relay instructions to his mate. I hovered, waiting for them to come back upstairs. They brought a stretcher and blanket. While the older man sorted out the equipment, the bearded one talked to me.

'We'll take her into Detox. She done it before?'

'I don't know,' I said. 'Will she be alright?'

He nodded. 'She'll be alright – more than I can say for her liver. She not taken pills or 'owt?'

'I don't think so.' I glanced round. I hadn't seen any small tablet bottles. 'Which hospital?'

'The Infirmary. You her next of kin?'

'No.'

'Neighbour?'

'No, I just met her.'

'Tonight?' He was puzzled.

'Recently. She rang me tonight.'

The other man grunted gently as he eased Nina onto the stretcher.

'You coming to the hospital? We could do with a few details and that.'

'No, I can't.' I found a pen and tore a blank page from my diary. Wrote down Nina's name, my own and my phone number.

'You won't know her N.H.S. number then?' said the man, adjusting the buckles on the stretcher.

'No.' Stupid question.

'She's probably BUPA, furious when she wakes up on the ward.' He cackled.

When they'd gone, I stood in the hallway. I wanted to go home. I wanted a stiff drink, a long sleep, to give in to the fatigue. But there was a broken window to sort out. I rummaged round the storeroom itself but there weren't any tools there. I'd noticed another door tucked under the stairs, so I tried that. It was unlocked. Stairs led down to a basement room. It was kitted out like a D.I.Y. catalogue. Shiny tools hung neatly in rows. Nails and screws were stacked in boxes, graded by size. Sheets and lengths of wood stood to attention in one corner. No off-cuts, no sawdust. I doubt whether any of it had been touched since they'd bought it. Well, dusted maybe.

I found a bit of plywood that I thought was about the right size, selected nails and hammer. It didn't take long to hammer it over the frame outside. I hurried, in my anxiety to get away. It was a bodged job but at least the hole was covered up. Back inside, I wrote a note in case there were any callers (cleaner, close friends or even Jack back sooner than expected). I left it by the hall phone. There were a bunch of keys there and they fit the front door. I went out and locked up. Stood for a moment, just breathing in the warm night air, a faint trace of night scented stock in it. Heard a barn owl 'kerwic'.

Fang was still barking intermittently. He might need food and water but I wasn't going to go anywhere near the animal. Bloody dogs.

I got in the Mini and drove to the bottom of Nina's drive. There I stopped. I hadn't planned it but it seemed the right thing to do. I slipped a felt pen in my pocket and slid out of the car. Walked quickly round to Fraser's gates and through them into the shrubberies at the side of the drive. I wove through the rhododendrons and camellias till I reached the lawn that surrounded the forecourt. There were four cars and a minibus parked there. I wrote down the registration numbers on my forearm with the pen. Then I retraced my steps. Who was calling on Fraser tonight? Unfortunately, I don't have a direct line to the police computer but there was one name I could fill in anyway. One of the four cars was a white Mercedes. So, was Eddie Kenton there for business or pleasure?

I had a rush of elation once I was homeward-bound. I fished out an Otis Redding tape and stuck it on. Joined in with a vengeance. All the fears I'd been sitting on since Nina had rung could be faced now. Nina was alive. She hadn't been attacked. There was no big conspiracy; I hadn't had to find another corpse, just a dead drunk, and I was so grateful to her. I sang out loud, 'Young girls they do get weary...'

Half-way home, I remembered Diane. My stomach plummeted. I should have been there hours ago.

'Diane, it's Sal, I'm so sorry. I got a phone call from this woman. She'd drunk herself unconscious – not when she rang me, but nearly – and...'

'Sal, spare me the sordid details. You could have bloody well rung me.'

'But... yes, I'm sorry, I didn't think.'

'I know.'

I squirmed at the chill in her voice.

'I don't need this, Sal, not on top of everything else. It's not fair. If you can't make the time, I'd rather you came out and said so. I need someone I can rely on.'

'I could come now.'

'And regale me with stories about your adventures tonight? No thanks.'

'I'm sorry, I don't know what else I can say.' Silence.

'Diane?'

'Goodnight.' She rang off.

I smarted with the injustice of it. Did she really think I was so shallow? Was it just her depression talking? My fists were clenched. I couldn't keep still. No way was I going to sleep, in this state. I wanted to run, to hit something, to dance myself senseless. I was full of energy again, dizzy with adrenalin.

I pulled my cycle from the shed and set off down the backstreets. Turned into the park and pedalled fast round the outer paths. I passed a couple of dog-walkers, spotted a huddle of teenagers under the climbing frame in the playground. Caught a whiff of sweet smoke.

At the far side of the park, I joined Platt Lane, a long straight road, not too busy. I pedalled hard, pushing myself as fast as I could. When I reached the end, I took a right. It didn't much matter where I went. It was the speed I wanted. I kept up the pace. My calves and buttocks clenched with the effort. My chest burned.

I was red, gasping and bathed in sweat when I walked unsteadily into the kitchen.

'Well,' said Clive, straightening up from the fridge, 'just look...'

I was beside him in a trice. 'Don't say it, Clive,' I jabbed my finger at him in warning, 'just don't say a fucking word.'

CHAPTER THIRTY FOUR

'What makes wind, Mummy?'

Six-thirty. A host of worries swarmed in on me like parasites. Diane, Nina, Fang. That voice on the phone. Getting out of bed, I felt as though I'd been fed through a mangle. When I tried to bend to put my socks on, the muscles across my lower back screeched in pain. It was a day of picking up pieces. I dropped the kids off and walked round to the Dobson's. It was ages since I'd been to the office – its new cheap and cheerful look still felt unfamiliar.

I rang Stockport Infirmary and found out that Nina Zaleski would be discharged by early afternoon. I asked them to tell her I'd bring clothes and give her a lift home.

I rang Mrs Williams. She was hopping mad, having tried to speak to Miller; she'd been told he was unavailable and had been fobbed off with Sergeant Boyston.

'He couldn't tell me a thing,' she said. 'He didn't even seem to understand why I was complaining. I told him I wanted the Inspector to contact me as soon as he's back.'

As soon as I rang off, the phone bleated at me. I snatched it up, unnerved by the sudden noise. It was work. Bliss. Paid work which would help offset the horrible details in the bank statement that had come that morning.

My client was a worried employer. He ran an electrical goods shop. Someone on the staff was siphoning off stock on a pretty regular basis. I arranged to call and discuss the details on Wednesday afternoon, when the shop was shut.

I spent an hour putting the files from the salvageable pile in order in the cabinet. An old one that I'd created in my first flush of optimism, when I'd started the business on the Enterprise Allowance Scheme, was marked Equipment Guarantees. Inside was my camera warranty, well past the expiry date. I binned that, crossed out the title and wrote VAT in big letters. Surely that would bore the pants off anyone who might come looking? Into it, I put a note of the car numbers I'd copied from my arm, together with a short biography of all the characters connected to the search for Martin Hobbs. For prudence's sake, I altered names and glossed over details.

Norman Tebbit – rich, Gaelic, high-tech empire, cold fish, maybe living with...

Peter Pan – no home of his own, hiding or hidden?

Jack Duckworth – business with Norman, ex-film director, white car.

Kirk Douglas – charity champion, connection to Norm? Money?

I bracketed those four together. At the bottom of the page, I added Tinkerbell – light-fingered friend of the Artist (dead) and the Suspect (dead).

Grumpy – rubbed out the Artist? Hooked the Suspect. Frightens Tinkerbell, and me!

I realised that Janice connected to the top via Martin and to the bottom via Derek, the Suspect. And that Martin was still the key to it all – he linked the two groups.

I jotted down a few other questions and observations,

including the warning I'd received.

On a fresh sheet of paper, I wrote myself a note in large capitals: THE LETTER – NOTHING ELSE. An admonition to keep on the right track. Like talking to a brick wall.

The sky was full of the promise of thunder. Sulky clouds, tinged violet, moved into place. The air was stifling, a headache lurked at the nape of my neck.

Along Old Hall Lane, the bin-bags crouched in little piles, waiting for the refuse van. A daft idea formed and, without taking time to assess it, I stopped the car at the pile nearest to Fraser's and Nina's, nipped out and slung the lot in the boot. Only when I was back in the Mini, did I risk checking to see if anyone had seen me. The street was deserted. My blush faded and I drove on to Nina's and deposited the rubbish round the far side of the house.

I unlocked the door and went in. Fang roared into action from behind the kitchen door. Upstairs, I searched through drawers and cupboards till I'd found underwear, a stylish turquoise tracksuit and some white leather sports shoes. I paused on the way down to peer out at Fraser's. No cars there today. I'd go round with the letter once I'd brought Nina back.

Finding the hospital was a doddle, finding a parking space a nightmare. At last I spotted someone leaving, on a side street, and sat patiently while they loaded assorted bags and babies and moved off.

Nina was alone in a dayroom, the television on. She wore a paper hospital gown. Her face was the colour of oatmeal. When she saw me, she looked embarrassed. She covered it quickly with an expression of world-weariness.

'Sal.' A brittle smile.

'Clothes.' I handed her the pile. 'I've come to give you a lift home.'

She sighed and nodded. She got up slowly and walked to the door. When she'd gone, I turned the television off and turned the chair round to face the windows that looked out onto buildings and, beyond those, fields and trees. The sky glowered darker and a flash illuminated the landscape. I counted four before the thunder broke in a rich growl. Large drops of rain followed, splashing as they hit.

I was mesmerised by the time she returned. I didn't hear her come in. She touched me lightly on the shoulder and I started.

'You need to sign out or anything?' I asked her.

She shook her head.

I hadn't brought her a coat. That made two of us. By the time we reached the car, the rain had mottled our clothes and drenched our hair.

'I suppose I should thank you – for last night,' she said dryly, as she fastened the seat belt.

'It's not compulsory,' I said. 'How do you feel?'

'As though they put lye in the bottle. And pretty stupid. I'd appreciate it if we could just forget the whole thing.' Tough lady talking but out of the corner of my eye I caught a twitching jaw muscle that told me she was hurting.

The rain was so heavy, it was hard to see the way.

'I have a confession to make,' I said. 'Well, two, actually.'

'Go on.'

'I smashed a window to break into your house last night and I left Fang shut up in the kitchen without any dinner.'

'Best place for him. He'd have ripped your throat out if you'd tried anything else.'

When we reached the ranch, I showed Nina the damage. She told me to wait in the lounge while she sorted Fang out. After a few minutes she called me through. She'd cleared up the mess he'd made but even the disinfectant couldn't hide the smell. He was just finishing some food. A large, dirty-white animal with thick fur and a solid body. He growled softly at me while he finished his meal.

'Is upstairs a mess?' Nina asked.

With a rush of embarrassment, I realised I'd just left the bedroom after the ambulance had gone and I hadn't done anything to clear up this morning.

'I don't know.'

It wasn't too bad. A puddle of dried vomit, the fruity smell of spilt alcohol. But I felt it would be tactful if I went, left her to clear up herself.

'I'd better go,' I said. She followed me onto the landing.

'What about next door? Do you still want to know about Fraser's movements?'

'Yes. I was going to try going round now. Does he usually park the car in view?'

She moved past me and looked out of the window. 'Not always. He has a garage round the far side. He could well be at work now.'

I thought about it. 'I don't want to be recognised,' I said, 'if he is there.'

Nina stood back and screwed her eyes up, examining me. 'I have just the thing,' she said. 'This way.'

I followed her through to the second bedroom, which was used as a dressing room. Walk-in wardrobes lined one wall and full-length mirrors covered the one opposite. She crossed to a chest of drawers and pulled out a bleached blonde frizzy-perm wig. A red pvc zip-up minidress was next. Nina insisted on the pillar-box red lipstick and the long lash mascara. While she finished me off, back-combing the wig, she told me how she'd trained as a beautician. But all her training couldn't mask the fact that her hands were shaking too badly to do the make-up.

I surveyed myself in the mirror. Shoes were a problem. My tatty trainers hardly fit the image and Nina's feet were two sizes smaller than mine. She was all for me teetering in strappy mules, with my heels hanging off the back, but I insisted that I needed to be able to run.

'Shame you ain't got bigger boobies,' she said. 'Draw attention away from those feet.'

The final touch was a soft gold leather bum-bag, into which I folded the letter from Janice Brookes to Martin. It was still raining. Nina found me a red brolly.

Feeling like a right nerd, I made my way down Nina's drive, along the road a few yards and into Fraser's, taking the route through the bushes to avoid rattling the gravel. I tiptoed round the side to the garage. It had a steel door – not even a keyhole to peer through. But, round the back, there was a small meshed window. I jumped up to see in. No car.

Back round to the front. I pushed open the golden letter box and peeped in. Palatial entrance hall, rich rug on the floor, vase of lilies, doors off, nothing moving. I turned so my ear was at the slot. Faint murmur; a tele, radio? I waited. Running water started then stopped. Someone was home. I straightened up, wincing a bit as I renewed acquaintance with my torn muscles.

I rang the bell loud and long, heard it trilling through the house. Waited, rang again, waited. After the third attempt, I listened again. The radio had been turned off. Quiet. I moved away a few yards so I could look up at the house for any sign of life. Gave the bell one last try.

I didn't hear the car. Not until it swept round the last bend into the turning circle. It swerved to a halt, spraying gravel. Fraser Mackinlay jumped out.

'Yes?' he barked. 'What do you want?'

'Good afternoon, sir.' I pulled my lips apart to show my teeth. 'I'm in the area looking for clients.' I tried for a broad accent, all Coronation Street. 'Home beauty treatments, facials, extensions, waxing...' I don't know whether it was the trainers that blew it, but Fraser's eyes raked me up and down, then he lunged.

I dropped the umbrella and ran, kicking up gravel as I went. I skidded as I rounded the corner and one leg went scooting out to the side. I dug in with the other, to regain my balance, and felt the sickening wrench of my weak ankle. Fraser had gained on me. He could move fast. As I took off again, I knew I wouldn't make it. He was at my heels and my windpipe was hurting with the exertion and the punishment from last night's cycle ride. He was right behind me now. He grabbed for me, his fingers tightening in the coarse hair of the wig. He held tight, stopped, expecting me to jerk to a halt. I sailed on. I heard him shout in dismay.

I had the advantage now and didn't dare relax my pace. Thank God for the trainers. I ignored the pain in my ankle. I reached the gates and turned onto the pavement, ran past Nina's. I sensed Fraser had stopped. When I judged I'd created enough distance, I looked back. Just in time to see him fling the wig to the ground and wheel away from the road.

I trotted another mile before I found anywhere with a public phone. A big theme pub, Tudor beams and microwave dinners. I'd no money, but I begged some ten pences off a party of office workers who were pissed enough to be feeling generous.

I got Nina's number from Directory Enquiries.

'It's me, Sal. I'm at the Black Bull Tavern on Middlewich Road. Can you come and get me?' I felt awkward calling for help from someone who'd near enough poisoned herself within the last twenty-four hours – she must be feeling lousy – but there was no-one else I could ask.

'What are you doing there? What happened?'

'Fraser chased me.'

She thought it was funny. 'Didn't catch you, then.'

I described the drama on the drive back. Nina hooted with laughter. She was still pale but seemed to have some of her old sparkle back. She was sucking mints, her hands were steady. I assumed she'd been back at the booze.

I ducked down as we neared the house, only emerging once we were at her front door. Back in the dressing room, I wriggled out of the red sheath and into my damp jeans and sweatshirt.

'Do you think he knew who you were?' she asked.

'I don't know – hope he doesn't treat all his callers like that. I suppose once the wig was off he got a pretty good look. And if he's that paranoid, he'll remember me from the other day. I'm sorry about the wig.'

'No problem. It always gave me one helluva headache.'

It was after three; I'd be late for Maddie. I pulled the letter from the bum-bag.

'What do you want me to do about Fraser?' Nina asked.

'Nothing. He'll be on red alert now,' I said. 'Don't

even bother watching, unless you happen to be passing the window.'

The green lights were on my side for a change. I reached school just in time. I limped through the playground and drew a lot of sidelong glances from other parents. Maddie was in her surly mood. I let her be and we drove over to Tom's nursery. I was gasping for a drink and almost faint with hunger. I felt smelly, too, after all that exercise and the fear. I craved a pot of tea, beans on toast (had we any bread?), a fierce shower.

Tom was in the home corner. He burst into tears as I moved towards him. I knelt down at his side. 'Tom, what's the matter?'

He shrank away from me, clung to the nursery nurse. What was it? Anxiety clawed at my stomach. I looked at her over his head. She pointed at my face, mouthed the words.

Oh God. No wonder they'd stared in the playground. I was still tarted up to the nines.

CHAPTER THIRTY FIVE

The storm really got going around tea-time. Digger set up a whine that grated on my nerves. Gusts of strong wind joined heavy rain. Out of the kitchen window, I could see the plants taking a battering, whipped this way and that, heads bowed with the weight. Maddie's trike and Tom's car scudded round with the strongest blasts. I pulled on my cagoule, slipped a pair of scissors in the pocket and went out there. I put the toys away in the shed and weighted the sandpit cover down with stones. Then I cut a handful of pinks and snipped off every sweet-pea in sight. Cut and come again.

Ray knocked on the window and crooked his fingers like a handset. It was Mrs Williams.

'I got hold of Detective Inspector Miller,' she said. 'Took me most of the day.'

'What did he have to say?'

'He apologised – after a fashion. Blamed it on his juniors. Can't say it was exactly heartfelt. Could do with a course in public relations, that one. He treats me like I'm threepence short of a shilling. Probably thinks if you've got grey hair you've no grey matter. Anyway, he wouldn't tell me straight about the forensics, not what they're after nor when it'll be ready.'

'He probably doesn't know himself, but he'd hate to admit it.'

'Well,' she continued, 'after pressing him a bit, he agreed to let me know if anything definite came up.'

'Good. How are you?'

She sighed. 'Oh, alright, I suppose. I just wish it were all over. I'm going down to stay at our Natalie's for a few days, tomorrow. There any news your end?'

'Well, I tried to see Martin today but I got chased off by the bloke who owns the place. He definitely doesn't like callers. I'll have to tread carefully if I go back there.'

'You'll try again, won't you? I've been thinking about that boy and that letter. That's all she left to him – all she got a chance to give him. I want to make sure he gets it.'

'Yes.' There wasn't much else I could say.

The sweet-peas were a cluster of colour, every shade from the palest pink through to deep violet and striking fuchsia. I filled little jars with them and dotted them through the house. When I came back into the kitchen, the pinks had filled the air with their scent of sweet cloves.

I could take them round to Diane. A peace offering. There were still a couple of hours before the meeting with Clive.

Ray was happy to swap bedtime duty, though Maddie kicked up a protest. I invited her to watch the storm with me before I went. We turned the lights off in my room and gazed out, counting in between rumble and flash. One loud crack had us both shrieking with delight and shock.

I parked a few doors down from Diane's. The narrow street was lined with cars at that time of day. Behind the lacy net curtains, little ones were being put to bed and the small rooms tidied up. At this time of year, if it hadn't been raining, the kids would have been out on the street, mums would bring out chairs and sit on the dusty pavement, swapping tales and shouting warnings to their offspring. They'd all grown up together round here. Diane was an incomer, regarded as a 'student' by the neighbours, who pitied her lonely existence, as they saw it, and were plainly bemused by the bright abstract prints she made.

As I unclicked the seat belt, a car drew up alongside me, blocking the narrow street. Oh no, an irate resident perhaps. One of those people who insist on parking right outside their own front door.

I got out of the car and the passenger leapt out of the other car and came towards me.

'Have I got your space?' I called.

He looked incredibly upset. It was only a parking space, for heaven's sake. I opened my mouth to offer to move, if that's what he wanted. He leapt the last yard onto the pavement and thumped me full in the face. Suns burst in my eyes, trailing wires of pain from my nose. I was on the floor, my hands cupped over my face, making little yelping noises. Pain exploded in my belly, my ribs. Kicking me. I curled to protect myself. I could hear his breath coming in noisy gasps as he kicked my legs and my arms. He stamped on my head; my skull and ear ground against wet paving stones. I think he just did that once. I could taste iron, sweet and salt. There was a pause. Then a blow to my kidneys, sharp and hard, which sent a deep, bruising pain rolling through my abdomen.

'Come on, you wanker.' A shout.

I waited for the next blow. Nothing. Sick boiled up and spurted from my nose and mouth. It was nothing to do with me. I wasn't there.

I was wet, the pavement was wet. I was lying on the pavement. He must have gone. I opened my eyes. The left one swam red. I closed it. I could see quite well out of the other. A tuft of grass growing between the paving stone and the kerbstone. And just there, a neat white turd. How come some dogs do white ones? There were feet. Two. In Mickey Mouse socks with ears that stuck out at the side and red plastic sandals.

'What yer doin'?' A high piping voice. 'Yer've been sick. Have you got a nosebleed?'

I tried to lift myself up but nothing worked.

'Can you get Diane?' My voice worked. It sounded so ordinary. 'She's at number twenty-three.'

'Alright.'

I closed my eye.

'Sal? Oh my god.'

'I brought you some flowers,' I said, 'but I don't know where I've put them.'

Things were a bit hazy after that. All I wanted was to dive into sleep, where the hurting couldn't follow, but they kept waking me up. Lifting me into the ambulance, making me stand up for the X-ray, asking me to look at lights, turning me over to stitch my ear and cheek. They kept me in overnight. I was mildly concussed.

Comes from having your head stamped on.

At some point, I'd agreed to report it to the police. The following morning, people started crashing trolleys around at six am. By the time a policewoman arrived at nine-thirty, I was ready for another night's sleep.

Her questions made me feel wobbly. Added to that, I couldn't give a decent description of my assailant – young white man dressed in casual clothes. Nothing memorable, no memory of the make of the car – maybe it was maroon or blue. No, I didn't know him, no, nothing was stolen. But...

I told her about the threatening phone-call, the

paint. I explained that I thought Smiley had me beaten up, to warn me off. I told her to pass it all on to Detective Inspector Miller at Bootle Street. She raised her eyebrows at that. Name dropping again.

'Perhaps you need to take out an injunction against this man?' Yeah, then I'd really feel safe. I nodded. Closed my eyes. Go away. Let me sleep.

There were a dozen of them round my bed. The one with the receding hair-line muttered something at me, plucked the chart from the bottom of the bed and fired questions at the others. When they moved on, I called a nurse over.

'When are they sending me home?' I asked. 'Do I need to see the doctor?'

'You just seen him.'

'But he didn't tell me anything.'

She nodded. 'I'll see if I can find out for you.' I heard her exercise sandals clop against the lino, as she made her way back to the nurses' station at the end of the ward. I was just dozing off again when she returned.

'We're keeping you in for another night,' she said. 'Just a precaution.'

'What have I got, apart from the stitches?'

'Three broken ribs, bruising to the coccyx, superficial lesions.'

I knew she meant cuts. 'What about my eye?'

'Burst blood vessel – it'll soon sort itself out. Looks worse than it is. The stitches will come out next week, the ribs just need a bit of time.'

I asked for more painkillers and got them. And slept. They woke me up and plonked a plate in front of me; grey curls of flesh, yellow re-heated mash.

'I'm a vegetarian.'

'Well, there's nothing down here,' retorted the woman with the trolley.

'Nobody asked me,' I explained feebly.

She banged the plate back on the trolley. 'There probably won't be any left now,' she complained.

Well, it's not my fault, fuckface.

A few minutes later, a new plate was slammed down on my tray. The same yellowing potato accompanied now by a watery cauliflower cheese. The cauliflower had disintegrated into a grainy puree and the sauce had a sharp, sick smell. I was hungry but the smell made me gyp. As soon as she was out of sight, I put the tray on my locker and curled up under the covers.

Early afternoon. Ray came, bearing some wholemeal bread, fresh cheese and a bowl of three-bean salad glistening in its dressing. Plus a carton of freshly squeezed orange juice. Heaven.

'You didn't bring Maddie.'

'At school. I thought it'd be best to carry on as normal.'

I bit off some bread. 'What did you tell them?'

'That you tripped and banged into a wall.'

'That old favourite.'

'And I told my mum you were mugged. You okay? Looks nasty.'

'It hurts. These are really sore,' I pointed to my cheek and my ear, 'and I've three broken ribs.'

He nodded. 'We came down last night but you were out of it.'

'I don't remember much about last night.'

'So what really happened?'

As I told Ray the sequence of events, I found myself getting angry, outraged at the injustice of it.

'The fucking bastard, he rings me up, issues threats, so I do what he says. I don't go near and what happens? – he still does me over.'

'But it wasn't him – this Smiley bloke?'

'Not in person, no. But I bet he set those goons on me, without even giving me a chance to do what he wants.' I was getting aerated; the people at neighbouring beds began to cast glances my way.

'You must report it, Sal.'

'I have.' Injured tone. 'I gave a statement this morning.' I concentrated on the salad for a while. Then I asked Ray to bring Maddie in for visiting that evening.

'But you're coming home, aren't you? That's what the nurse just told me.'

'No, they said they wanted to keep me in another night.'

'Hang on.' Ray walked down to the nurses' station and came back with one of the nurses I didn't know.

'I thought I was staying in,' I began.

'Well, as there's been no complications, Doctor's happy for you to be discharged this afternoon.'

'When was that decided?' I asked. I was puzzled at the sudden change.

'I'm not sure,' she said. 'I've just come on shift. But if a patient's doing well enough, doesn't require any special treatment...'

Light dawned. 'You need the bed, don't you?'

She avoided the question. 'If there's any concern, you just ring in. And you'll have your out-patient's appointment next week. Excuse me.' She smiled brightly and escaped.

'Don't tell me you want to stay here.' Ray was appalled.

I shrugged. 'At least someone else does the sheets and clears the rubbish up. Oh, shit.'

'What?'

'Can you ring Nina Zaleski for me? The number's in the address bit of my diary, in my bag.' Suddenly, I was confused. Where was my bag? 'I don't know where my bag is, Ray, I didn't take it to Diane's.'

'Calm down, I'll find it. So, I ring this woman and say...'

'I left some rubbish at the side of her house. Tell her not to chuck it, I want to go through it.'

Ray had a peculiar look on his face. I laughed, then gasped as the stitches tugged round my cheekbone.

Ray would come back for me at five. I told him where to find my clothes.

'My mum's offered to help out for a couple of days.'

'Oh.' My stomach dipped with disappointment.

'She means well,' he said.

Maybe. Well, the kids would enjoy it and Clive would go all smarmy.

'The meeting, last night, Clive...'

'He didn't show.'

'What?' I didn't even get the satisfaction of having stood him up. 'This isn't on, Ray. We should just give him notice.'

'And lose all the money he owes?'

'You think he's going to pay?'

'Yeah, he bloody well is.'

I shook my head. 'No chance. He's up to his eyes in debt. Where's he going to get that sort of money from? We should just cut our losses.'

'No way.' Ray was getting steamed up, the skin round his lower lip white and taut.

'Ray, he isn't worth it. ' I put my hand on his forearm. 'He's a little shit and I don't want to waste any more emotional energy dealing with him.'

'Where are we going to find eight hundred pounds?'

'It's not that much.'

'It is. Six hundred pounds rent, the rest in bills – more, if you include this quarter's.'

'Oh God, not now.' I held up my hands.

'Okay.' Ray pushed back his chair and picked up the empty salad bowl. Told me he'd be back about five.

I wanted a shower and asked for a fresh robe. There wasn't one. The nurse managed to dig out two hand towels, stiff with months of boil-washing. I shuffled to the bathroom, feeling unsteady on my feet. My weak ankle had returned to normal size. I guess it couldn't keep up with the competition.

I surveyed my face dispassionately. The inch-long cut on my cheek, with its neat black stitching, looked ugly but I'd been told the scar would be very faint. There was bruising around both my eyes and the left one still had its maze of red spidery threads and small clots across most of the white. I couldn't see my ear, which had been torn and stitched. The hair around there was harsh with dried blood and dirt.

I undressed and it was then that I caught a glimpse of my body, reflected from the full length mirror and back into the one above the basin. Bruises; huge savage purple and yellow mottles on my thigh, above my buttocks. Looking down, another the size of a saucer below my breast. I looked away.

In the cubicle, I turned the shower on full, hot as I could bear it. Under cover of the streaming, steaming water, I gave in to the pressure that had been swelling like a balloon in my chest. With my fists balled, I mouthed all those age-old clichés, railing against my pain, my outrage and sorrow. Over and over again. It's not fair, it's not fair, you bastard, you bastard, you fucking bastard, it's not fair.

CHAPTER THIRTY SIX

With an unusual sensitivity, Maddie treated me with great love and attention on my return. It wasn't just in the way she was physically careful, sitting beside me rather than clambering on my lap, but also in the quick glances I noticed, where she seemed to be checking I was still okay. Her solicitude made me feel all teary.

I'd no energy and I was tucked up and sleeping before nightfall. When I finally hauled myself out of bed, eyes wincing at the harsh daylight, I was perversely pleased at the way my body ached. If I was physically in pain, it didn't leave as much space for worrying about the deeper hurts, the anxiety and fear below the surface.

Downstairs, the house was a tip. At least Nana Tello and I didn't compete over housework. She loathed cleaning. I'd no need to worry about sticky shelves and a smelly fridge.

I had tea and toast while she talked about the crime wave, about the Ordsall riots, the Moss Side shootings. She went through all the acquaintances she had who'd ever been mugged or burgled. She blamed the parents, she blamed the teachers, she blamed godlessness and the lack of National Service. She never mentioned poverty or inequality. Then she began to lecture me about not looking after myself, out at all times of the day and night, these places...

'It was broad daylight. I was walking a few yards

from my car to Diane's door – what should I have done?' I demanded.

'Well...' She was stuck for an answer. Her eyes shifted about, looking for a safer topic. 'Clive's a nice boy, you lucky to get a lodger like that.'

'Clive's a little shit, actually. We're gonna chuck him out.'

'Sal!' She exploded.

'I'm going back to bed,' I said. 'I feel sleepy.'

She clicked her tongue. Her face set with offence. I was too cross with her to apologise.

I wasn't sleepy. I didn't get into bed. Instead, I sorted out my drawers. I reunited pairs of socks, cleared out knickers with holes or dead elastic. I folded T-shirts and sweaters, put aside some for jumble, others for dusters. I cleared out my jewellery box. I dusted the clutter of little bottles on my shelf by the mirror and hung up the heap of clothes on the chair by the wardrobe. My thoughts fluttered about. I avoided trying to concentrate on anything. I lay down again and listened to the rain, the blackbird and the chatter of the magpies. I slipped into sleep and woke stiff and tense, with fragments of an ugly dream dissolving into obscurity.

Knocking at my door. 'Come in.'

'Sal, I brought you tea.' She held up a mug.

'Thanks.' I wriggled up to a sitting position. My ribs hurt like hell. 'I'm sorry about before.'

She sucked her teeth. 'You should be,' she said. 'It's bad for a woman, this language.' She put my tea down and began to smooth the edge of the duvet with her hand.

'We are asking Clive to go, though.'

'Why?'

Didn't Ray ever tell her anything? 'He doesn't pay

231

the rent or the bills. He's unreliable, he lies...'

'He's young,' she said, her voice dripping indulgence. 'He has to learn.'

'Yeah, well, we're teaching him a lesson.'

She sighed. So did I. She couldn't see beyond Clive's gross flattery. While I could imagine the savage way he'd caricature her to his friends. The crazy Italian Mama with the thick accent.

Tears came from nowhere and dripped in my tea. I put it down, astonished.

'Oh, there, now lovey.' She pulled my head to her bosom. I cried a bit but the jerking hurt my ribs. I quietened and pulled back.

'I don't know why I'm crying,' I said.

''Cos they hurt you; you hurt, you cry.'

That simple.

'Mrs Fraser cried for weeks and they didn't mess her face up like they do you. I said to her, you cry, you cry all you like. Now,' she stood up and put her hands on my shoulders, 'I'll get you some nice food, you see.'

I waited till she'd closed the door before giving in again to soft little sniffles of self-pity. Easier on the ribs but, even then, the way I screwed my face up tugged at the embroidery.

Invalid food Italian-style was a rich tomato soup followed by a creamy macaroni cheese pie. I ate like it was mid-winter and I was a navvy. Nana Tello beamed with pride. We were at peace for all of two hours. Till the kids came home.

Ray had gone to Asda. The rest of us were watching children's television. I went to make drinks and caught the remarks as I came back into the lounge.

'Knees together, Maddie, that's right.' Maddie was perched on the edge of the sofa, knees and ankles pressed together.

'You don't have to sit like that, Maddie.' I tried to keep my tone light. Nana Tello glared.

'Nana said.'

'Well, I don't think you need to bother about it.'

'She's showing her knickers,' Nana hissed at me.

'She's four years old, for Christ's sake.'

She drew breath sharply at my blasphemy but ploughed on. 'There's a lot a funny people about.'

'I know, but that's nothing to do with how Maddie sits or what she wears – don't start blaming her.' It was the old 'she asked for it' mentality. I was tempted to chuck in Martin Hobbs as an example, but I didn't want to escalate the argument. I could see Tom looking worried. 'I'm going in the garden.'

The rain had stopped, everything was sodden. Fresh sweet-peas decked the canes. The grass needed mowing as soon as it dried off and I was up to it. I pottered round, dead-heading window boxes and tubs, making a mental note to tidy up the rockery, where periwinkle and alyssum were fighting for space.

I'd been hoping to hear from Inspector Miller. Surely he'd take my allegations a bit more seriously, now I'd been duffed up? I suppose he was busy making the case against Derek Carlton; a minor assault like mine would be low on the list. And it wasn't actually Smiley who'd jumped me. It still seemed grossly unfair that Smiley had sent his dog-men after me without even waiting to see if I'd heeded his warning. I guess I expected even villains to play by some sort of rules. Naive.

My mind turned from work to money. The lack of it. If Ray was right about Clive's debts, then I needed to up my production level. Get more work. My stomach lurched. Work. I should've been at the electrical goods shop, seeing the man about suspected pilfering. Shit. I tried to ring and got the ansaphone. Left a grovelling apology and begged him to contact me again if he thought we could do business. Kept it vague enough so it wouldn't alert any potential pilferers to the nature of my job. Pilfering always smacks of missing biros and envelopes, but this bloke's losses were running into hundreds a month; microwaves and VCRs going walkies.

Oh, well. My advert would be in at the end of the week. Maybe now was a good time to reapply for Housing Benefit. Given the paltry level of income over the last few weeks, I'd probably qualify again. Or should I go for family credit? I couldn't get both, and family credit meant free prescriptions and dental care. I didn't want to wallow in my poverty. It was time to start thinking positive and looking ahead. I could follow up the ad in the paper with a few cards in shop windows.

The trouble was, I was still holding onto the letter to Martin Hobbs, an obligation hanging round my neck like an albatross. What could I do now? He hadn't come to the door when I'd called last time. There'd definitely been someone there, radio playing, water running. I needed some proof he was there, then perhaps I could send the letter by recorded delivery. Make a copy for safekeeping? It was time to do some muck-raking.

I rang Nina.

'What's with the garbage, Sal?'

'Sorry. I thought if I went through it I might be able to tell if Martin was staying there. You know, different cigarette packets, frozen dinners for two, maybe even correspondence to Martin. If you could just hang on to it for a while?'

'How long is a while? If the weather gets any

warmer it is not going to be very pleasant.'

'I know. It's just that I've had...' – what would Ray have said? – '...a bit of bad luck.'

'So I hear. Your husband said you were mugged.'
'He's not my husband.'

'Well, that's stupid. If he dies, you have a whole heap of legal trouble to prove you should get the house and...'

'No, you don't understand. We just live together, we're not having a relationship.'

'Oh, I'm sorry. So, are you hurt?'

'Bit shaken up, cuts and bruises.'

'Mmm.' I knew she wanted the bin-bags shifting, but no way was I going off to oblige until I was capable.

'Actually, half the rubbish is yours. I just grabbed everything near the gates. So you could work out which is which and chuck that.'

'And go through the rest, while I'm at it?'

'No, I wasn't suggesting...'

'But that would be quicker than waiting for you to do it.'

'Well,' – she was right – 'yes.'

'Right. So what you want is anything that points to who is living next door, particularly anything suggesting our missing teenager?'

'Yeah. If you can bear it.'

'I'll let you know,' she said dryly and rang off.

Diane came round that evening with a litre of red wine and a bag of black olives, done Provencal-style with herbs. She was sporting a lovely midnight-blue tunic with a meandering cream and gold print on it (one of hers) and had earrings to match, but she looked tense round the eyes and her laughter was a mite too hearty. We adjourned to my room, away from interruptions, and settled into the easy chairs by the bay window. With the curtain open, we could see the

235

sunset ripple day-glo colours in and out of the scattered clouds.

I told Diane the gist of what had happened before she found me on the pavement and recounted to her my recent escapades trying to reach Martin Hobbs. She liked the bit about the wig. She was convinced that Fraser and Eddie Kenton were probably using Martin to make porno movies.

'Well, that would explain why they were both so hostile to my visits,' I said. 'I know Kenton's walked that way before but Fraser doesn't strike me as a porno merchant. He's no need of the money and he's so... starchy.'

'Maybe that's how he relaxes.' She raised her eyebrows at me.

'Well, it's all supposition and it's nothing to do with me, especially now they've got someone for Janice's death. I need work I'll get paid for.'

I didn't want to talk about me all night. 'Barcelona,' I said.

She screwed up her face and puffed out her cheeks.

'Come on, all the grisly details.'

'Oh, Sal, it was a disaster from start to finish. I had my bag nicked the first afternoon and Ben went on about how careless I'd been with it, then I started with cystitis, awful, I was pissing blood...'

'Wait,' I shrieked. 'Start at the very beginning, don't miss anything out. The airport...'

'Okay,' she filled our glasses and took a swig, 'the airport.'

The practical cock-ups of the holiday had become funnier with the passing of time but when she got to the part where she and Ben discussed ending the relationship, she came over all tearful and I could see how raw the wounds still were. I went and put my arms round her. When she'd finished crying, I passed her the box of tissues and refilled her glass.

'I'm sorry about the other night,' I said, 'not turning up and not phoning. It honestly just went right out of my head. You're really important to me, you know. I don't want to mess you about.'

'Oh, stop it,' she said. 'You'll set me off again.' I grinned, chewed on an olive.

'Has my mascara run?' she asked.

'Yeah.'

She stood up and went over to the mirror, used tissue and cream to wipe away the navy streaks.

'The trouble is,' she said, 'it's always the same. The relationship starts off brilliantly and goes downhill from there on in. And they always want more, they want to take over, they want me cooking tea every night, they want marriage or babies. I thought men were supposed to be scared of commitment. I just keep thinking it's always going to be like this, always.' Her voice started getting squeaky. 'And I don't think I can bear it.' She crumpled again. I went and hugged her again. Tears tickled my own nose in sympathy.

We drank more wine, ate more olives. I told Diane about my clashes with Nana Tello. She told me about her work – her latest commission was going well. Her eyes sparkled as she talked about it and she waved her arms about in big sweeping gestures. By the time we'd emptied the bottle, our friendship was back on line.

I saw her out and waited on the back steps while she unlocked her bike.

'And remember,' she said, as she snapped on her lights, 'next time, there's no need to go battering your head on the pavement – an apology will do fine. Talk about attention-seeking!'

CHAPTER THIRTY SEVEN

Friday was Manchester weather. Endless soaking rain
that fell from thick, steely skies. I'd slept well till nine,
waking refreshed, and the sight from my window
didn't have me diving back to bed.

I was ravenous but I wanted a treat for breakfast.
Something to welcome myself back to the world.
There was a fiver in my purse. I drove to the health
food shop and bought a Greek-style Bio yoghurt and
some nuts. In the greengrocers next door I bought a
selection of fruit and a bunch of lilies. Back home, I
stuck the lilies in water and put them on the kitchen
table. Then I sliced up some banana, apple and grapes,
mixed them with the thick, creamy yoghurt, poured
honey over that and a sprinkling of nuts. The final
touch was a glass of freshly squeezed orange juice.
Serious pleasure.

As I finished, the phone rang. I gave the number.

'Is that Sal?'

'Yes, who is it?'

'It's Leanne, right, I wanted to...'

'You've got a bloody nerve.' My stomach clenched,
my face got hot.

'What d'you mean?'

'You know what I mean. What are you doing, ringing
to see if I've got the message? Well, I have, loud and
clear, and you can tell Smiley his fucking goons put me
in hospital and you can also tell him that the phone

call would have done the job. There was no need to send in the clowns... so,' I was running out of words and breath, 'so you can just fuck off, Leanne.'

'It's not my fault, is it?' Surly innocence.

'I don't give a toss whether you went running or he came asking, all I know is, within hours of me leaving you, he's threatening me, and my child, on the phone and next thing I know I'm beaten senseless.' I was screeching by then, shaking with renewed outrage. 'So you can just go and fuck yourself.' Eloquent. I hung up.

I wanted to break something, lash out. Digger slunk past. Clive couldn't have timed it worse. I was sorting out the cutlery, crashing handfuls of metal around, when he bounded into the kitchen.

'God,' he said, 'what happened to you?'

'I got beaten up.' I could see from his eyes he was weighing up whether to make some clever dick remark. He didn't get chance.

'Clive, we want you to move out. I'm giving you notice now, a month, but if you can find somewhere sooner, we'd be delighted. And we'd like you to settle the rent and the bills – I think it's about eight hundred pounds so far. Ray's got the exact figures.'

'You can't throw me out, I haven't done anything.'

'Precisely. You've done sweet f.a. for as long as possible, you haven't contributed anything to the running of the house and we're sick of it.'

'You can't make me leave.' His chin came up. 'I've got rights, you know.'

'I doubt it. Tenants pay rent. You seem to have stopped. I think you've forfeited any rights.'

'Look, look.' He waved his hands up near his ears – it was all too much, man. 'Okay, I got a bit behind and I missed a meeting, but this is way over the top. We can work something out. I'll pay it off a bit at a time.'

'It's too late, Clive. You've blown it. I can't trust you anymore. You'll have to leave.'

'Where can I go? It's impossible renting these days. I'll end up on the streets.'

'Oh, I don't think Daddy would let that happen, do you?' Below the belt maybe. Clive couldn't help having a rich father he never saw.

'You'll be sorry for this,' he began to shout, pointing his index finger at me, 'just wait and see.' He moved closer. 'I'll get you back for this, you cow, you just wait, you cunt.'

The prickle of fear hadn't a chance. I was still boiling from Leanne and here was the red rag.

In a trice, I had Clive by the collar. I pushed my face up against his, smelt sweet aftershave and stale tobacco. 'Don't you dare threaten me, you little shit.' Even I was impressed at how scary I sounded. 'Don't you ever speak to me like that. Now, get out.' I shoved him away.

'Dearie me, what's the matter?' Neither of us had heard Nana Tello come in. She stood, aghast, a bag of shopping in each hand.

'Clive's just going,' I said. 'He's off to find somewhere else to live.'

'Oh,' she said to me coldly. She turned to Clive. 'You could try the shop windows,' she offered brightly.

'Aw, piss off Grandma,' he said, as he made his exit.

She drew in a sharp breath. Lifted the carriers onto the table. 'You've upset him,' she accused me.

'Yes,' and then I felt the bubbles rising, a ridiculous giggle that took me over completely. 'Yes,' I gasped, doubled up as the laughter shook my ribs, 'yes, I suppose you could say that.'

CHAPTER THIRTY EIGHT

In the late post, I had another note from the Victim Support Scheme. I wondered if they'd noticed it was the same person they'd written to just the week before. I was impressed with their efficiency. I'd heard rumours that they were going to have their funding cut. Was nothing safe?

Bev rang to see about meeting up for a swim on Sunday morning and going back to their house for lunch. I told her about my injuries. I didn't really want to bare all my bruises at the baths.

'Bit of gentle stretching might be good for you,' she said. I wasn't sure, nor were my ribs. I accepted lunch and said I'd confirm the swim on Sunday morning. I asked if Harry was there. I wanted to tell him what Smiley had put me through.

'He's out,' said Bev. 'Another shooting in Moss Side, last night.'

'Oh, no. What happened?'

'Some little girl got caught in the crossfire, she's in intensive care. One of the youths involved is dead. Harry's been there since first light.' Bev sounded pissed off. With the situation or with Harry?

'It just gets worse,' I said. 'Kids with guns.'

'They reckon you can pick one up for fifty quid, less than a pair of trainers.'

I made the sort of noises expected and rang off.

Ordsall and now Moss Side. Just down the road, but it still felt unreal – as though it were all happening in someone else's city.

I fished out my cagoule, found my bag, made a sandwich and filled a flask. Nana Tello was in the lounge, pouring over the racing papers, ringing hopefuls with a stubby pencil. I told her I was off to the office. I'd have to talk to Ray about her staying – if I tried to tell her that I could manage fine now, she'd take umbrage.

Within an hour of getting to the office, I'd had two calls in response to my ad in the paper. A solicitor wanted three lots of papers serving on people and would pay nicely to get them off her hands and a woman wanted me to check whether her husband was really working late so many nights. The solicitor would have the papers ready first thing Monday morning and I arranged to visit the worried wife the same afternoon.

I opened two new files with the relevant details and allowed myself a cocky grin as I dropped them in the drawer of the filing cabinet.

I played with figures for a while; working out how much rent I owed the Dobson's; ringing to check on insurance rates for minimum contents cover (two plastic chairs, a phone and a distressed filing cabinet); checking back with my invoices to tot up what I'd earned over the last couple of months. I tried not to let it get me down. It convinced me to call at the post office for a Family Credit form as soon as possible.

I took the letter addressed to Martin out of my bag and propped it up by the phone. Then I unpacked my lunch and ate it, gazing all the while at the letter.

It was proving impossible to deliver by hand. If I sent it by registered delivery, it could always be intercepted and signed for by Fraser Mackinlay. Fraser had consistently denied me access to Martin, denied he even knew him. I opened my Blue Riband, bit off a chunk, took a sip of coffee and thought. My mind went to the group who I'd seen with Martin at the night-club. I could hardly go back and ask Eddie Kenton to confirm whether Martin was staying at the house in Cheadle. But what about Bruce Sharrocks? I'd still not found anything to connect him to the others. If I asked him straight out, played the innocent, pretended I knew Fraser too, perhaps? But not over the phone. Easier to weigh up his responses face to face.

I rang his secretary to confirm that Mr Sharrocks would be in his office today. She was expecting him back from lunch at one-thirty. No, I didn't want to leave a message.

I got to town a little early. I had a credit card in my pocket. The bank, obviously enjoying the draconian charges, hadn't repossessed it. Feeling poor made me glum, spending a bit would cheer me up. The sales were on – they always are. I picked up a baggy cotton-knit top in cornflower-blue for myself, a pair of shorts each for Tom and Maddie and a pair of pyjamas for Maddie – all her other ones had shrunk while she'd grown. They no longer met at the waist or covered ankles and wrists.

I reached Albert Square at one-thirty precisely. The Town Hall is a great building; lovely creamy stone, carvings, clock tower. Inside, it's all Victorian gothic, pillars and inner courtyards, marble floors. Any possible beauty is overridden by heaps of heraldic mural and fresco work and truckloads of gloomy portraits of local aldermen.

I asked the porter, in his ornate wooden den, the way to Social Services. With one eye on his crossword, he directed me to the fifth floor in the Town Hall Extension. I crossed the small side street and found my way in and to a lift. No marble pillars and brooding oils here.

I knocked on a couple of office doors as though I'd every right to and was soon told which belonged to Sharrocks. I knocked and went in. He was there, behind an imposing hardwood desk. There was a painting of a sailing ship on one wall and a display cabinet full of model ships on another.

He half rose from his chair. 'Can I help you?' I saw the hint of curiosity as he saw my bruised face, but he rapidly hid it.

He was larger than I'd remembered, broad-shouldered, a thick neck. His hair was thick, the colour of mustard, leonine around the craggy face. His chin was comic-book square, with a dimple just like Kirk Douglas. And his voice was familiar.

'I'm looking for a friend of mine.' I paused deliberately, uncertain about revealing too much.

'Yes, well, I think you've come to the wrong place.' A slight lisp, Mancunian accent. 'As you can see, there's no-one here but me.'

I couldn't place it, but I'd heard that voice recently; not over the last few days, more like weeks. Think.

'I'll try next door,' I bluffed. 'I know she said Social Services.'

'Ask at reception,' he smiled. 'They'll be able to help.'

I forced a smile in return. 'Thanks.' My mind stumbled on towards placing the voice. It hadn't been in person. A phone call. That faint sibilance, the light timbre. I opened the door and closed it again behind me.

Barry Smith. Barry Smith, that was it. He'd rung to

arrange an appointment. He never showed up. I'd sat waiting in my office. Waiting. And there was something else...

I made my way back out onto the cobbled square. That day, when he'd rung, it was the day before I'd found J.B.'s body, it was the day that Leanne had seen Smiley rushing away. The day of his death. And I'd been safely out of the picture. Twiddling my thumbs and waiting for a bogus client. Barry Smith aka Bruce Sharrocks.

Oh, shit. I broke into a run. My ribs hurt. I was forced to walk quickly instead. I stood at the bus-stop, feeling like a target. When I got off the bus near home, I felt a sweep of relief that no-one else had followed me. I paused at the front door, looked up and down the street. No parked cars with men reading tabloids in them, no funny characters leaning on lamp-posts.

And no-one home. There was a note from Nana Tello saying she'd gone home, that Nina had rung and that Ray would be getting the kids. My armpits stank. I stood under the shower until the smell, and some of my paranoia, had washed away.

When I heard the doorbell go, it came flooding back. I put the chain on and called through the glass panels. 'Who is it?'

'Pete. Is Clive in?'

'No.' I left the chain on and opened the door, stuck my face through the crack. 'Was it you that rang before?'

He nodded.

'I'm sorry, I did pass on your message.'

He gave a big sigh. Tossed his long hair back away from his face. 'Do you know when he'll be back?'

'No. He's hoping to be moving out. He might not be here much longer. I'll tell him you came.'

I tore a piece out of Maddie's scrapbook and printed the message in huge letters: PETE CAME ROUND – HE WANTS HIS MONEY. I pinned it to Clive's door. I didn't think Pete could hold out much hope, but at least I'd done my duty.

Nina was in when I tried her.

'Garbage report,' she said. 'Hang on, I wrote it all out.'

'Was it disgusting? Where did you do it?'

'In the garage.' She stretched the word out with her American drawl. 'With a scarf tied round my face, rubber gloves and a can of air freshener.'

'And?'

'Disappointing.'

'Oh no.' My heart sank. I'd really hoped this inventive line of enquiry would give me the proof I wanted.

'Nothing in the way of letters to Martin,' she said. 'Forms, nothing like that. Just garbage really. Except the condoms.'

'What?'

'Well, it takes two to practise safe sex. And there were a dozen in the bags. Someone's having fun.'

'You counted them.' I blanched at the thought.

'I take my work seriously.'

It didn't prove anything really. Just that someone in that house had used condoms in the previous week.

'What else?'

'Vegetable matter, chop bones, chicken joints, take-away cartons, eight wine bottles, two whisky, beer cans, lots. I didn't count those.'

'Not one for re-cycling, our Fraser.'

'Dead flowers, film cartons...'

'Video?'

'No, those little yellow ones for photographs. And

one of them's a chocolate junkie. Lots of Mars Bar wrappers, those bite-size ones.'

'That could be Martin. Teenagers are often heavy sweet eaters, aren't they?'

Nina went on with the list. Like she said, it was rubbish. The bottles and the condoms made sense when I thought back to the night I'd seen all the cars outside Mackinlay's. Party time. Eddie there, showing his movies, or maybe even making one. Speculation. It could just as easily suggest Fraser had a drink problem and a lively libido. Monday night could have been a business meeting.

'That it?'

'You want more?'

I laughed. 'What did you do with it all?'

'I bagged it up and took it to the tip, along with the clothes I'd been wearing.'

I thanked her.

'Yeah. I kinda wish I could've found something important,' she said.

She had. But neither of us knew that then.

CHAPTER THIRTY NINE

The kids were asleep. Ray was in the cellar. It was twilight when the doorbell rang. It never occurred to me to put the chain on that time.

It was Leanne. As soon as I glimpsed her – egg-coloured hair, black T-shirt, sullen face, I pushed the door. She was quick. Stuck her foot in the way before I could close it.

'Open the friggin' door,' she complained.

'Get lost, Leanne. You're not coming in.'

'Open the door. You've got it all wrong, yer daft cow. You're hurting my foot.'

I relented, sighed and stepped back. She came in huffing her shoulders. Started to roll her eyes to heaven. Then she got a proper look at me.

'Fuckin' hell.' Note of respect in her voice. I blushed.

'Anything broken?'

'Ribs.' What did she care? 'How did you know where I lived?'

She pulled her mouth to the side. 'Was on your library ticket.' Ah, yes. My purse.

'What do you want? What do you mean, I've got it all wrong?'

'Can we sit down or summat? I hate standing up.'

I led her through to the kitchen and we sat at the table.

'I didn't tell him, right,' she began, 'about you coming

round.'

'Oh, yeah.'

'I didn't.'

'How do I know you're telling the truth?'

'You don't.'

There was a pause.

'If you didn't tell him, then how come I get a phone call that same afternoon, why did I get beaten up?'

She shrugged. 'How do you know it was Smiley?'

I sighed. 'I don't Leanne, it's an educated guess.'

'Maybe he had someone following you.'

I'd thought of that. He certainly had by the time I was visiting Diane. But before then? I shivered. Maybe Leanne was telling the truth. It was hard to judge. What the hell, I was in no mood to apologise. I pushed back my chair.

'I didn't come about that,' she said. 'Not just that.'

'Oh?'

'It's Derek. They're going to pin a murder on him, you know, that woman that was found on the motorway...'

'Well, they're looking for evidence.'

'But he didn't do it. He'd never do stuff like that.'

'He was using crack, Leanne. You said yourself it was doing his head in. People get violent.'

'He'd have used his shooter, his gun. He wasn't a fighter.'

Oh God. Did all these kids have guns?

'All I know is they're waiting for forensic reports. If it wasn't Derek, they won't find anything.'

'They'll find what suits them. Be easy for them to set him up. He can't prove them wrong now, can he?' She pulled a crumpled packet of Benson and Hedges from the waistband of her skirt. Lit up.

'Why would they want to do that?'

'Tidies things up. They've got the killer. He's black, he's a user – everyone's going to believe he done it, aren't they?'

'Can you give him an alibi? She was killed the Sunday night, the day before we went to J.B.'s funeral.' Three weeks ago. And ten days after that, they'd pulled Derek from the Mersey. How long had he been there?

'No,' said Leanne. At least that was honest. 'He wasn't around. I was going to tell him about J.B.'s funeral, so he could come with me. But I didn't see him. I never saw him after that.' She pulled hard on the cigarette and I heard the soft rustle of it burning.

'Did he know J.B.?'

'Yeah, they was old mates. They grew up together.'

'I thought J.B. was in care?'

'He was. So was Derek. They were both at Hanley Court. That's where I was for a bit. That's where I met Derek.'

I had a sudden prickling at the nape of my neck.

'Did you ever hear of a man called Sharrocks?'

She paused, the cigarette a few inches from her mouth. Looked me in the eyes. Was it a trick question?

'Yeah.' Cautious.

'Bruce Sharrocks. He's mixed up in all this, I think. He made a phoney appointment with me, kept me out of the way the day J.B. was killed.'

'We called him Mr Bollocks,' she said. She was gripping the edge of the table, her fingers pinched white. 'He was the boss at Hanley Court – till he got promoted.' There was more to come. I could see it in the dull glare of her eyes, as she looked beyond me to the past. 'We thought it'd be alright then, him in the Town Hall. But he had to come and visit. It was like his brothel, see.'

The silence was shattered by the breeping of the phone.

'I'm sorry.' I slid away and answered it.

'Hello?'

A young, gruff voice asked to speak to me. I told him he already was.

'It's Max here, Max Ainsworth. You came and talked to us at St. Matthew's, about Martin Hobbs.' Oh yes, Max. Sitting on his own in the playground. The only one who had any concern for Martin.

'It's about Martin,' he went on quickly. 'He's just rung us up. He's in real bother. He wants me to meet him, take him some money and clothes and stuff. He was in a right state. Kept saying they were after him, that they'd kill him. I thought you'd want to know, want to come.' Max's voice was heavy with concern.

'What did you say?'

'I said I'd do what he said. He wanted to see us at Heaton Park. We went fishing there once. There's this old monument, like an arch, near the boating lake. He said to meet there.'

'Have you got a car?'

'No, a bike, motor-bike.'

'You better let me sort this out,' I said. 'If someone really is after him then it could get nasty. There's no point in us all going.'

'Oh, no,' he said firmly. 'I promised. I don't let me mates down. I'm coming. I'm not chickening out now.'

I could tell he wouldn't budge. I knew of a petrol station on one of the roads that skirted the park. We arranged to rendez-vous there. My heart was fluttering when I put down the receiver.

Leanne was smoking, leaning up against the worktop, when I went back into the kitchen.

I made a clumsy attempt to thank her for telling me

what she had. She brushed it away. 'Forget it.'

'Did any of you ever complain?'

The drop-dead look said it all. 'Who to? The boss?'

'Well, social workers or...'

'I don't want to talk about it.' She launched herself away from the side.

'I'm sorry, I've got to go out,' I said. 'Martin's in trouble.'

'What's happened?'

'I don't know, but he's running away from someone. I'll drop you in town.'

'I want to come with you.'

'No,' I said.

'Martin knows me,' she said. 'He's not going to trust you, is he?'

Maybe she'd got a point. But did I trust Leanne? Enough to let her come along?

'I don't know,' I said. 'I'll think about it on the way.'

I told Ray where I was going and why.

'You're crazy.' He flung down his chisel. 'Your stitches aren't even out and you're off in the dark to find some kid who's on the run. Ring the police, Sal.' The temper he'd been holding onto finally slipped loose. 'For Christ's sake, grow up and think about what you're doing.'

'I will ring the bloody police,' I shouted back, 'and don't talk to me like I'm deliberately courting danger. I'm not going to sit here and let some schoolboy play heroics all on his own. I'll ring them now and, with any luck, they'll be there before me.' I stalked across the room and pulled the door to behind me. There were so many wood chippings littering the floor that the damn thing wouldn't even slam properly.

'Where's the toilet?' Leanne was waiting in the hall. I told her, then dialled the police.

The desk sergeant was less than helpful. I'd no crime to report, so he couldn't squander police resources. In the end, I asked him to contact D.I. Miller as a matter of urgency and tell him where I was going and why.

'Tell him someone is trying to kill Martin, that he's got information of vital importance to the police.' Okay, so I was being prodigal with the truth – but it was a pretty good hunch.

CHAPTER FORTY

Leanne was quiet on the drive into town. That suited me. I was trying to grasp what the new information meant. Sharrocks had been abusing children in his care. J.B. and Derek were dead. Because of that? Leanne was still very much alive. Maybe she was next? Did Sharrocks know Smiley? How did any of that tie in to Janice's murder?

It was still warm but damp too, a misty drizzle which turned the streetlamps into fuzzy, orange balls. We drove down Oxford Road. I turned right at the BBC studios and cut through UMIST and over to Piccadilly. I still wasn't sure whether Leanne would be an asset or a liability. On balance, I thought I'd better leave her out of it. I pulled up outside the old warehouse.

'I'll drop you here,' I said. 'I don't want too many of us chasing around after Martin.'

'I want to come.' Her voice was intense and she sat very still as she spoke. 'Martin knows me. I won't get in the way.' In the pause that followed, I looked in the rear-view mirror, watched people walking towards town for a night in the clubs.

'Please, it means a lot to me.' That threw me and I let it affect my judgement. I agreed and made her promise that she'd do what I asked. I'd be calling the tune.

'I just need to get something from the squat,' she said.

'What?' I became suspicious.

'I need to change my tampon,' she retorted. I could hardly argue with that.

'Get a move on, then.'

She was quick, I'll give her that. She came back with a thin nylon jacket over the top of her T-shirt, all puce and lime-green. She brushed the beads of damp from her hair. Pulled out her cigarettes and lighter from her high-tops. I wound down my window, heard the snick of the flame and saw the flare of light.

'Martin won't be expecting us,' I explained, as I pulled away, 'just his mate Max. I don't want to frighten him off. We'll get Max to do the talking first and explain that he got in touch with me.' Leanne nodded. 'The important thing,' I said, 'is to get him somewhere safe.' I hadn't thought where, yet. I was hoping that the police would come through on that one.

Max was there, helmet under his arm, astride his bike in the forecourt of the petrol station, when we arrived. He still wore thick glasses but his uniform had been replaced by biking leathers and he'd had his hair cropped close since I last saw him.

I hooted the horn and waved him over. Opened the back door and he climbed in.

'Hiya. What did your folks say about all this?'

'Nowt,' he said, 'they think I'm off to the late show at the Cornerhouse.'

'This is Leanne, this is Max.'

She threw her head round and tossed off a greeting. Max mumbled something in response.

'I've explained to Leanne that Martin doesn't know we're coming. You're going to have to reassure him.'

'What's Leanne doing here?' he asked.

Good question.

'Martin stayed same place as me when he came to Manchester. He'll talk to me,' she boasted. 'He doesn't know her.' She nodded in my direction.

'But Max talks first,' I reminded her. 'Martin asked for Max.'

We drove over to the park entrance and parked the car. The gates were locked at dusk. Leanne and I climbed up onto Max's shoulders and over, jumped down the other side. Max, helped by his height, was able to climb over unaided.

As we walked into the park, the sound of traffic receded. There was no lighting and the cloudy sky obscured any moonlight there might have been. It was still drizzling. We approached the colonnade. Four columns and a tower either end, supporting the crosspiece. By daylight, I remembered sandy stone, carvings near the top. Now it was a vague silhouette, its outline shifting in obscurity.

'Martin, it's Max. Are you there? There's two other people here; Sal Kilkenny , she's a private detective, she'll be able to help; and your friend, Leanne. Martin.'

No response. I strained to hear breathing but couldn't. But I sensed that someone was there besides the three of us.

'C'mon Martin,' Leanne shouted. 'What the fuck's going on?' I grabbed her arm to shut her up. There was a rustle to our left and Martin stepped out from behind the bushes. His face was haggard, as though fear had weighed the flesh down. I was struck again by how slight he was. There were marks on his face, dirt or bruises. He was shivering. He wore a thin white T-shirt and dark pants.

'Who's after yer?' asked Leanne.

He shuddered.

'Come out of the rain,' I said. There was some cover at the base of the towers, old entrance-ways, like large sentry-boxes open on two sides but offering reasonable shelter. I stepped in. Martin and Max huddled against one wall. Leanne stood in the middle of the space, arms in her jacket pockets.

'Is it Smiley?' she said.

'Yeah, and the others.'

I thought of the two who'd caught up with me. 'Which others?' He rubbed his face.

'Were you staying with Fraser?' I asked.

Martin laughed, a mirthless sound. 'He locked me up. I had a collar, like a dog. He wouldn't let me go. He didn't touch me, you know. He liked the girls. They wanted me for the pictures and the videos. I said I didn't want to, I promised not to say anything but he said they couldn't afford to take the risk. He locked me up.'

'And you ran away. Is that why they're after you, Martin?'

He swung his head from side to side as though he couldn't fathom it out.

'What happened with Derek?' Leanne spoke softly. What the hell did she mean? I waited.

'Tell us about Derek,' Leanne insisted.

'No,' he protested, 'no, no.' The shaking became more pronounced. He was remembering something he'd rather forget.

'They think Derek killed Janice Brookes,' I said, 'the woman they found on the motorway.'

'He didn't, did he?' said Leanne. 'It was someone else, wasn't it? Someone else at that house. Was it Smiley?'

Why the hell hadn't she told me that Derek knew

Martin, knew about the house?

'I can't tell you.' He broke down, making squeaky little noises. 'They'll kill me, they'll kill me.'

'You've got to tell us,' said Leanne, anger sharpening her tone. 'Derek was my mate, I want to know. He didn't do, it did he? Martin?'

'Oh, fuck.' A spasm shook his body and he pressed himself back against the stone slab. I followed his eyes. Leanne had a gun. She was pointing it at Martin.

My mouth went dry. 'Leanne.'

'Shut up, I'm talking to Martin.'

'Don't, don't,' Martin whimpered.

'Tell us.'

'We had to help. Derek, he was running for Smiley. He was round now and again, errands.' The phrases came out staccato, little bursts of information punctuated by his shivering. 'It was in the hall. There was an old curtain. We had to roll it up. The body, this woman's body. Mr Johnson was there, giving orders.'

'Who's he?' I asked.

'Smiley's boss,' said Martin.

'Go on.' Leanne waved the gun. I glanced over to Max. He looked wary, tensed like a frightened animal. I knew the sensation.

'Derek was freaking out, he didn't want to do it. Smiley was stringing him out, saying he wouldn't get his stuff and that. Crack. He gives him a bit to keep him going. We put it in the car. It's her car. Derek has to drive it. Mr Johnson says it's fine. Leave her, the body, on the motorway. Bring the car to Smiley. Don't forget the curtain. Mr Mackinlay asks about the curtain but Smiley says he'll arrange a little fire. Put it in an empty flat in Hulme. Get it torched.' He stopped abruptly.

'So, Derek drove off and you didn't see him again?' I

said. 'Leanne, put that bloody thing down, will you?'

She ignored me. 'Derek didn't kill her, did he?'

'No.' A whisper.

'Who killed her, Martin?' I kept my voice gentle. He rocked back and forth. 'Who killed her?'

'They'll do me in,' he said.

'No,' I said. 'We're going to make sure you're alright.'

Max put his hand on Martin's shoulder.

'It was one of the parties. They were filming. All the little kids were up in the bedrooms. I was in the lounge with Mr Mackinlay and this visitor. He's telling me what I've got to do – with the little girls, when it's my turn. I never wanted to do it.' He looked up at me, grief on his face. 'I was just working the clubs a bit. Mr Mackinlay, he says it'll be like that but safer. A nice place. He didn't say about kids – some of them were that small. One guy, he brought his own kids there...' Into my mind flashed the picture I'd seen from Nina's window; the white minibus, the clutch of cars, another party.

'What happened?' said Leanne.

'Everyone was pissed, really pissed. Mr Sharrocks comes down for another bottle and the bell goes. There's two blokes from London not arrived yet, so he goes to see if it's them. I couldn't see anything. There was screaming, a woman. Mackinlay goes out and comes back and says to stay out of the hall. Tells me to wait with the visitor. This bloke, he just goes, he could tell there was something wrong. Mr Mackinlay rings Mr Johnson.' Martin swallowed and rubbed his eyes. 'Mr Sharrocks comes in then. He's all covered with blood. He says, 'She was hysterical, I can't bear hysterical women.' Mr Mackinlay tells him to shut up and Mr Sharrocks says, 'She was onto us, she'd come for her boy. I did it for all of us.' He's going on and on.

Mr Mackinlay slaps him and he's quiet.' Martin looked up at me. 'But I know now, I know. They're never going to let me go. They'll find me.'

Leanne's face was blank. All expression wiped out. She lowered the gun and put it in her pocket. That's why she'd called in at the squat. For a gun, not a tampon.

'How did you get away?' Max asked in a hoarse voice.

'Bathroom window. I've been planning it, waiting for a chance.'

I turned aside and gulped fresh air. Pushed away the pictures conjured up by Martin's story.

'Come on,' I said. 'We've a car over at the gates.' Then I heard footsteps. So did Martin.

'Someone's coming,' he said. And my guts dissolved.

CHAPTER FORTY ONE

'Wait here.' I stepped out from the foot of the colonnade and walked over to the path. Squinting into the gloom, I made out a figure. As he drew nearer, I recognised the combination of spectacles, moustache and long stylish raincoat. I began to breathe again. Detective Inspector Miller. Relief. The cavalry had arrived.

'It's alright,' I called back to the others. 'I know who it is.'

I walked over to Miller.

'You got my message. Martin's here, and he knows who killed Janice Brookes. It wasn't Derek Carlton – he was set up. There's more besides. But I think we need to get him to safety, he's petrified. Convinced that the people involved will kill him to keep him quiet.'

Miller nodded. The cynical look hadn't left his eyes. He'd still got me labelled as an interfering neurotic but at least he'd come when I needed him.

'I'll just explain who you are,' I said. 'He might bolt if he doesn't understand.'

I crossed the wet grass back to the others. Martin was still shaking, his eyes darting to and fro. I placed my hands on his shoulders and looked him full in the face.

'Martin, the police are here.' He jerked. 'It's okay, I've told them roughly what's happened. The rest can wait. They'll find a safe place for you. They'll be able to protect you and make sure the right people are sent down for this. Understand?' He gave a small nod. Max, at his side, remained still and quiet.

Leanne leant back against the wall opposite, narrowing her eyes.

'Okay, Inspector,' I shouted.

Miller walked forward into view, a few yards in front of us.

'No,' Martin said softly, 'no.' He screamed in desperation. 'That's him, that's Mr Johnson.'

Oh, shit. My heart kicked at my breasts. I saw movement from Leanne, as she darted forward, then I reeled as the sharp, cracking sound pierced my ear-drums. Miller hit the ground and Leanne ran off between the columns and behind the monument. I struggled to make sense of what was happening. I could smell the bitter scent of gunpowder. My ears were singing.

'Oh, shit,' said Martin. 'She's killed him.'

I moved, then froze at the sound of footsteps running on the path. Another man appeared. He wore a dark suit, a light shirt. He looked as though he was laughing. He stopped beside Miller and dropped onto one knee.

'Smiley,' Martin said. I felt him swoon beside me and slither down the wall, till he was crouching at our feet. I looked at Max. Saw my own fear staring back at me.

Miller murmured something and I heard Smiley answer no. Then Smiley handed Miller his glasses and helped him up. Miller brushed down his coat. He was unhurt. Leanne had missed; he'd just been playing safe. The two men quickly covered the ground to where we were. Stood framed in the entrance. No-one spoke. My right knee was jerking. I hoped they wouldn't notice.

'You've hurt your face,' said Miller.

'Sticking it where it's not wanted.' Smiley stepped inside.

'Who's this?' Miller gestured to Max.

'He doesn't know anything,' I said. 'Let him go.'

'We're not stupid, Miss Kilkenny,' said Miller.

'Think murder's clever, do you?' I retorted.

Smiley breathed in sharply, then brought a gun out from his suit, held it up against my head, cool on my temple. I felt absurd relief. It wasn't a knife, he wouldn't cut me like the other one had. It didn't last. Giddy with fear, I heard my mouth running on.

'People know we're here, you know. What are you planning to do? Kill us all? Bit over the top, isn't it? Four corpses.'

'Oh, it'll be front page,' said Miller. 'Crack Addict Massacre. We'll piece it together. Hobbs, a runaway, lured you all up here. Said he was in trouble.' Miller tilted his head to the side as though he was dreaming up the next bit. 'But he wanted money, he needed to get a fix. You refused; there was a scuffle. He flipped. The three of you were shot at close-quarters, your pockets emptied. We found Hobbs in the city centre, a couple of hours later. He'd managed to score. He made a verbal confession on the way to the nick, told us where to find the gun. He still had some of your property in his pockets. Sadly' – he paused and smiled. I smelt mint – 'sadly, before we could get the police doctor to him, he'd gone into a drug-induced coma. He never recovered.'

'Just like J.B.' My bowels were churning. 'How did you fix his overdose? He'd never have let you near him with a needle.'

'I like the old-fashioned ways myself,' said Smiley. 'Take someone by surprise, give 'em a good whiff of chloroform. Few seconds, they're out of it. All the time in the world, then. Set it up just right.'

'Why?' I said. 'He found out about Sharrocks. He realised Martin had got mixed up with a paedophiles' ring. That was it, wasn't it?'

'A little knowledge is such a dangerous thing,' said Miller sarcastically.

'You wouldn't be told,' said Smiley. 'You ignored the paint; off you trot, bothering Mr Kenton. He wasn't pleased. So I rang you, to make things clear.' He leaned even closer to make his point. 'What did you do, stupid cow, you go off sniffing round Mr Mackinlay. Well, when he let us know, I had to send the boys, show you we meant business. But you wouldn't drop it, would you?'

I resisted the urge to explain; that I thought I had dropped it – I hadn't realised it was one big conspiracy. I imagined them all on their car phones complaining about me, while I lumbered around.

I got flippant then. 'You're giving me a headache,' I said to Smiley. He clicked the trigger. My bones ran soft. I darted a look at Max and he winked. I couldn't believe it. He did it again, a slow deliberate wink. He'd cracked.

'Get the girl,' Miller instructed Smiley. 'I'm getting piss wet out here.' Smiley moved the gun from my head, edged away and swung out through the back of the tower. Miller stepped in, slid out his own gun and trained it on me.

'You better sort out which one you're using,' I said, 'or it'll bugger up the forensics, won't it? Did you get the results you wanted on Derek?'

He gave me a warm smile. 'Turned out nicely. Fingerprints on the steering wheel, hair on the dead woman's clothing. We can place him in the car. That's all we need.'

'What's in it for you?' I asked. 'You like raping children too?'

His jaw tensed. The gun slammed across my cheekbone, heavy enough to jolt my jaw and neck. The burning turned to numbness. I put my hand up and felt for damage. The stitches were split, the wound had burst open. It felt sticky.

'I'm a rich man,' Miller said. 'Perversion doesn't interest me. Money does. I'm not about to give that up.' He was on the payroll. A cop who could sort out any difficulties with the law. That would go for the pornography they were producing, as well as the abuse. He could even turn his hand to a stupid mistake like murder.

Max began to make a huffing noise, covering his glasses with his hands. The sound echoed in the damp air. I leaned over towards him and put my arm round his shoulder.

'Very touching,' muttered Miller. 'Smiley, what the fuck are you playing at?'

As he yelled, Max pulled my head close. 'Get down,' he whispered. I began to slide down to Martin's level. A flash of anger stopped me, half-way down. He was about to pull some stupid macho stunt that'd get us all shot. Before I could straighten up and caution him, I saw Max's leg flick out. His foot, his trainer, kicked hard at Miller's hand. I heard a snapping sound. Miller gasped and the gun flew up. Max kicked again, at his balls now. Miller groaned and began to double up. Max's hand flew out and slashed at his windpipe, the other hand at his shoulder. The force sent him keeling over backwards. When he hit the ground, I heard the air woof out of his body. Max rubbed at his hand.

'Judo?' I asked. Oh, you wonderful boy.

'Aikido,' he grinned. 'Regional finalist. Where'd the gun go?'

I shrugged. 'It's so dark. Is he dead?'

'Bloody hell, I hope not. He should be out for a couple of hours, though.'

I shuddered. A gunshot rapped out somewhere behind us, making me start. Leanne or Smiley? We waited in silence. There was the sound of footsteps running, shoes not trainers. My heart was thumping in my ears, muffling other noises.

Smiley appeared, gun in hand. 'She's taken off, scared...' He stopped short when he saw Miller, approached slowly, swinging round and back like a paratrooper in a film.

He knelt down and put a hand to Miller's neck.

'He's dying,' I bluffed. 'You can't save him now. Max's a karate expert; he's ruptured his kidneys and damaged most of the internal organs. He's bleeding to death from the inside.'

He shook Miller. 'You're lying,' he screeched.

'Without Miller, there's no way you can make it work. Who's going to falsify the confession, put the gun in the right place, arrest Martin?'

I was irritating him. 'Shut it.' He shoved the gun down in the direction of Martin. 'This'll have his prints on. I can make him O.D. here. It doesn't matter, they can figure it out.'

'They'll know it stinks,' I said.

'It doesn't fucking matter,' he shouted in desperation, the gun waving in his hand. He fought for calm and levelled the gun at me. I wouldn't beg. I'd pleaded before, with the man who held a kitchen knife to my throat. I'd begged and he'd stuck the knife in anyway.

I licked my lips. The buzzing in my ears grew louder. I wouldn't be able to go swimming with Maddie.

There was a click, then a crack, and Smiley jerked to the side. He staggered back a couple of steps, then stood teetering on his feet. I smelt cordite again. He levelled the gun and squeezed the trigger gently.

I was slammed back against the stone. The shot rang out. My arm sang with pain. The ground drifted.

Smiley dropped to his knees. The gun slipped from his fingers. I couldn't see where he'd been hit. Leanne came running.

'He thought I'd gone,' she said. 'Now I've got him.' She knelt in front of him and placed the muzzle up against his forehead.

'Leanne, no,' I croaked.

'You killed Derek,' she said, matter-of-fact. The gun clicked. There was a dreamy look in Smiley's eyes.

'He couldn't swim,' he said. 'We had to keep Sharrocks out of it.'

She nodded. 'He supplied the kids. Did you ever go to the parties, Smiley? We used to have them at Hanley Court or we'd go off in the minibus. Special games we had to play.' Her voice was so low I could only just hear her. 'Secret games. Always lots of visitors. We got sweets. Mars Bars. He always brought Mars Bars.'

Someone likes chocolate – that was what Nina had said – lots of Mars Bar wrappers in the rubbish.

'Leanne.' I leant forward.

The explosion made me recoil.

'Oh, Jesus Christ.' Max ran over.

She was still kneeling beside Smiley. Blood was spurting, a pulsing fountain where his head had been. I could see his brains, smell the hot iron scent.

Max moved to pull Leanne aside.

'Fuck off.' She flung his hand away. Stumbled to her feet and began to run. There were dark patches on her hair and her jacket.

'Leanne!' I struggled to get some volume. 'We'll tell them what happened. Wait, it'll be alright.' She disappeared from view.

I could feel shock, its open arms ready to claim me. But I needed to get safe first.

'Martin.' I edged over to him and ruffled his hair. 'Martin, we have to go. Smiley won't bother us now. Miller – Mr Johnson's – passed out.' Martin looked up, eyes groggy.

'I'll bring him,' said Max. 'Can you walk?'

'Yes.'

My feet were a long way from my head. If I watched them, it was easier to make them move where I wanted them to. I could hear Max beside me, panting, as he carried Martin. The drizzle had stopped. My face was wet. I wasn't crying, was I? There was something important I had to tell Max. My mind slid around the edges of it.

There was the Mini. But the gate was shut.

'Oh, no.' Max had forgotten too.

My right palm was wet. I turned it over, made out black, trickling along the creases.

'You go,' I said. 'Ring an ambulance, take the car.'

'I haven't taken my test, yet.'

We both laughed. A moment of delirium.

'My keys are in this pocket, can you get them?' I was too weak to wrestle in my jeans pocket. Max sat Martin up against the gate, then retrieved the keys.

I remembered what was important. 'Max, ring Harry. Don't talk to anyone else. Tell Harry I'm hurt, tell him we need Y Department. The police are mixed up in it. Don't talk to anyone till Harry's here.'

'What's his number?'

I reeled it off. Gingerly, I lowered myself down next to Martin. The gate shook as Max clambered over and leapt down the other side. I heard him drive away.

It was quiet, not much traffic now. The numbness had spread up from my arm and shoulder. I couldn't feel the right side of my face. I heard a siren sing-song in the distance and, a little later, the chocker-chocker of the police helicopter, down to the south towards the city, where the sky was bleeding mandarin. Should be up here mate, I thought. It's all happening here.

The siren sound got stuck in my ears, whining on and on. I was thirsty. I could taste metal, smell blood. Martin stirred. I reached out for his hand. It was small, smooth, the nails ragged. It felt nice – this hand in mine. I wanted to cry. I felt warm piss leak through my pants.

'Martin,' I whispered. 'Are you there?' He was quiet.

I heard a dog bark once, a long way off. I thought of Digger. Then there was nothing.

CHAPTER FORTY TWO

They called it a graze. Christ, I hate that euphemism.
They said the same thing when I had Maddie. If you
weren't actually torn limb from limb, it was just a
graze. Unmitigated bloody agony, more like.

But even grazes heal with time.

Justice sure isn't swift. It's March now. The grape
hyacinths are out, eight months have passed, winter's
come and gone and the trial still hasn't started.

The police spent days interviewing us: Max, Martin
and myself. Going over and over our story. They didn't
like what they were hearing. Harry got us a good
solicitor. She was there all the time. Calm and clear.
Making sure it was all above-board.

Bruce Sharrocks and D. I. Miller were remanded on
bail.   Eddie Kenton got sent down. They seized some
of his video collection. He was shipping it as far as the
Philippines, using Mackinlay's business network.
Mackinlay made himself scarce. Left the country.
Probably chartered his own bloody plane. Some place
where there's no extradition treaty.

It made front page in the Evening News for a night:
Charity Boss faces Murder Rap – Child Sex Ring
Exposed. There was never a peep about Miller's
involvement. Funny, that.

They haven't caught up with Leanne. Not yet. I hope they don't. It's not as if she's a threat to society – more the other way around.

Martin's still in a mess. They've got him in a special hostel. He gets counselling and help to sort himself out. I went there once, to take him the letter from Janice. I warned his worker first, had her standing by. It was the hardest thing I've ever done. The sound he made, when he realised what I was saying, still churns me up thinking about it. I left Mrs Williams' number with them. I don't know if Martin ever got in touch. I like to think he will one day. He could do with some of that love.

I've gone off Harry. He's still a good friend, but the little frissons of lust have dried up. Back in September, Bev took me on one side and told me she'd some news. Divorce, separation? I pictured Harry moving into the top flat.

'The reason I've been so edgy,' Bev was saying.

I'd become a stepmother. Harry's boys could visit every weekend...

'I'm pregnant. We're having a baby,' she beamed at me.

I think that's when I lost it.

And Clive? About three weeks after I'd issued the ultimatum, I surprised him and a woman friend loading his stuff into the back of a car. He introduced Gina. Her eyes sparkled with delight. I wondered whether to warn her but self-interest won out. He didn't leave a forwarding address. We never saw a penny. Ray dropped a few dark hints – must be ways of finding out where he is... I didn't rise to the bait.

The squat's gone now. Part of the canal re-development. I went back when I was feeling up to it. I was hoping to rescue one of J.B.'s sketches. I was too late. There was nothing left. Just this big hole, piles of rubble and twisted metal being pushed around by bulldozers. I stood and watched.

One of the labourers noticed me, called across. 'You looking for someone?'

'No,' I shook my head and smiled. Turned back towards Piccadilly. 'No, not any more.'